The Cross on Cotton Creek

D L Havlin

The Cross on Cotton Creek

Copyright © 2012 D. L. Havlin
ISBN 978-1-943789-61-0

All rights reserved. No part of this book may be reproduced or transmitted in any form or by any means, electrical or mechanical, including photocopying, recording by any information storage system, without permission in writing from the publisher.

All performance rights to this novel are retained by the author. No adaptation of the material in this book may be used for stage, television, film, radio, or any other performance form, unless written permission is obtained from the author.

This book was printed in the United States of America by Taylor and Seale Publishing, LLC, Daytona Beach Shores, Florida, 32118.

This novel is a work of fiction. Names, characters, places and incidents are the product of the author's imagination and are used fictitiously. Any resemblance to actual persons, living or dead, events, or locales is entirely coincidental.

Taylor and Seale Publishing, LLC
2 Ocean's West, Suite 406
Daytona Beach Shores, FL 32118

Dedication

To the people who have made the most contributions to my development as a writer: Robert W. Fulton, PhD,
Bev Browning, Chet Collins, Babs Brown
and my wife, Jeanelle.

Other Titles by D L Havlin

Bait Man

Bully Route Home

A Place No One Should Go

The Hangin' Oak

Blue Water Red Blood

September on Echo Creek

Story Time-R

Acknowledgements

For years I read acknowledgements in books with little or no appreciation of what they represented. After over twenty years of writing, I read them with understanding and reverence. Anyone who writes has had others make contributions to their successes and mitigate their failures. I've benefitted greatly from *many* peoples' assistance in *many* different ways.

I owe a continuing debt of gratitude to my mentor/editors, Robert Fulton, PhD. who forged some raw material into a writer, and Babs Brown who has been and continues to be my watch dog, barking loud and long when my work lacks in any area. Authors Bev Browning, Veronica Helen Hart, and Robert B. Parker, agents Mary Sue Seymour and Anne Hawkins provided me with encouragement when my confidence was waning and kept me at the keyboard.

I owe special thanks to Taylor & Seale Publishing and to its Editor-in-chief, Mary Custureri and to V. H. Hart, her Senior Editor. Their belief in my work and encouragement is greatly appreciated. Obviously, you wouldn't be reading this book without Mary and Taylor & Seale.

I've been blessed with many excellent "test pilot readers" during my career. The list has grown too long to mention them all, but there are several that have been with me for a long time. Chet Collins, Linda Kay Solinger, Paul Owens, Carol Robb, Nancy Rogge, Gloria Andrews, Linda Hilliard, and Pat Cole don't spare criticism or praise … if it's earned.

Finally, I reserve my largest, most heart-felt thank you for my loving wife, partner and do-all assistant—Jeanelle. Without her support, encouragement, understanding and tolerance I'd have abandoned writing long ago.

Chapter 1

November 26, 1954

"Why go there the last part of November? It's pretty close to the date your great-great-grandfather made his promise, Landry. And, generally speaking, I've taken the day after Thanksgiving off . . . least ways, the last several years." Landry Dawes the fourth spoke to Landry Dawes the fifth as their car sped along Georgia Highway 16 between Monticello and Eatonton. They'd left their farm northwest of Eufaula, Alabama, at 2:30 AM that Friday to drive 210 miles to their destination. Their goal was a place four generations of Dawes had visited every five years to honor a solemn promise made by their ancestor during the Civil War. Not once during the ninety years since the first Landry Dawes made the commitment had a descendent defaulted on the original Landry Dawes' word.

The boy yawned and stretched his long arms to the top of the 1950 Ford. "I just wondered." It was his first time accompanying his father to do a task that eventually would become his. "We gonna stop for breakfast?" The eighteen-year-old required copious quantities of food to satisfy his lean, 6' 2" body's constant complaints. His next meal was always an issue.

"Yes, there's a little restaurant I always stop at. It's on the corner where we turn off this road to go to the church." The father raised his eyebrows. "Well, to the brick pile that *was* the church."

The boy leaned against the passenger side door and looked at his father quizzically. "Why did Great-great-grandpa buy that place? I know about the family stuff—the family honor and all that. But, why buy it?"

"Maybe it's the good deer hunting or the fact there's 240 acres that go with it." The father laughed and shrugged his shoulders. "Maybe he wanted to be a Georgia Cracker."

"An Alabama man that wants to go to Georgia to live? When pigs fly. And, Dad, you've always said none of our family ever gave a hoot for hunting deer. Hell, we've got white tails all over our place and Great-grandpa's . . . and we've got four times the land. You and grandpa only hunt quail and dove. Why don't you sell it off or lease the acreage?"

"I might one of these days." The older man thought about an envelope and notebook enclosed in the car's glove compartment. Selling was more than an economic decision. Dawes Sr. took his eyes off the road long enough to evaluate the look on his son's face. It was serious, not the smart-assed look that sometimes ruled his teenage persona. He'd planned to tell the boy why they visited the place every five years and performed their task at the church ruins, but it wouldn't hurt to start his talk as they drove. Landry Sr. looked back at the road. "What do you know about the War Between the States?"

"You mean about Great-great-grandpa being in Wheeler's Cavalry? You always talk about that at reunions. His sword and all . . . ."

"No. What do you know about the war itself? Do you know the significance of the place we're going?"

"Don't have the slightest idea." The boy stretched his legs and stared out the windshield at the first cool grays of the coming dawn.

"They don't teach much in school anymore," the elder Dawes snorted. "Ever hear of Sherman's March to the Sea?"

"Oh, yeah! Sure."

"Well, you're driving over land, right now, that part of Sherman's army passed over ninety years ago."

"I guess it was a whale of a battle, wasn't it?" The boy looked into the dense woods through which they were passing. The battles fought in Virginia's forests flashed in his mind.

"No, it wasn't. After the Battle of Atlanta, which was a hell of a long fight, the Confederate General, Hood, took most of the rebel army and went north to Chattanooga. Hood's idea was to threaten Sherman's supply line. He figured he'd force the whole Union Army to chase him. It didn't work. Sherman had three times the men the Confederates had so he split his army in two. He sent General Thomas north to deal with Hood with one half and took the 62,000 troops he had left and turned them loose on the 13,000 men commanded by General Hardee and General Wheeler who tried to defend this area. Sherman's soldiers were battle trained troops. A lot of the Confederates were militia made up of old men and boys. It wasn't so much of a battle as it was a war on the civilians.

Sherman's troops robbed, burned, and destroyed everything on their way from Atlanta to Savannah. His men covered a sixty-mile wide area like locusts. The less disciplined among the Yankees raped and murdered civilians. There were a lot of scavengers that followed behind Sherman's army that were worse."

Why didn't they just destroy the Confederate soldiers? There weren't that many."

"It's the concept of total war. Sherman believed that the war, any war, isn't over until the people fighting it are faced with such horrible times they lose the will to fight." Dawes senior squinted as the headlights from a lone approaching car half blinded him.

"Oh, like what we did to the Germans and the Japs?" The boy's tone was light and carefree.

Dawes' answer wasn't. He'd spent time in the Pacific before a Nambu machine gun ended his time in the hell called World War II. "Yes, exactly like that." He blinked as the car zipped by, fighting blind spots from the car's headlights. After his vision cleared, he grumbled, "Damn it, we've passed right by the restaurant and road." He slowed the car, found a farm lane and turned the car around. Dawes looked at his watch. It was 7:45. If he remembered correctly, the place called "Flora and Fanny's good food" should have been open almost two hours. The small restaurant's lights blinked their welcome as the first glow of sunlight came to rest on the building's walls, walls that desperately needed a coat of white paint. The ladders tied on top of the Ford the Dawes rode in pointed at the parking lot with a half-dozen pick-ups and autos sitting on its gravel.

* * *

The young waitress didn't look much older than the boy, but it was evident through her sharp-eyed look that she was much his senior in all worldly ways. "Mornin' ya'll." She slipped soiled and beaten-up menus in front of the Dawes. "You boys want some coffee?"

"Yes, ma'am." Landry Sr.'s speech suddenly adopted a much more pronounced drawl. The boy smirked at his father as the girl wiggled away.

"You're a big enough hick without pretending to be more of one." The boy grinned at his father. "Besides, I don't think Mom would like you flirting with the help."

Landry Sr. laughed, "Your mother knows how much I like red heads." He held his hand up to silence any retort. "I was just before answering your question about why our family keeps up with this ritual. Where was I when we stopped the car?"

"You'd explained what Sherman did and why all the people in his path hated him and his troops. How even many of the freed slaves despised the Yankees. You were getting into the details of what happened when Sherman came through this area and, I'm guessing, how our family got involved." Young Dawes looked at the menu. "I hope they put cheese in the grits."

"It's been five years since I was here, but the sign outside is the same. I kinda think the same folks still own this place. Back then, you could get about anything you wanted in your grits. Probably still can." Dawes took a breath and got back to telling his tale. "Hmm, I think I was talking about what parts of the Union army marched through here."

"Yep."

"General William's Twentieth Corp was the closest. They were part of Sherman's left wing . . . that was under General Slocum's overall command. There was some space between the main columns. Sherman covered that area by giving orders to send out patrols from each column to keep in touch. And, of course, there were bummers working behind the lines."

Landry junior looked bored until the term "bummers" was used. He asked, "What are bummers?"

"It's what Sherman's foraging troops were called. He sent them out to confiscate supplies and lay waste to everything they couldn't carry. When troops are given that kind of order, things often get out of control, particularly in fringe areas like this was. It was a group of bummers that are a big part of the story. Those Yankees and what they did to friends of your Great-great-grandfather; friends he made when he stayed at the church, are what make what we do special." He looked at the menu and waved his hand, silencing his son. "Let's get ready to order. The ham and redeye gravy was real good last time. I'm going to get that and an omelet, biscuits, and grits. What are you getting?"

"Three eggs over-easy, the ham and gravy, bacon, toast, and grits."

"No biscuits?"

"Not hardly, don't nobody make 'em as good as mom." Landry Jr. lost focus on his breakfast choices when the girl approached the table toward the end of his statement. The waitress' low cut blouse replaced his breakfast order as the center of his attention. She carried their coffee, cream, and sugar to the table, using them as deftly as a stripper would use fans to tease male observers. Having perceived young Dawes interest, she posed provocatively as she placed the cups and saucers in front of the father and son. "You boys know what you want?" She smiled at the young man as she spoke, hoping for the largest possible tip, but willing to forego it for a bit of fun.

Mesmerized, the boy stared at her, speechless. It was his father who said, "I'll take the omelet. Ham and redeye. Biscuits and grits with plenty of butter. By the way, do the same folks own this place that did five years ago?"

"Sure do! Same family has run this place for over forty years. Flora has passed on, but Miss Fanny comes in to yell at the cooks . . . 'least four times a week. Everything on the menu will taste just like it did last time you came 'round." The waitress was enjoying young Landry's preoccupation with her looks. "What about you, *young 'un*?" The inference was unavoidable, and the boy's face turned crimson. His eyes quickly dropped to the menu.

"I'll take three eggs over-easy, ham and gravy, toast, bacon, and can I get cheese in my grits?"

"Sure. Cookie will put anything you want in them." The waitress wrote notes on her order pad, turned theatrically and headed for the door to the kitchen. Landry watched as she walked away.

"Don't swallow your tongue, boy!" His father laughed. "She's playing with you." He paused, "Where were we?"

"Bummers did something."

"Yeah. Your Great-great-grandpa got wounded during a rear guard action at Lovejoy's Station a couple days after Sherman launched his march. That was around November 16th

or 17th. He was taken from the battlefield by buddies; they bandaged his wounds, brought him to here, and dropped him at the church. The pastor and his wife took him and others in and helped nurse them until they were strong enough to move on. Another wounded man was staying there and he became very good friends with your Great-great-grandpa."

"Were they both part of Wheeler's Cavalry?"

His father shook his head. "The other man was part of Hood's Quartermaster Corps. Hood had to leave part of his supplies behind. Hood gave orders for a detachment from that Corps to take what they could salvage and get it to Savannah. They burned the rest. Great-great-grandpa's friend was one of the officers who were in charge of doing that. He was supposed to report to General Hardee who was positioned on the coast." Landry senior paused to collect his thoughts. "Anyway, the preacher kept both of them hidden in the basement of the church. Dealing with the Union troops was a crap shoot. Some behaved well, took prisoners, respected women, and left the folks they raided with enough food to scrimp by on. Others . . . they killed every rebel soldier they came across, raped every woman they met, and stole or destroyed everything."

Landry senior interrupted his narration. Four men, obviously locals, entered the restaurant and stared at the two Dawes who were complete strangers, intruding into their rural domain. The Dawes would have done the same if the four entered their small hometown eatery in Eufaula. Strangers aroused curiosity in small communities; there was normally little else happening to be curious about. After they seated themselves, exchanged some words with the waitress, and she provided them with a newspaper, the men lost interest in gawking at the unknown visitors.

"And?" Landry Jr. brought his father back to the conversation.

"Oh, yeah . . . Anyway, the two of them were at the church for some weeks. They both began to heal, but Grandpa Dawes got well quicker. When it got time for your Great-great-grandpa to leave, he felt indebted to the preacher and wanted to know what he could do for him before he left. The pastor said at his age it was hard to get up on the church roof to paint the cross. He feared that if it didn't get a good coat of paint every five years it would rust away. Your Great-great-grandpa promised he, and all his descendants would keep that cross painted. He figured that was the least he could do for the preacher saving him from capture and probable death."

"Are ya'll the ones that paint the cross?" The girl had returned, her arms cradling the multiple plates containing their breakfast. It was her turn to show an amazed expression.

"Guilty," the senior Dawes answered.

"Oh, wow!" She looked surprised and excited. The waitress carefully, but quickly, placed the items in front of the father and son then hurried off to the table where the four men sat. Landry Sr. watched for a second as the men at the other table stared at he and his son while the girl spoke to them, gesturing wildly with her hands as she talked. He looked down at his breakfast. "Let's eat this before it gets cold.

Chapter 2

November 16, 1864

Landry Dawes opened his eyes. There was no difference. He was dead. Everything remained black. He wished his twenty-two years of life had been better spent, at least better spent in God's eyes. Hell. He would go there. Maybe he'd already arrived. Without thinking about it, he moved his leg. It responded. As rational thought crept back into his mind, he realized the weight of some object covered him, at least his upper body.

Landry tried to push what restrained him aside; his right arm responded, but his left screamed in pain and was incapable of movement. Searing waves swept over him followed by nausea. He groaned. Somewhere in another world he heard a familiar voice say, "Dawes is alive! Pull him out from under that horse."

He felt hands grab his cavalry boots while others relieved the weight pressing down on him. A voice said, "Now!" Immediately after people pulled on his legs, the excruciating pain in his arm was joined by an equally severe pain in his lower chest. Blackness remained as he passed out again.

* * *

When he woke again, it was because cold rain was drenching his bloody clothes and his tortured body. After a few seconds, he realized he was tied across a horse's back, bouncing up and down as it trotted, each jarring step sending shocks of pain through him. He moaned and opened his eyes. Some crude form of a splint held his left arm and it swung free. His right wrist had a rope tied around it and the hemp disappeared under the horse's belly. Red clay mud and water puddles relentlessly swung past. Someone next to him shouted, "This here one's a movin'. He ain't dead yet."

Another voice responded, "He ain't gonna make it to the coast. We'd best make for Hurley's place. They'll take care of him." After a few more steps, Landry fell back into peaceful, welcomed, unconsciousness.

* * *

"Bring water, Marian."

Landry tried opening his eyes. A blurred image bent over him. He was laying on his back on something soft. A bed! He smiled at the image as it came into clearer focus. Tall and gaunt faced, the man's concerned expression was reassuring in some strange manner. His clothes, there was something about his clothes. It wasn't a uniform. Dawes struggled with his confused brain . . . it came to him. "You're a preacher man," he rasped out. Through a strange flickering light, his surroundings were sharpening.

"Yes, you're right, son." The man wiped Landry's brow with a damp cloth. A woman appeared next to the man— she held a glass in her hand.

"I'll hold him up some. You help him drink." The preacher moved toward the head of the bed, placed his hands beneath Landry's shoulders and gently raised him from the mattress. Dawes saw the glass move. It touched his lips and the cool liquid felt good in his mouth. The woman's hands were careful not to allow too much to flow down his throat. She said, "Let me know when you've had enough." After a few more sips, Landry blinked and moved his head slightly.

The glass moved away as quickly and smoothly as it had appeared. Landry managed to say, "Thank you."

The man eased Landry back down to the bed's surface. He asked, "What's your name, son?"

"Landry Dawes."

"Where you from, Landry?"

"My folks have a farm outside of Montgomery, Alabama, sir." Landry's head was clearing and he was able to observe his benefactors and his surroundings more carefully. The preacher was a man in his fifties or more, tall with narrow shoulders, and he gave the appearance of being frail. His face was prune wrinkled, he had a full beard that shrouded much of his face and suspended a large pointed nose. Hazel eyes shone from deep sockets.

Landry assumed the woman called Marian was the preacher's wife. She had a soft, round face, with pale blue, wide-set eyes, its most remarkable features in an otherwise unexceptional countenance. Her short body was neither heavy nor light. The brown sack-style frock covered her in a manner that made it difficult to discern much about her figure. A sad-faced smile seemed permanently etched in place under her light brown hair.

It was then that Landry noticed the walls around his bed were red clay. The "ceiling" consisted of floor joists; he was in a cellar. He blinked a few times until his eyes found steps leading to an open trapdoor. The questions in his mind must have shown in his face, for the preacher quickly answered them. "Son, we have you down here so if a Yankee patrol comes by we can hide you. There have been several in the area. They don't all respect churches as sanctuaries. Our parishioners have told us some Union soldiers are shooting Confederate stragglers without benefit of question. And that also is true of those who assist them. So, you see, keeping you down here is for both your and our safety."

"I understand and thank you."

"I'm Reverend Marcus Hurley. This is my wife, Marian." The woman nodded and smiled wider.

"How did I get here, sir?"

"Men from your cavalry unit brought you to us. The trip to Savannah is a long one and there was concern they might be forced to fight their way through. One of them knew me and my wife. They asked us to see after you." Reverend Hurley stood erect, his head just inches from the wooden floor beams. "You are fortunate. The man who set your arm and saw to your wound was a doctor's assistant. The bullet passed through you and hit no vital area. You have lost a lot of blood, but the break in your arm isn't a bad one and the wound was cleaned and bandaged using liquor to keep it from putrefying. You should be on your feet in a day or two and ready to travel in a couple weeks. We'll get you some clothes and find out."

An excited female voice came through the trap door opening from somewhere above. "Missa Marian, deys folks a comin' on da road." After a few seconds of silence, the woman screamed, "Oh . . . Oh . . . Oh . . . Dey be da Yankee soldiers!"

The preacher nodded to his wife. She started up the stairs immediately. Hurley began extinguishing candles that Landry didn't notice until they lost their light. Before Hurley blew out the last one, he said in a low tone, "Don't worry." It was dark. The skinny frame of the pastor was silhouetted in the light coming from the trapdoor opening—until it closed and the world went black again.

***

November 20, 1864

"I think it's safe, sir." The corporal swayed in his saddle trying his best to keep his exhausted body on his horse.

Stephen McKenney hoped Corporal Evans was right. He was relying exclusively on the man's knowledge of the area to get them past Milledgeville. Georgia's state capitol was sure to be teeming with Yankees. There would be no way to get his wagon load of important materials, papers. . . and gold, through to Hardee at Savannah by parading down normally traveled roads. Union troops controlled them all. Sherman's Army moved faster than his commanding officer, Colonel Garren, said they could. Lieutenant McKenney was in charge of the valuable wagon of crucial goods because of that miscalculation. The Colonel Garren paid for his mistake with his life.

The five wagon column that left Atlanta November 13th packed with supplies was down to one; the sixty men assigned to guard it, reduced to seven. A day after Howard's Army of Tennessee brushed aside Wheeler's cavalry at Lovejoy Station, a reconnaissance group of Union cavalry caught up with the little column. In one of those small unit actions that fail to make history books, the sixty-man detachment fought valiantly as both sides fought to virtual annihilation. Fourteen confederates were left to continue. Colonel Garren was one of the first to die, as were seven of the mules pulling the wagons. In McKenney's opinion, the animals were the far greater loss.

The forty or so soldiers in the attacking Union patrol died to the man with the exception of three or four who fled at the first shedding of blood.

McKenney's inherited command had been reduced to two wagons, over-packed with what the Lieutenant deemed the most critical portion of the original load. Items abandoned were burnt. The column's remainder forged onward on the Milledgeville Road, going from the leisurely pace Colonel Garren had sponsored, to a break-neck race to the rear McKenney demanded. This proved almost as calamitous. The overloads and pace strained the poor mules up to, and past, the point of dying. One animal succumbed; one was left behind as it was more of a hindrance than use. The load was reduced to only the most essential of items, its size limited to something that their one remaining mule could pull without killing it. Smoke rose from the second pile of abandoned supplies when McKenny had left them.

"How close are they, Corporal?" McKenney asked.

"They's small patrols all 'round. I think we can sneak past them. But, I don't think there's any way a gettin' past Howard's or Slocum's columns. They's just too many of them."

"Can we get and keep in front of them and turn south?"

The corporal shook his head, "Ain't no way, sir. Even if you had two, no, four good mules, rested up and all, we couldn't. Howard's got men close to Macon. Goin' north ain't no better. General Kirkpatrick's across the Oconee River I hear tell from a farmer I talked to. That means they's ten to twenty miles out front of us on both sides. We're lucky they's keepin' to the main roads, mostly. We need to stay low and hope we can slip out behind them somehows."

"That's what we'll do, Corporal." Stephen watched his scout who was blinking his eyes to keep awake after forty-eight hours without sleep. The man would fall from the saddle fairly soon if he didn't get rest. Chances of getting away from the Union troops without his knowledge of the area would go from slim to none. McKenny had quickly learned to accept the little corporal's council. The six men he'd sent out, against the corporal's advice, to try to locate some element of the Confederate Army, met an undetermined fate, for five never returned. One had tried—they found his bullet-riddled corpse next to his horse on one of the back roads Evans was guiding them over. "Is there a place we can hide the wagon and get some rest? Maybe wait until they pass us completely? Someplace close?"

The corporal took a deep breath. "If'n we can get the wagon there, I know a good place a few miles from here. They's some real heavy woods over by Cotton Creek. Lots of pines are mixed in so's we can stick the wagon back in it. It's south of Eatonton and the main pike goin' through there, say six miles. I'm sure the Yankees are all over that road."

"Okay, you can take us to the spot you said we can hide, Evans." McKenney looked at the heavily wooded crest of a hill where they had stopped. "It's only an hour or two until dark, let's wait. Get some rest."

"You sure, sir?"

McKenney knew what Evans was concerned about. The last time everyone had slept, one soldier had walked off, deserted, reducing their numbers to seven. "I'll stay awake,

Corporal. Besides, this spot gives us a little cover to keep from being seen and, at least, it's possible to defend." He called out to the rest of his men, "Dismount and get a little rest. We're moving after dark."

The men swung out of their saddles wearily and without comment. They were demoralized, tired . . . ready to go home. They'd seen enough dead men and burnt houses. There was little to keep them with him. That little thing was honor.

***

November 21, 1864

Cold rain, accompanied by a biting wind, came with darkness. Though it made them all miserable, Stephen knew it reduced the probability of meeting Union patrols. The rules of war declared the winners sheltered and slept in such weather; the losers shivered and slithered away. As an added precaution, Lieutenant McKenney waited until after midnight to start his little troop to the hiding spot Evans had spoken about. After getting four hours sleep before the puddle building up around Evans woke him, the man seemed completely revitalized. As they began moving, and before the corporal rode off to scout the way, he was confident and optimistic. Though McKenney had managed only a couple hours sleep after Evans awoke and stood watch, he felt amazingly refreshed.

The last thing Evans said after he gave Stephen directions and before he galloped off was that it shouldn't take more than two hours to get to the spot. He said he would check back every little while to keep his lieutenant apprised of what was ahead. After a half-hour he returned, still smiling and up-beat.

The wagon creaked along in the steady rain without problems. When Evans raced up the second time, everything had changed.

He snapped off a quick salute to McKenney and blurted out, "Sir, they's about thirty Yankees camped out on the trail up ahead. Less 'an a half-mile, I'd say."

"Damn!" The lieutenant looked around. There was an open field on one side of the road where the wagon stood and scattered woods on the other. "Is there any way to get around them?"

"No good way. We'd have to go back a spell an it'd add five, maybe six miles, and I ain't been over that way. It might be crawlin' with Blue Bellies, too." He shrugged his shoulders. "The best bet we got is to go on. They's another wagon trail up about 400 yards short from that Yankee camp. With it a raining and all, we might sneak up and get on it. That would actually be shorter, but it ain't hardly passable."

McKenney didn't hesitate, "Let's get moving forward, Corporal." The rest of the men had gathered around the wagon. Stephen looked at them and said, "Men, stay as quiet as you've ever been, if you want to live." He jiggled the reins and the wagon started forward.

***

Evans waited just below the crest of a small hill. He motioned them forward with a frantic circling of his arm. As the wagon got close enough to the top of the rise, Stephen could see a couple ruts leading off to the left. That had to be the trail Evans spoke of, for he could see tents and a sheltered campfire a few hundred yards further down the road. Evans confirmed the ruts were the new route when he pointed to them. As McKenney passed him, Evans whispered, "The sentry's asleep." When the wagon reached the turn-off and Stephen tried to guide the mule on to the side-trail, the animal balked. It stood stubbornly after only going several feet down the road. McKenney tried whistling and ordering the animal as loudly as he dared. The mule wouldn't move.

The lieutenant knew the breed well, for his father had twelve on their farm in Virginia. He tied the reins to the wagon seat, jumped down to the ground and quickly trotted to the mule's head. He removed his jacket and covered the animal's eyes, grabbed the mule's halter and said, "Yoooo, mule." The animal started forward, trusting that its master would lead it to safety. Walking would slow them down, but there was no other choice. Evans rode up and said in a gassy whisper, "Sir, this here goes back to the main road in a ways. The road makes a sharp turn and this makes like a triangle short cut. Where it comes out is almost at the spot I'm a gonna hide us."

"Good, Evans. You stay behind, get out of sight. Be sure they didn't spot us. After we're in those woods far enough we can't be seen, you come, hear?"

"Yes, sir." Evans led his horse to the roadside behind a copse of trees.

McKenney tugged on the halter and walked as fast as he could convince the mule to move. The ruts were not as bad of a road as Stephen had visualized based on Evans remarks. It hugged the top of the hill's ridge and led toward the woods. He glanced at the Yankee camp. If a Union soldier looked at the hill, the wagon and his small troop would be silhouetted against the gray sky. However, no movement or alarm came from the soaked white canvas tents. The first trees on the heavily forested hill side were still seventy yards away. It seemed as though it was taking forever to get to its curtain, a curtain that would obscure them from the Union troops' vision. Fifty yards—forty yards—thirty yards, the camp remained still. Twenty yards. Ten yards. Stephen believed for the first time they'd make it. He led the mule behind the trees on the woods' fringe. When he did, the trail suddenly became narrower and dropped at a severe angle. He was descending into a low area, either a bog or a creek run. McKenney looked back at the wagon. It was pushing against the traces causing the mule to stride awkwardly in the increasingly soft, slick red clay.

They struggled downward. The trail made a sharp curve along the hill side causing the wagon to slide sideways. Stephen held his breath, but the wheels gripped the soil enough to avoid a disaster. He weaved along the hillside for fifteen minutes, each minute his concern about his enemies lessened and his fears that the trail would become impassible increased. The five men who rode their horses with him saw their mounts hooves slip in the slop. Around another bend, a young pine had toppled across the trail. Though only four inches in diameter, the heavy woods on either side meant that the mule would have to step across the fallen timber and pull the wagon over it. The slope would make crossing that sapling precarious at best.

"Okay, mule, you need to see where you're going to get over this. Don't do anything crazy when I take my coat off of your head." Stephen positioned the animal in front of the log. He slowly lifted the garment from over the animal's eyes. The mule's pupils had a wild look in them, but it stayed still and seemed to settle down. McKenney stared at the pine. Would it be possible to move it? He was about to have his men dismount to try pulling it out of the way when Evans trotted up.

"Hey, Lieutenant," Evans saluted as he spoke, "Those Yankees are saddlin' up. About half of them. They didn't look to be in no hurry, but we best move on . . . *fast*."

That made up McKenney's mind. "Corporal, go get on the mules nose and lead him." Rest of you, except Wilson, get down and help me get this thing across this pine. Wilson, ride back up the trail a couple turns and watch for Yanks."

Evans walked the mule forward, the animal stepping over the log nervously, but without balking. As the wagon wheels approached the pine, McKenney yelled, "Stop." He motioned to his dismounted men. "All of you on the downhill side with me. When the wheels get to the tree, lift and push."

Stephen positioned himself at the front edge of the wagon, his men standing behind him, all preparing to strain their backs to get the wagon over the impediment. "Okay, Corporal, move him!" The wagon lurched forward, jarred against the tree, and crept upward. McKenney leaped forward in front of the wagon and said as loudly as he dared, "Everybody, *now*!" Groans from the men accompanied the wagon's upward thrust. It came across hard and fast, knocking Stephen to the side and to the ground. He felt tendons tear as his knee was forced backwards. The lieutenant tumbled out of the way and watched helplessly as the wagon's rear wheels rode up and over and the front wheels turned. The wagon rolled onto its side, spilling its contents on the ground.

When McKenney tried to stand, he found his knee wouldn't support his weight. As far as he could see, all his men escaped injury but him. He immediately knew what he must do. Corporal Evans was beside him in an instant, helping support him.

"I saw what happened, Lieutenant. Sit here and I'll find something to help support you." Evans helped him back to the ground. Within seconds, he returned, pulling his belt from his pants and carrying two inch thick limbs that were approximately three feet long. He said, "Give me your belt, sir." Within moments, Evans had fashioned a brace on McKenney's leg.

"We can pull the wagon over with the horses, sir."

"We don't have time, Evans. If we did get it over, it'll take a couple hours to fix that," he pointed to a wheel lying, detached, on the ground, "And a couple more to gather things up and reload it. You help me over there. I'll tell you what I want you to take to Savannah."

"What do you mean?" Evans said nervously. "No, I ain't leavin' you here."

"Yes, Corporal you are, 'cause those are going to be my orders to you." McKenney nodded his head toward the spilled pile of material next to the rolled-over wagon. "Get me over there. I'll tell you what I want you to try to get to Hardee."

***

Lieutenant Stephen McKenney was resigned to spending the rest of the war in a Union prison or being killed. He didn't have a preference. After instructing what packages and packets were to be carried via horseback and assigning them to the individuals that would go with Evans, there remained two very large, very heavy boxes. The corporal asked, "What do we do with those, Lieutenant McKenney?"

The officer scanned the area until he saw a bramble thicket 150 feet uphill in the heavy woods. "You and the men move them up there and hide them the best you can." He watched Evans and the others struggle with the weight of the steel bound boxes. They disappeared behind the brush. Within minutes they returned with Evans following behind, trying to erase any trace of their walk up the hill.

Evans walked back to McKenney carrying a stick that was five feet long. "You sure about this, sir," he said. He handed the walking stick/crutch to Stephen. "Want me to put a blanket on the mule?"

"No, that poor animal is so lame from the spill it ought to be shot. Just leave it wander. We can't take a chance on the noise."

"We can ride double."

"No, Corporal. That would just make it sure that two of us didn't get there instead of one. You ride back and get Wilson. Then ride like hell."

"I done sent Bernard back for Wilson. They gonna meet us at Griswoldville. There's a small garrison there. Wilson knows the area and says he knows how to get into the town's defenses."

Stephen wrapped his arm around the stick and took a step. The "crutch" allowed him to keep enough weight off his leg to hobble along. He said, "It'll work."

"Lieutenant, there's a place for you to go. You keep a headin' down this here trail. Look over top of the woods to the right. When it gets light, you look for a white cross a stickin' up on a steeple above them trees. You go to that. The reverend will take you in. He's a real good man. It ain't that far. You might want to go a distance and hide until light. You look for that there cross."

McKenney nodded. "I'll do that. Now, Evans you get moving. Darkness is your friend. Good luck."

Evans stiffened and saluted, "God be with you, sir." He rode off with the four men that remained of the sixty. Stephen was alone. When they were out of sight, he went to the upset wagon and sat on a portion of it. After surveying the area around him for a hiding place and considering how difficult it would be to move around with only one functional leg, he spit and said, "Ain't no way." If the Blue Bellies caught him before light, they caught him. He'd wait where he was until the sun came up. As he tried to make himself comfortable, the rain abated. Stephen mumbled, "Maybe, just maybe."

Chapter 3

First Light, November 21, 1864

A shot of pain woke Stephen McKenney. An awkward movement twisted his knee and it protested vehemently. Light was beginning to stream through the pines and naked deciduous trees. McKenney went from semi-conscious to hyper-alert. Where were the Yankees? Nowhere! Union troops hadn't followed them after all.

It took a few minutes to organize his thoughts. Evans mentioned a church where he might find help. Down the trail . . . look for a cross . . . yes, he remembered. He moved and his knee screamed, "No!" Where was the tree limb Evans had given him? The walking stick had fallen next to him, but was within reach. He took a few minutes to muster his resolve for he knew what was coming. Picking up the stick caused him to move his knee, the pain nauseated him.

Anger coursed through him. Dumb, it was so dumb to have stood in front of that wagon. He cursed, strained and pulled up on the wagon and stood leaning against it. The knee throbbed within seconds. It increased as he thought about what was next. Stephen knew his attempt to find the church would be a painful one. After several seconds postponing the pain he knew he'd experience, he took the first step. It was as excruciating as he expected. He hobbled another step. And another. Maybe he was getting used to the pain, but it didn't seem it was as bad as the first. He improved his grip on the walking stick, took a deep breath and started down the trail. After every three or four steps he glanced at the tree line hoping to see the steeple and cross. It was clear the pain wasn't going to abate but so much. He needed a positive to grasp. Steven thought, *At least the Yankees weren't hauling me off to Libby Prison.*

He'd traveled a quarter of a mile when one of his searches above the tree tops disclosed a smear of white through the branches. Another twenty paces and he could see the cross elevated above the tree-line. It sat on bricks that must be the steeple of the church Evans told him about. He decided to leave the trail and walk straight toward it.

***

Landry asked, "Mrs. Hurley, can't I do something to help?" Dawes was used to working hard, doing his share. Being a patient didn't fit his behavior pattern. His wound and arm were healing and he was ready to do something to earn his keep.

"The good Lord knows I appreciate you constantly asking to help, but you need to heal, young man." Marian cut slices off the ham sitting on the table in front of her.

"Please let me do something."

Mrs. Hurley saw the exasperated look on Landry's face. She tapped her knife on the table. Marian looked at the splint on his arm and the spot on his shirt that covered his bandaged wound. "I guess you could fetch a few little pieces of wood from behind the house. Now . . . you be sure you just bring three or four *small* pieces in. They're for the stove and cooking. Don't you dare pick up that go devil and try splitting kindling. Promise!"

"Yes, ma'am." Dawes beamed. He felt the first few drops of guilt drain away.

***

Landry whistled as he walked to the piles of firewood that heated the rectory and provided fuel for the cooking stove, a stove that was Marian Hurley's most prized possession. Last night's rain had disappeared and the cold breeze that followed the front took its place. Dawes wore a long sleeve shirt and trousers donated by a parishioner, his uniform having been discarded as an unnecessary danger. The forty-degree temperature chilled him, but he didn't mind a bit. He wanted to make use of every opportunity to repay the Hurleys for taking care of him and sharing their meager food supply.

Landry surveyed the 200 feet to the back edge of the cleared area behind the church. It sloped upward, shedding the previous night's rain. Cotton Creek didn't gurgle its usual greeting. The overnight run-off had swollen it to the top of its banks and its waters produced a gentle roar. He glanced at Cotton Creek Road which separated the creek from church property. According to the preacher, many Sunday churchgoers parked their buggies and tethered their horses in the low bottom between the creek and road. He hoped that it wouldn't flood. The church's front yard was small, so the selection was as much from necessity as choice.

Landry shouted, "It's gonna be a beautiful day." No one was there to answer, but it had to be said. He looked back toward the west. The sky was clear, a light blue unmarred by the few clouds that were disappearing to the east. Early morning sunrays shone against the red brick wall of the church, its stained glass windows, and the buildings two unique features: stained glass skylights and the huge white cross perched high above on a steeple constructed of a four foot square solid column of bricks. The skylights were to, "Allow the light and truth of the Lord to shine on his people," a fact which Pastor Hurley was fond of pointing out. When the church had been constructed fifteen years before, its builders declared the reason to make the steeple and cross so sturdy was to make them as indestructible as the church's message. That was why they placed a huge steel cross on top instead of the usual wooden structure. The symbol was designed to be there in perpetuity. It towered high above the trees in the surrounding heavy woods.

Landry reached the stacks of wood, determined to resupply Mrs. Hurley's needs for kindling for a couple days. There were dozens of pieces that would easily fit in the stove and form good cooking embers. The splint on his left arm would serve as a good cradle for the kindling. He selected pieces of oak, turning his nose up at faster burning red gum and poplar. Landry was intent on picking the best pieces of stove wood, temporarily forgetting his circum-stances as an enemy combatant behind his opponent's lines. A noise in the woods somewhere behind the stacks of firewood reminded him with the force of a cherry-red poker applied to his flesh.

He froze, turning only his head ever so slowly to stare into the maze of tree trunks. The leaf covered ground and the late fall die-back of underbrush made looking for its source much less difficult than if it had been summer. Only a few patches of olive drab and pine green remained on the slope behind the church. His deer hunting eyes detected nothing, but he remained motionless. His ears told him the creature, four or two legged, was almost directly behind him. He determined it must be hiding behind one of several large tree trunks or was lying in a patch of blackberry vines that formed a tan hump sixty feet back into the woods. That was if his imagination wasn't playing tricks on him.

Clinging to the half-dozen sticks of kindling, he took several strides in each direction trying to get a better angle to see behind the trees. Subconsciously, he grasped one club sized piece of wood, just in case. Though Landry strained his eyes, he could see no trace of any animal, not even one of the squirrels that frequented the woods. He returned to the pile of kindling and resumed his selection process, but with a heightened awareness of happenings around him.

Landry had added a couple more sticks to his arm-load when a crashing in the underbrush electrified him. He looked up in time to see something crash downward into the blackberry vines. Moans came from whoever it was, for it was most certainly human. Dropping his load of wood, and readying his club, he carefully approached the tangle of vines. As he neared, he heard the moan again and saw a man dressed in a Confederate officer's uniform. A crude splint was attached to one of his legs, a leg whose knee was swollen to the point of bursting the gray fabric around it. The officer lay face down in the thorny vines. Landry tossed away the club.

Dawes grabbed the man's shoulder with his good arm and gently turn the man over, cringing as the needlelike thorns tore at the man's flesh on his face and neck. The man's blue eyes were open, and he blinked at Landry. The officer's expression was more of curiosity than filled with pain or fear. Dawes realized he couldn't free the man from the blackberry vines, lift him, and get him back to the church. "I'll be back with help," Landry said and took a step away. He remembered he was still a member of the Confederate States Army. He turned, saluted, and added, "Sir," then trotted to the rectory for help.

***

"I don't think it's broken," Marcus Hurley said as he gently moved the knee.

"Aaaaaaah," Stephen McKenney groaned, stiffened his leg, and pinched his eyes shut.

Hurley shook his head. The knee cap was on the side of the young lieutenant's leg. The swelling, blue, purple and black colors gave evidence of massive internal damage and bleeding. There was little he could do with his limited medical knowledge. He doubted the man would ever walk without the assistance of crutches or a cane. Hurley shook his head again. What to do? Should he move the knee cap back into position? Would that help more than it would hurt? Though it didn't appear there was a broken bone, he couldn't be sure. What to do! Hurley spoke to himself as well as the man. "You need professional medical help. That's a bad knee. A bad . . . *bad* knee. But, if I go get a doctor to look at your leg, I can't be sure that he won't turn you into the Yankees, Lieutenant. There have been orders issued that no civilians are to harbor Confederate Troops. We're supposed to report you. Of course, I won't. But, I can't promise a doctor wouldn't."

"You can trust what he says, Lieutenant." Landry Dawes looked down at the man lying in what had previously been his bed. He was flanked by Marian and Louise, one of the Hurley's three black servants. But, not slaves.

Landry remembered how adamant Marcus Hurley was when he said he didn't believe in slavery. He was a man of the cloth. He couldn't understand how any man of the cloth could own slaves. He couldn't understand how any *Christian* could own slaves, for that matter. Hurley stopped short of audibly doubting the sincerity of others professed faith, but not by much. He'd acquired the blacks because of severe injustices reported to him. After he purchased the slaves, he promptly set them free. Four had chosen to go North; three remained with him. Hurley, the son of a wealthy Charleston merchant, was not without financial means.

"I'd prefer not to go to a Union prison, Reverend." McKenny shifted slightly and winced in pain. "If you think you can do something for me, I'd rather try that." His words brought Landry back from his thoughts.

Marcus looked at the leg and took a deep breath. As he stared at the leg, he said, "Louise, go get Samuel." The girl practically ran up the cellar steps.

"Sorry, but you'll have to stay down here. There aren't quite as many soldiers passing by since the Yankees have moved toward the coast, but there's enough still going up and down the road that it isn't safe for you to be out since you can't walk." Hurley realized how that sounded and quickly revised it to, "That's until you can move on your own."

Louise returned bringing a tall, thin black man with white hair and features that spoke of his many years. Hurley said, "This is Samuel. He's the best veterinarian in five counties. He took care of all the animals on the largest plantation in these parts for thirty years. He's patched up many a field hand. He can do more than I can. Samuel, will you see what you can do for this man?"

"Yessa, I sure'll do my best. Let me take a good look." The old man bent over the leg. Within a few seconds he whistled. "You done bent dat knee backwards, didn't ya?"

"That's pretty much what happened," Stephen said.

Samuel probed the swollen flesh with his fingers, bringing moans, groans, and low curses from Stephen while he flinched in pain as the examination progressed.

"Hain't good. I cain't lie 'bout dat." The black man stared at the knee. "Don't got no broke bones, I think. But everything in dat joint a holdin' them bones agether is messed up." Samuel looked in McKenney's eyes. "I got to get it back like its s'posed to be, knee cap and all, but it's gonna hurt like Hell fire."

"Do it," McKenney said.

"Does you have any a da devil's water, Reverend?" Samuel asked.

"Whiskey?"

Samuel nodded.

"No, but I can get some quickly."

"It a save him a heap of hurtin'." Samuel grinned, "I knows where there might be a little while you's getting' dat other." He went to the stairs. "Be back, right fast."

***

McKenney consumed enough rum and vile corn moonshine that he passed out. Even in his intoxicated state, the pain of having the knee cap moved back into its proper position snapped him from his stupor, while Dawes, Hurley, and the two women held the lieutenant as immobile as possible. Within a few minutes, the liquor did its part and Stephen lapsed back into unconsciousness. The women made trips back and forth to Cotton Creek for its cold water to be used in compresses to reduce the swelling. Eventually, hours of effort took effect. When the swelling was reduced as much as circumstance would allow, Samuel made a cast by wrapping wet newspapers around the knee, placing a coat of flour paste over the paper, and repeating the process until a half-inch cylinder encased the damaged knee.

Each time the lieutenant began to show signs of sobering, Reverend Hurley or Samuel would force enough liquor into him to prolong his stupor. It took a day and a half for the cast to cure and Stephen was kept in a state the most drunken sailor would envy during the process.

When McKenney woke up, it was on the third morning he'd been stashed in the church basement. His eyes fluttered open, he saw the man who had discovered him lying in the blackberry patch. Stephen's head began pounding, heralding a monumental hangover. The one called Dawes was whittling on a piece of wood. When he twisted in bed to get a better view of what the man was working on, his knee objected. Stephen murmured, "Uhhhhhhhh."

Landry looked at McKenney, smiled, and called to someone in the church, "He's awake. Tell Mrs. Hurley." Dawes laid down the crutch top on which he was working. He nodded his head in the direction of McKenney's knee. "That thing still painin' you a lot?"

Stephen looked down at the blankets covering his body. His eyes widened when he realized he was naked under the patchwork quilt. He asked, "Where's my clothes?"

"I don't know. The women folk did something with them when we stripped you. I wouldn't worry on it. The trousers aren't much anymore. We had to cut most of the left leg away to get at the knee. Besides, you're kinda big and heftin' you around wasn't easy for any of us, me with an arm that isn't right and the women being so much littler than you."

The question was in the lieutenant's eyes.

"A body has to do what a body has to do." Dawes laughed.

McKenney's face turned a brilliant red.

"Reckon we didn't get proper introduced when we pulled you out of those blackberry bushes. I'm plum sorry for cuttin' you up so when I turned you over, but those scratches are healing good. Anyway, my name is Landry Dawes out of Alabama. It's a long story, but I ended up in Wheeler's cavalry." He stopped to snap an informal salute. "I'm a private and I know you're an officer and all . . . but things being how they are . . . well, I don't mean no disrespect."

"None taken, Dawes. What part of Alabama?"

"Waters Corners. That's about fifty miles south of Montgomery. It's just a spot where two dirt roads cross. My Pap has a farm there. Ain't much, but I love it. I'd break my other arm if'n I could go to sleep and wake up there tomorrow."

"I know how you feel. Stephen McKenney. I live in Virginia, in the Shenandoah. Down the river, between Haymarket and Woodstock. It's a beautiful place." Stephen's face clouded. "There's been a lot of fighting around our place. The Yankees marched across it at least once. They got whipped by a bunch of VMI cadets. I get letters from my mother. She doesn't say, but I think something bad happened.

She doesn't write as much since my little brother was killed at Gettysburg. She . . ."

"It's good to see you awake." Marian Hurley was carrying a tray as she hiked her skirts enough to keep from tripping on the cellar steps, but not so high they could see her ankles. She carried plates with eggs, bacon, corn bread, and grits. A steaming cup of coffee was nestled in between. "Let's get some food in you instead of that horrible liquor."

Chapter 4

November 28, 1864

"Reverend Hurley, that was sure a mighty fine sermon yesterday," Landry Dawes said. His arm had healed enough to allow him to use a broom and he swept the church floor daily as part payment for his self-imposed debt.

Marcus Hurley took time out from putting another coat of varnish on the pews. "Thank you, Landry. A preacher always hopes he'll be heard."

"It's a darned shame you didn't have Lincoln and Jeff Davis a listenin' to you. We'd end this thing. Turn those swords into plow shares like you was sayin'. I'd be back to Alabama and huntin' deer instead of huntin' my fellow man, right soon."

Hurley dipped his brush in the bucket, rubbed the bristles on its side, but hesitated before he placed another stroke on the seat. "It isn't that easy, I'm afraid. It's gone too far. There will be untold pain and agony before this is over. Even more than there's been so far. When hate becomes so firmly entrenched and when the peoples' leaders become part of it, the end is bad, indeed."

"Well, those were powerful words. I'd have to believe they'd a had hard time a walkin' out of the door and away from the cross on top of this buildin' without finding a way to end this war." Dawes stopped swishing the corn broom over the floor.

"Thank you for your belief in God, for He's the one that makes it happen." Hurley finished stroking the brush over the seat, straightened, placed the brush in the paint can, and arched his back. "I'm afraid my knees and back aren't made for this part of the Lord's work."

"I can do that just fine. I'll finish this later." Dawes leaned his broom against a pew and walked over to the row where Marcus was kneeling. "Ain't no call, you doin' that." He extended the hand not hampered by the cast to Hurley.

The preacher grinned and took Dawes hand. "Okay." Landry helped him to his feet. "Thank you," Hurley said, adding, "You and Stephen are doing your best to spoil Marian and me. The two of you try to do everything. When you leave, we won't know what to do. You need to let us toil for our own good."

"Reverend, while I'm here, let my twenty-two-year-old knees do what your sixty-year-old knees can't, so you can use your sixty-year-old brain to think of things that my twenty-two-year-old brain doesn't."

"Okay, Landry, but you don't have to try to do everything."

Landry's face became serious, "Reverend Hurley, tell me one thing you cain't do, one that's important to you, I'll do it."

Marcus Hurley realized that it was more important for Landry Dawes' soul to do something for the church than he visualized it would be for the brick building they stood in. He thought for several seconds, then said, "There is one thing. Samuel and my old legs have a hard time with heights. The cross on top of this building is very difficult for us to paint. If you could do that before you leave us, I would be very thankful."

"How often does it need to be painted?"

"If you paint it, it will be five years before it needs it again."

"Reverend Hurley, before I leave you, I'll paint that cross. And, I'll tell you what's more: *For as long as the cross stands over its steeple—me and mine will come here and paint it every five years.*"

"Hush," the Reverend said sternly. "Our Father says for us not to swear oaths."

Landry looked at him evenly. "I ain't swearin'. I'm just *sayin'*."

***

"Mista McKenney, they's a bunch a bad folks a runnin' 'round here. Scallywags and Scavengers and Bummers. Some's of 'um is jist bad men. They done killed all the peoples over to the Barker's Plantation." Samuel shook his head. "The Mista, his Missus, an all five of his chillin. All the field hands and the house folk, killed them too. Stole everything there then burnt anything left, house, barns, even the pole sheds."

"Doesn't the Union Army do anything to stop it?" Stephen heard story after story of the horrible terror spreading across the Georgia countryside. He stopped shelling corn. McKenney looked at the road running in front of the church from where they were seated on the rectory's front porch. He'd seen the rag-tag ruffians cruising the red clay, their horses' hooves carving evil into every place they rode.

"No, suh. They's tellin' everybody we brought it on ourselves. They ain't liftin' a finger to stop it." Samuel shook his head sadly. "A bunch of 'um is black folk gone bad. I heerd they burnt down three churches over to Milledgeville. Killed everybody, too."

Stephen felt anger building. He asked, "Samuel, do you know where my gun and sword are?"

"Uh-huh."

"Can you get them and put them in the cellar by my bed?"

Samuel nodded.

***

"Mrs. Hurley, the corn's all shelled. It's in a sack on the porch." Stephen hobbled across the kitchen floor on his crutch, making staccato taps as he walked.

"Thank you, Lieutenant McKenney." Marian continued fussing with some mason jars, cleaning them and storing them for reuse next year. She glanced at him then quickly took a second look. "You're moving much better. Is the knee starting to heal?"

"It hurts less. It doesn't take much weight, though. I wouldn't be able to get around if it wasn't for this thing Dawes made for me." He waved the crutch in the air.

"I hope it gets stronger soon." She smiled and went back to cleaning jars. McKenney loitered, looking for the right words to approach Mrs. Hurley. Marian sensed something was bothering her guest. "Did you want something? Maybe a piece of corn bread? There's some in the box on the counter."

"No, ma'am. But thank you, anyway." He saw the questioning look on her face. "I just . . . well, Samuel told me that there are groups raiding plantations and churches. I'm concerned for you and the Reverend. Landry and my presence here puts you in more danger than if we weren't. I think we should move on."

"Now, how long do you think you two would last out on the roads? The Yankees would pick you up quicker than a cat would pounce on a one-legged mouse. You boys should stay here until you have a decent chance to evade the Yankees."

"Mrs. Hurley, if anything were to happen to you and your husband because of me being here, I don't think I could live with myself."

Marian put the wash rag in the wash tub, turned, and leaned against the work table. "I'm not the person to talk to about this. You should talk to Marcus. See what he has to say."

***

"What if they come? What are we gonna do, Stephen? You say we should go. I don't think you can right now." Landry sat on a chair next to McKenney in the little cellar. "The last thing I want to do is endanger the Hurleys, but will they really be safer if we leave? From what I hear tell, the scavenger groups don't need no reason. They're thieves and murderers. Most of them are groups of deserters and outlaws. They ain't anything to do with the Blue Bellies. If they come here, we could help defend the Hurleys. Marcus and Samuel cain't do nothing."

Flickering light from the lone candle cast eerie shadows on the two men's faces. McKenney shook his head, "Landry, that's the valiant thing to do, but foolish. What can we do against ten to fifteen well-armed men? We don't have enough weapons. Even if we did, we might get lucky and kill *half* of them. That will just make them furious and certain they'll kill everyone here."

"That don't change things. First, you can't go yet. That leg wouldn't let you go ten miles on foot. If you *was* to get a horse, how'd you get on or off? And, we both know all we can really do is pray the Hurleys will be okay. There ain't any way to know if'n the bummers will come here. The Hurleys have nice stuff, preachin' folk or not. Sooner or later those vultures will get wind of it. You know what's gonna happen. Honest, I'd rather be here to *try* to protect them."

The lieutenant sat quietly for several seconds. He sighed and looked straight into Dawes' eyes. "I have another reason for leaving. Landry, I trust you, and I need your help on this. There is something I have to get back to Hardee or whoever is commanding our troops. My leg isn't healing like I hoped. Will you help?"

"Yes."

"Tomorrow, I'm going to give you some directions to go to the woods where the wagon overturned. I told you that much. There are two boxes I had the men hide. I want you to see if they're still there." He paused and said in a low voice, "Landry, half of Hood's funds for supplying his army's troops are in them. Most of its gold, not Confederate bills. If it's still there, I've got to try to get it to Hardee."

"Ohhhh, shit!" Landry turned pale.

***

The directions McKenney gave Dawes were excellent. Landry was able to walk to the site in less than fifteen minutes in the next morning's fresh, cold air. The wagon was turned over, three of its wheels pointing to the sky, the fourth lying at its side, but the supplies that McKenney said he'd find were gone. Parts were missing from the wagon; enough to make its use impossible. Someone had chopped up and removed the pine tree, opening the trail. There was little evidence of traffic other than that. There weren't any wagon tracks and few hoof prints.

Landry positioned himself where McKenney had instructed him to stand; at the front corner of the wagon. He looked up the hill. Though there were a number of thickets scattered in the woods, the one Stephen had described was obvious. Dawes walked up the hill, climbing over fallen timber and avoiding thick patches of dried weeds. When he walked behind the thicket, he didn't see the boxes until he took a second look. Corporal Evans had done an excellent job hiding the cache. He'd sprinkled brown fallen leaves over the boxes, placed a fallen limb over them, finally put a sprinkling of dried weeds on top. Landry carefully removed the camouflage so he could recover the cargo. Dawes tried lifting one by a handle on its side. He could barely budge it.

Landry straightened up and whistled. It would take three strong men, maybe more, to move it. The good news was it was still there, the bad; it was likely to stay . . .unless . . . He thought about the burlap sacks stashed in the cellar. It would take a lot of trips, but he could carry a little at a time. Eventually, he'd be able to get it back to the church. He replaced the camouflage and started down the hill. Dawes was half-way down when he heard a noise in the woods behind him. He stooped over, moved behind some tall weeds, and slowly turned to apprehensively look up the hill.

Dawes sighed with relief. The noise was from a mule wandering down the hill toward him. Probably the one Stephen said was pulling the wagon. The animal spotted him and quickened its pace. It had "CSA" branded on its side. It was happy to see him and was looking to be fed. The halter was still in place. With the mule carrying the loads, it would greatly reduce the time the transfer would take. Landry saw this bit of good fortune as an omen. He looked skyward and said, "Thank you, Lord."

***

"That's the last of it," Landry said.

McKenney and Reverend Hurley looked at the two foot high stack of burlap sacks. Hurley and Stephen were covering the pile with additional empties. Soon the three quarters of a million dollars in the bags below were covered with a thick layer of tan-brown cloth.

"Reverend, I promise I'll have this out of here as soon as possible." Stephen hobbled over to the chair that served as the only furniture in the tiny cellar. He winced as he sat down while placing his crutch on the bed.

"I understand the need for this . . ." Hurley's voice trailed off. He didn't look happy.

"Soon, I promise." The lieutenant realized the responsibility he was asking the others to share. He just didn't feel he had a choice.

***

The swelling in Stephen's knee had decreased to the point the cast was not providing the support required for healing without risk of reinjury. Samuel and Marcus removed the old one. "If'n you was a horse, you'd done been shot," the old black man said as he shook his head. True, the swelling had greatly reduced. Now, the severe nature of the injury was much more apparent.

"They's not a heap I's can do. Sep makin' it stiff as it can be." He left and soon returned with a handful of thin slivers of wood about a foot long. "I be a hopin' this works."

He began dipping the newspapers in a bucket of water while Reverend Hurley added ingredients and stirred the flour paste to the right consistency in another bucket. Samuel began the careful build-up of the cast. When the project was half complete, he skillfully placed the wood in the cast to reinforce and take pressure off the knee. When he finished the cast it was a half again as thick as its predecessor. He looked at it and nodded. "Dis works with horses an' cows. I sho hope it helps you." He stood and moved the left-over material to one corner of the cellar. "You's need to keep sittin' resta da day. Maybe da next day."

"I will. Thank you very much, Samuel." McKenney adjusted his body to get more comfortable without endangering his newly minted cast.

Samuel beamed and said, "You's welcome. I gotta go help Missa Hurley, now." He disappeared up the cellar stairs leaving Stephen and Marcus alone. Hurley gathered the sack of flour and bucket and started to leave.

"Can you stay for a moment?" Stephen asked.

"Sure, Lieutenant." Hurley returned to stand next to Stephen. "How may I help you?"

"You've helped me far too much already, Reverend. I feel I've put you in danger by just being here. This," he pointed to the pile of bags, "just compounds it. I talked to your wife about leaving. She said I should talk to you."

"Isn't it obvious you can't leave? Besides, I don't believe that your presence here puts us in additional danger. If the

Union people knew you had stopped here we'd be in trouble, it's too late for avoiding that, but they don't know and won't. As far as the outlaw groups roving around, your being here doesn't mean a thing . . . one way or the other. They just want to rob and kill. And, even so, I'd still insist you stay here."

McKenney took a deep breath. "I was talking to Dawes. He said he's coming back to paint the cross on top of the steeple every five years. I want to do something like that for you. What can I do? What would you really want of me?"

Reverend Hurley sat down in the chair next to the bed. He sighed. "You're determined?"

"Yes, with all my spirit."

After remaining silent for several seconds, the reverend said, "I'm going to ask something that may be very hard for you to do, Lieutenant."

When Hurley hesitated, McKenney prompted, "I'll do anything."

Marcus' sad smile spoke as definitively as his words. "Some things that may seem very easy can become very hard, and I fear I'm going to ask one of those from you. You are a fine man, Lieutenant. You're honest, high-minded, and honorable. So, what I'm going to ask you may trouble you. This war is over. The Confederate leaders haven't acknowledged that, I don't know if they realize it or not, but it is. I see the death of more men, the foolish destruction of property, the prolonging of the southern people's agony, when the South can no longer win, as sins. I will ask that you no longer lead men in battle, that you'll never kill another man. No matter what the situation, no matter whether you perceive your honor will be lost, no matter how threatened you or those around you are—that may be very hard."

Stephen sat silently, thinking about the words Hurley spoke. He looked down at his hands, turned them over so he could see his palms then folded them in his lap before speaking. McKenney didn't look at the preacher as he spoke. "I know what you're saying is true. And, if two-thirds of the Confederate Officer Corps told you what their minds told them, they'd tell you we eventually will lose. But, that isn't what their hearts say. It isn't what my heart tells me. But, I asked." The lieutenant looked at Reverend Hurley, searching for his eyes and fixing them. "I asked you what you would require of me, and what you asked, I will do."

Hurley nodded. "I believe God has a plan for all of us. I don't know what that plan is for you . . . or for me. Or Dawes. Or Marian. Or Samuel. But, I do know he's brought us together for some purpose. We'll live with it, or maybe even die with it, but whatever the outcome, it's been ordained this way. I take great comfort in that."

The two men looked at each other in silence. Each felt they had become part of a train on a track and that they must ride it to the end. As if throwing a log in the boiler to start the engine moving, Marcus said, "I'll ask Marian to bring your supper here. You shouldn't risk damaging your cast before it's completely cured." He climbed the stairs, an air of finality filling the void his leaving created.

Chapter 5

December 6, 1864

"They'll be thinkin' of gettin' ready for Christmas in Alabama . . . at my home." Dawes lay on his half of the bed and stared at the ceiling. The flickering light of two candles illuminated the cellar. Late Fall's shortened days put the two roommates in bed early and with time to waste prior to sleep overtaking them. "I sure hope they ain't goin' through what the folks around here are."

Stephen lay on his side; the candle on the chair next to the bed was pulled up close to him to provide enough light to read the volume of *Hamlet* in which he was engrossed. He showed no sign of hearing Landry speak to him.

Dawes looked at his friend. McKenney wasn't snoring, a sure indicator he wasn't sleeping. "You asleep?" Landry asked. There was no response. He gently nudged Stephen, "Hey, don't you wonder what's goin' on at your home?"

McKenney sighed, folded over the corner of the page he was reading, and rolled onto his back. "I guess so. The thought of what might be happening there bothers me so much that . . ." He didn't finish his thought.

"If it helps you any, anything that's happened there is probably long over. One of Wheeler's staff clerks told us Sheridan pulled out in October. Last I heard, Early was ready to begin a campaign to regain control of the valley for us."

"Landry, we've been up and down that valley fighting the Union since the beginning of the war. The war just doesn't end there. And, we don't have old Stonewall to whip their generals like we did back then. I hope you're right, but I'm afraid the same thing that happened here is happening there."

"Well, we see less and less of the Blue Bellies around here. There's only been one group through here in the last four days." Landry shook his head. "I know what you're goin' to say. They're just rumors. I ain't sayin' the scavengers and bummers *aren't* bad. But, don't you think they're following Sherman? Hell, they've stole most everything worthwhile around here."

"The Hurleys have nice stuff and there's some silver in the church, I'm concerned that—"

"Boys!" It was Samuel's excited voice. He stood at the open trap door. "Blow out dem candles, deys Yankees at the house, they'sa comin' here." The trap door slammed shut. They heard Samuel slide a rug over it.

Both men blew out their candle. Darkness encased them. They heard the old black man's quick shuffling gait as he left the church. Landry murmured, "Damn!"

"Shhhhhhhssssssiiiiiiissssssss," Stephen hissed.

The blackness was so complete that Landry couldn't see his hand in front of his face when he held it a few inches from his eyes. He could hear Stephen's breathing. And . . . nothing else. Minutes dragged on. He was sure that something had happened to the Hurleys. But, there hadn't been any shots fired. The soldiers could've bayoneted them or killed them with sabers. He whispered to McKenney, "Do you think we should go check on the Hurleys?"

"Shhhhhhhssssssiiiiiiissssss."

"Damn, Stephen."

"Shhhhhhhssssssiiiiiiissssss."

Landry fidgeted around then thought about his cavalry saber under the bed. He reached down and felt around until his fingers touched the sheath. He grasped and maneuvered it until he found its grip and guard. When he withdrew it from the scabbard, there was a long metallic sliding sound.

"Shhhhhhhsssssssiiiiiiiissssssssss."

Silently, Landry laid the sword on the bed next to him. He felt Stephen moving, straining, his breathing becoming labored. He knew McKenney was attempting to get his pistol from under his side of the bed. Finally, he relaxed and his breathing returned to normal.

Nothing happened. There was no noise. Nothing. His nerves were taut as violin strings. Landry was sure an hour had past. He was about to suggest again they see if the Hurleys were okay when he heard the muffled sound of the church's front door open. The sound of boots scrapping and tapping the wooden floors overhead advanced toward them. He heard low voices engaged in conversation. Judging from the number of step sounds above them, there were several men in the group. He heard someone call out, "There's no one back here."

One heavy set of footsteps approached. Landry's hand felt for the saber and he felt Stephen's body stiffened next to him. The "Thump, thump, thump, thump," of boot heels passed directly over them. A deep voice said, "Do I look like a preacher in the pulpit?" There were several laughs. Another voice said, "Those folks was lying to us. Ain't no Rebs here."

"What about taking this?"

The deep bass voice said, "No, leave their stuff here—for now."

The steps receded and the front door closed. Silence again. There was nothing to do, but wait.

***

After what seemed like two eternities, McKenney said, "I'm pretty sure they're gone. We can talk low." There was no response for many long seconds in the inky blackness. Landry finally said, "I guess I was wrong." He sat up on the side of the bed, slid off, and within seconds the sound of his saber sliding back into its scabbard rattled the darkness. It sounded much louder than normal. He asked, "Do you think the Hurleys or Samuel will be out before long?"

"Not if they're smart. We probably won't see them before morning. Remember what one of the men said about someone reporting we were here? Well, they believed it enough to come looking for us. If I were in charge, I'd leave a couple men to observe after I left . . . just in case it was true. It would be a natural thing for someone from the rectory to come out and check on us, and if they did, the Yankees would know we are here. I believe Marcus is just as smart. He won't take the chance. No one will be out until tomorrow."

***

"Until we find out who it was, we have to be extra careful. You both are going to have to stay down here most of the time. We know someone out there is an enemy. I think I'll be able to tell who it is in short order. If it's what I think it is, they'll be out here to see why they didn't get their fifty dollars. That's the bounty for turning in a Confederate soldier now." Marcus and Marian stood in front of their 'guests' who were going to be transformed into "prisoners" for an undeterminable period.

"Maybe we should get out of here—now." Stephen looked at Landry who nodded.

"It isn't possible. General Slocum has appointed a new military governor for this area. His name is Colonel Gore. I met him when we went into Eatonton yesterday. He strikes me as a man trying to make a reputation. He's established checkpoints on all roads and increased the bounty for reporting a soldier to fifty from twenty-five dollars. Martin Clebourne told me that one of Gore's staff officers got drunk and was walking up and down Eatonton's streets bragging that by the time Gore finished with the area, a rat wouldn't want to live here."

"Damn Yankees!" Landry said through clenched teeth.

"We must accept what we can do nothing about," Hurley said, then added, "for now."

"How did Gore react to you?" McKenney asked.

"He acted friendly. But, so can a rabid dog right before he bites. I believe the drunk. We must pray that as many of our friends and neighbors are spared as possible." Hurley shook his head. "And, we must do our best to help others, avoid provoking actions, and trust that the Lord will do what is best for us."

Stephen looked at Marcus quizzically for several seconds then said, "You answered me as a preacher. I'll ask again, how did Gore react to you?"

The two men locked gazes for several seconds. Hurley straightened to full height, took a breath, and exhaled slowly. "He sought me out for our meeting."

Their eyes remained engaged. The fact that this was *not* good did not have to be spoken. McKenney asked, "Do you know who the drunk officer that did the bragging is?"

"Captain Heinrich Holder. He's in charge of contraband confiscation," Reverend Hurley answered.

"In other words, he's in charge of robbing and raping," Landry said bitterly then quickly looked at Marian. "Begging your pardon, ma'am."

She nodded with only a slight frown expressing her distaste.

"Have you met this guy, yet?" Lieutenant McKenney asked.

Marcus nodded. "He was one of our visitors last night."

***

"I didn't think we'd find out quite so soon." Hurley shook his head as he spoke to Stephen and Landry. "I guess it proves that it's difficult to know how easily men can abandon what they believe in. The man showed up here this morning. He was shocked anything was still here. I could tell by his face; guilt was written across it, not by the fact he'd betrayed his fellow man, but by the fact he realized I was aware of it."

"Who is it?" McKenny asked.

"Howard Waltham. What is so ironic is that he was one of the most ardent of the secessionists in the county. Marian has never liked or trusted the man. I must learn to trust her instincts more in the future." Reverend Hurley kicked the cellar's clay floor with his toe, an action he substituted for cursing. "She feels he was instrumental in causing Jasmine to leave us."

"Who is Jasmine?" Dawes asked.

"Please, I'd rather not discuss that."

"What did Waltham say when he left?" Stephen changed the subject.

"That he and his family wouldn't be to church for the next couple weeks. He says he'll be in Atlanta on business."

Landry balled his fist and shook it. "I bet his business will be traitoring."

McKenney nodded and Marcus remained immobile and silent.

"I believe we must adopt a position that we can trust no one outside of our household. For the time being, you two must come to breakfast before the sun is up and to supper after dark . . . or eat here. It's a precaution that may not be needed, but I feel it *is* prudent." Hurley shook his head and put one of his hands on the shoulder of each of his friends. "Both of you have expressed your concern that your presence here endangers Marian and me. I fear it is the opposite. My outspoken feelings about slavery may have caused this strange vendetta by those who see me as somehow responsible for our calamities and see an opportunity to get revenge by using the Union to extract it. Samuel and I will see if we can find a way to spirit you out as soon as possible, because I believe it is inevitable that me and this church are to be taken down."

"Over my dead body," Landry said hotly.

"I've already asked this from the Lieutenant; now, Private, I must ask it of you. I ask you to refrain from killing another man in this war no matter what the provocation." Hurley's eyes implored rather than commanded Dawes to agree.

Landry remained silent, confusion and indecision on his face. He looked at McKenney. The lieutenant nodded. Dawes' eyes traveled to the red clay floor. He said softly, "I'll do my best."

"You must mean it," Hurley said.

Landry raised his eyes and glared at both Stephen and the reverend. "I said, I would." His words were spoken with anger, and dissatisfaction was written on his countenance, but there was no doubting his commitment or resolve.

***

December 14, 1864

"Hmmmmm, Yes'sa, I believes it can come off." The old black man felt Landry's grip on his hand. "It be hurtin' you?"

"No." Dawes chose to ignore the slight twinge a few inches below his elbow.

"Okay, Mista Landry, it'sa comin' off and stayin' off." Samuel grinned. "I'll get the saw an' a bucket a water and get dat rascal off der."

"Samuel, before you go, I need to know a few things: do you know where the ladders are? And, is one tall enough to reach the church roof?"

"Uh-huh."

"Does the Reverend have some white paint?" "Uh-huh."

"How about a short board," Landry held his hands three feet apart, "about like this, a hammer, some nails, and some rope?"

"I sho does."

"Good. I'm gonna need your help getting' those tonight."

Samuel frowned, "What cha gonna do?"

"Promise you won't tell?"

The old black man hesitated. He trusted Dawes. Samuel nodded, "Uh-huh."

"I promised the Reverend I'd paint the cross on top the church and I'm gonna do that thing before I leave."

"You fixin' a go?"

Landry nodded, "Yes, Samuel, I am, before I'm faced with something where I know I'll have to break my word."

***

When the sun rose on Thursday morning, December 15, 1864, two revelations were made by those living in the church and the rectory on Cotton Creek Road. The cross atop the steeple had a gleaming fresh coat of white paint drying in the dry breeze and first sun rays of the day. The ladder, can of paint, cleaned brush, coiled rope, and hammer lay neatly next to the church. The second was that Landry Dawes was gone. A note pinned to his pillow was simple. It said, "Thank you eternally. God bless you. Landry Dawes."

Chapter 6

November 26, 1954

"I don't know. Not for sure." Landry senior looked into his coffee's blackness as though looking for an answer to his son's question. "I've guessed at what the reason might be a number of times. Why he picked the time he did. . . to leave . . . wasn't passed down. Not in letters. Not in the tales that are told from father to son like I'm telling you now."

"You said not for sure. Do you have a theory?" young Dawes asked.

"Yes. I think he was pretty sure what would happen there . . . eventually. And, I believe if it did, he knew he wouldn't be able to keep his promise to the preacher. Great-great-grandpa was said to have had a temper and to have been very protective of his loved ones, so if he guessed that there would be problems at the church . . .well, he'd of killed as many men as was necessary to protect the Hurleys. A man's word and the whole concept of honor were so much more important then, it's difficult for us to understand. He'd given his word; he knew he'd have to leave to keep it."

"That's hard for me to figure, Dad. If he loved the Hurleys and if he thought something might happen to them, you'd think he'd say screw swearing he wouldn't kill anyone. I know I'd stay and do everything I could to protect them."

"Well, Landry, that's the difference in generations. What's important to my generation may not be to yours. Chances are you won't understand what some of your children believe. Different times present different challenges, needs, technologies, and we adapt to those changes." The father smiled and said, "Of course, my generation is always right."

"Sure." The boy snorted and smirked at his father. "I suppose you're going to tell me how Glenn Miller and Bing Crosby are better than the music I like to listen to."

"I'm glad you understand and acknowledge that." Dawes senior grinned.

"Would ya'll like your coffee freshened?" the waitress asked.

"That would be mighty fine. Son, you want more coffee?" The drawl was added again.

"Yes, ma'am," Landry said.

The waitress poured coffee into both of the Dawes' cups. "More cream and sugar?"

Both said, "Yes," simultaneously.

She disappeared briefly, returning with a small pitcher of cream. The girl picked up a full bowl of sugar from a neighboring table and placed both in front of the Dawes. The cocksure attitude had vanished and was replaced by a respectful, attentive air. She smiled, said, "Do ya'all need anything else?"

Both said, "No thank you," but she made no attempt to leave. It was obvious she wanted to talk.

"Can I do something for you, Miss?" Mr. Dawes asked.

The girl blushed and glanced away for a few seconds before returning her focus on the father. "I know it's none of my business, but I'm so curious. Are the stories true about what happened at the church and that's what's caused all the strange good and bad things that happen there?" The drawl had disappeared.

"What have you heard?" Dawes cocked his head to the side; no trace of a smile remained.

"It's kind of embarrassing—well, are you related to the man that started the painting?

"Yes. I'm the great-great-grandson." Dawes continued to show no emotion.

"The story is that your relative left the preacher and his folks before they all got killed and the Yankees burned the church. They say ya'll come back because you weren't there to help them. That your relative came back and buried them and swore an oath that causes the things that happen out there over the years."

Landry Dawes, Sr. leaned back in his chair. "That's the story, huh? Well, I don't know about all the things you're talking about that happened there, later. I can tell you a little about what didn't and did happen at the church that night. Would you like to sit down? It's gonna take some time."

"I need to talk to my boss." The girl hustled across the floor. Young Landry lost all focus on her words as he was mesmerized watching her; his father had not. His expression was that of a man deep in thought. When the waitress returned, a large, heavy-set, matronly looking woman wearing a cook's apron accompanied her. The waitress said, "This is my boss, Maylyn Autry. She's Miss Flora's daughter and is part owner of the restaurant. My name is Julie Smith."

"I'm Landry Dawes the fourth and this is my son, Landry the fifth. And, yes, the man who started painting the cross was the first Landry Dawes."

"Pleased to meet you both," the woman said. They both sat down. "I hope you don't mind me listenin' in." It wasn't a question.

"No problem." Both women's eyes were pinned to the elder Dawes face. Mr. Dawes returned their gaze, while young Landry sneaked peeks at Julie while trying to look disinterested.

"I've lived in this here county all my life, heard all kind of tales about the church, and ain't none of them that agree completely." The woman shook her head and exhaled. "That there place is important to many of us folks here about. I'd like to know the real story."

Landry nodded, "I can understand. I've heard a little of the stories about what's happened here in later years and I'm just as curious about them. Maybe we can both learn something."

Maylyn smiled, "That's a deal."

Mr. Dawes leaned forward. "Let's start with the parts of your version of the story I know didn't happen, Julie. My great-great-grandfather left here a week before the raid. He didn't know about what happened to the Hurleys and the church until he returned to paint the cross for the first time, five years later. Obviously, he didn't bury them. He returned to paint the cross because he told Reverend Hurley that he and his relatives would do it as long as it stood on the steeple because the preacher and his family sheltered him. That was what he did and what we do."

The women nodded, prompting him to continue.

"As far as the rest of the tale, I can only repeat what my ancestor was told happened. It's what's been passed down to me. He believed it was true because he knew most of the individuals and it made sense to him. And, he believed the account for another reason. One of the people that described the events ended up being his wife. The other was her friend."

"My goodness!" the woman said. "Was either of them a woman named Holder?"

Landry stared at Maylyn Autry for a few seconds before asking, "Was she related to you?"

"Oh, no. The Holders have always claimed they had a lot to do with trying to save the Hurleys and church from destruction. They have an old wood stove that was left to them in the Hurley's will."

"I can promise you, that isn't true."

"Oh . . . I just thought . . ."

"Precisely what happened inside the church that night won't ever be known. What the results were, certainly are. A friend of the original Landry Dawes, another Confederate staying with the Hurleys, witnessed who went in and who came out. He's one of the people that buried the Hurleys and the rest of those that lived at the church. I believe he's the one whose deed creates what happens at the old church site. The man's name was Stephen McKenney. The Hurleys learned that the Union commander knew that McKenney was hiding in the church and a patrol was being sent to apprehend him. McKenney had a very bad leg injury. He couldn't walk without a crutch, so he couldn't run. The Hurleys hid him high in a tree. When what happened, happened—he couldn't do anything—but watch."

"How horrible," Julie said.

"He didn't have a gun or anything?" Young Landry's interest had shifted from Julie to his father's words.

"No. He'd taken the same oath, well, given his word, that great-great-grandfather did; that he would never kill another man in his lifetime no matter what the cause. So, you see, even if he had a weapon he wouldn't have used it."

"I would have!" Young Dawes looked and sounded angry.

"I'm sure he wanted to kill every one of them. He could hear the women screaming in the sanctuary, saw the robbing of the rectory and the church. They took everything of value from both places. They even took Mrs. Hurley's stove." Dawes paused, looking at Mrs. Autry.

She raised her hand to her mouth, and mumbled, "Oh my!"

Julie snapped, "That shouldn't surprise you, Mrs. Maylyn. The Holder family is lower than the stuff at the bottom of the oldest outhouse in the county."

"Some things don't seem to change." Landry Senior stopped and sipped some coffee.

"I don't care what I'd promised the Hurleys." The son was incensed. "I'd have run each of the rats down separately and killed them. And, I'd have made them suffer. I'd . . . I'd . . . I'd have tied them to a tree and used an axe to kill them."

"No . . . you wouldn't have," his father said. "You might want to do that and worse, but when it came time, son, you couldn't. Good men don't do those things and I think you'll make a good man."

Landry junior shook his head angrily, but said nothing. He knew what his father said about good men was true and he was pleased his father believed he would become one.

"How did he bury them?" Maylyn asked. "With a bad leg and all."

"How did he even get out of the tree?" Julie said.

"I don't know all the details, just a few. What do I know? A friend of the Hurleys learned the raid was coming and was riding out to warn them, but the Yankees got there first. The church was still a roaring inferno when that person arrived. That's how Lieutenant McKenney got out of the tree. The two of them tried going into the church. The flames were too intense. When they were able, they found it wouldn't have made any difference. They found the murdered servants next to the door. Hurley and his wife were near the pulpit toward the rear of the church, dead—one shot and one cut down with a saber. Both were bayoneted to be sure they didn't live."

"The animals!" Mrs. Autry growled.

Mr. Dawes nodded. "They were. Those raiders represent the worst, most detestable element of war, the pain and injustice savaged on helpless civilians. Sherman's troops were among the most evil the world has seen."

"I wish I could have been there. I'd have done something." Young Dawes' face was red, his father's words arousing his southern heritage.

"You'd have made a good Confederate, Landry. I can see you in Picket's charge. A brave soldier, probably a dead one, but brave." There was no humor in Mr. Dawes' tone, expression, or words.

"What happened next?" Julie asked.

"I suppose that McKenney and the Hurleys' friend waited until the fire burned itself out. They pulled the bodies out, I guess, for I know they buried them. It was at the graveside that McKenney prayed that the deaths of his friends wouldn't be a useless sacrifice. The exact words weren't passed down, but Stephen asked that good people who visited the church would be protected and blessed, and evil ones punished. That's the history . . . as I understand what happened. And, no, I don't know where they're buried."

"What happened to that McKenney guy?" Julie had moisture forming in the corner of her eyes.

"Later, when he could, he decided he would go to the authorities to try to get justice for the Hurleys. His attempt never got made. A Yankee soldier killed him, claiming he had something to do with the death of the one Union man that died during the raid, but it was to cover-up what really happened. There is more to the story, but—"

"That's so terrible. Who told your great-great-grandpa about all that?" Autry asked.

"Lieutenant Mc Kenney's sister. He met her on one of his visits to paint the cross. They spent time together for a few days, exchanged letters and, eventually, got married." Dawes paused, unwilling to volunteer additional information unless pressed.

"That's just *so* interestin', Mr. Dawes. Do you mind if I repeat what you've told us? There are so many folks hereabouts that would just love to know this." The cook rose when the other waitress called to her for the third time during Landry Dawes' story.

"No, not at all."

"Are you painting it today?"

"Yes."

"Are you stayin' over?"

"No, we're heading home to Alabama tonight.

"Oh . . . Well, you might have some visitors at the church today. You said you'd like to learn about some of the events out there. I'll call some people that I think you'll enjoy talkin' to. Some of the tales are wonderful, some sinister, but, they're all fascinatin'." Maylyn walked away. "I hope you don't mind."

"That's fine." Mr. Dawes took a deep breath. He knew saying 'no' was futile.

"May I shake your hand?" Julie extended her white, soft palm and long, slender fingers toward Landry senior. Her eyes remained moist and tracks of tears glistened on her cheeks. Mr. Dawes took it, shook it, and looked at her questioningly.

"You see, there was a couple that lived near here. They'd been married nine years. Nine years. They wanted a baby, but the doctors said it was impossible. They went to Atlanta to all the fancy hospitals. Nothing worked. Then, one night, they went out to the old church." She smiled.

"And?" Mr. Dawes said.

"I'm the result."

Chapter 7

December 20, 1864

"Dey's nobody 'round. Mista Hurley say ta help you up so's you can get fresh air." Samuel struggled down the stairs, his old knees protesting every step. Since Landry Dawes left, moving from place to place was more problematic for Lieutenant McKenney. To keep from falling down the cellar steps, which he'd come close to doing once, Stephen needed minor assistance, or at least, observation when going up or down. Preventing any setback to his leg's healing process was necessary to avoid compounding his problem.

"Thank you, Samuel," Stephen said, as he put his book aside. He slid off the bed, got a firm grip on his crutch and hobbled to the stairs. His leg could support a little weight, not much, and it was stiff. Using it at all without the cast was out of the question. He'd tried the last time the cast was changed two days ago. McKenney knew it would never return to normal, but hoped it would heal enough he'd be able to ride a horse and walk with a cane. "Yous want me behind you?" Samuel asked.

"No, just hold my hand for the first step and last two or three at the top. I can hold on to the frame of the opening for the rest."

The old man obliged and Stephen reached the floor behind the pulpit, located ten feet in front of the cellar's trap door. Once on a level surface, McKenney could move about relatively well, though not quickly.

"Mista Hurley says, you be extra careful. Dey be lotsa Blue Coats and scavengers here 'bouts, now."

"Should I stay in the cellar?"

"No, sa. Jasmine be here. She be keepin' look on da road."

Stephen perked up; he'd heard the name several times, but to date, he hadn't seen this person who was more apparition than flesh. "She out on the road?" he asked.

"Uh-huh. But, she's a goin' directly. Jasmine's my grand-niece." Samuel looked toward the front door. "You wanna go outside? It's a might cold out der."

"I think I'll stay in here. At least, until lunch. Marcus lets me borrow books from his study. I'll read one of them."

"Does you need anything? A candle ta do your readin' by?" the old black man asked.

"Don't need one with those." McKenney pointed to the windows then up to the huge, heavy-paned, tinted glass skylights fashioned into the ceiling. Stephen had heard the story of how they were removed from a Charleston church that was rebuilt and Hurley's father had gotten them for his son. They turned the pews shades of red, green, blue, and yellow, along with the pages of the books he read under them.

"If'n yous tells me what color the book is, I'll fetch it for you."

"That's all right. I need the exercise." Stephen smiled at Samuel and pointed to a hymnal that lay on one of the pews. "Would you like to learn to read a little? I can teach you."

"No, sa. I'm an ol' dog. But, I'd sure like ta learn ta write my name."

"We'll do it this afternoon."

Samuel grinned and said, "Now tha's fine."

***

By the time the sound of a set of footsteps making a light scraping sound on the wooden church floors penetrated the fog *King Lear* surrounded him in, the person was only a few yards away. Stephen's head whipped around as he put the book down and grabbed his crutch. He struggled to his feet and gazed at the beautiful young woman now only a few feet from him. Immediately, he was captivated by her deep green eyes framed by sooty long eyelashes. She had long auburn hair that focused any male's attention on her hauntingly beautiful features. Her deep blue dress, in the fashion popular with plantation ladies of that period, covered all her light olive flesh except her hands, neck, and face. She smiled slightly and said, "Hello."

"Hello." McKenney felt awkward and self-conscious.

"Do you know if Reverend Hurley, his wife, or Samuel are around?"

"I haven't seen the Hurleys, but Samuel was here an hour ago." He found that he was trying to make himself taller and as little dependent on the crutch as possible.

Her pupils scanned him in a very impersonal manner. When she finished her three second evaluation, she asked, "How is your leg?"

"It's much better than it was, but I'm still not near normal." Though he tried, it was hard to tell much about the realities of her body other than she was tall, slender, and had good curves from the waist up.

"You are?" she asked. Her question's tone was one of confirmation, not inquiry.

"Lieutenant Stephen R. McKenney, Confederate States of America, at your service." Stephen did his best to make his crutch assisted bow as graceful as possible.

"Hello, Jasmine." Reverend Hurley spoke as he entered the front door. His countenance and voice were warm with affection.

Stephen was glad the girl had spun around to face Hurley. The shocked expression on his face would have said the words he was able to choke back, *you're not black*. It must be a coincidence. Jasmine was a common name. This girl had a lighter complexion than his. Her thin nose and thin lips were definitely not African. She had to be white.

"Hello, Reverend Marcus. I wanted to see you for a minute or two before I have to leave and I've got to go right away."

Hurley nodded. "We just came back from Aldus Smith's funeral." He shook his head sadly. "So many young men killed. It's a shame." The frown lifted from his face. "Marian said you'd been here when she saw the flour, coffee, and salt in the kitchen. Thank you."

The young woman waved one of her graceful hands in front of her. "It's nothing." She turned her head and looked at Stephen then back at Marcus. "Can we go out front?"

"Surely." Hurley smiled at the lieutenant. "Excuse us, Stephen."

Jasmine faced Stephen, cocked her head and tilted it forward, smiling ceremoniously as she did. "A pleasure meeting you, Lieutenant McKenney."

"The pleasure was mine Miss . . . Miss . . . ."

"Jones."

"The pleasure was mine, Miss Jones."

Marcus and Jasmine started for the door, but after they'd taken a couple steps, she turned and asked, "Lieutenant, will you tell my Uncle Samuel I said goodbye if I don't see him outside?"

"Yes, ma'am." Stephen attempted to mask his disbelief, but was only partly successful. Jasmine smiled and made a theatrical turn back to the door. She delivered a message.

***

"Did Jasmine's appearance surprise you, Stephen?" Hurley sat down on the pew next to McKenney after the young woman left.

Stephen stared at Marcus for several seconds before answering. "I'm sure you know it did."

"I'll explain it to you so it will spare Samuel the explanation, though there's no shame involved for him or Jasmine. Samuel, Louise, four others, and Jasmine were purchased by me because of Jasmine's plight. They all belonged to Howard Waltham. Waltham is from New Orleans. Some of the *gentlemen* from that area have a deplorable tradition. They select an attractive slave and make her a mistress. Then they take an attractive girl that results from that union and she becomes a second generation mistress. The sinful breeding continues. Jasmine is an octoroon, which means she is one eighth black. Several years back, when Waltham moved here, I spoke to him about stopping this sinful behavior. Jasmine was very young, only eleven, and bore him no children. But . . . he told me he wouldn't stop unless I wanted to buy her and several others he felt weren't useful to him. I'm sure he thought I wouldn't. I did, and I set them all free. Four wished to go North. I saw they reached Cincinnati safely. They have not done well, but remain there. Samuel, Louise, and Jasmine elected to stay with me. Samuel is too old to start a new life and Louise too frightened. Jasmine . . . Jasmine is neither. She's blessed with great intelligence. When she reached twenty-one, she moved into Eatonton. Jasmine took jobs, cooking, cleaning, and whatever else. She's done well for herself."

"Does she still live in Eatonton?" McKenney couldn't ask the question he was wondering about.

"Yes, close to it. She has a house and two acres right outside of town."

"How . . . does she . . ." Stephen unsuccessfully searched for words.

"She lives in a world apart," Hurley said. "She doesn't fit in either society well. She was raised by us as our children would have been. But, as long as she stays here, the white world is forbidden to her. Jasmine identifies with that society, not the black one. She seems happy, but I know some things are very, very difficult for her. It helps that she is well liked in the community." Hurley paused and placed one hand on Stephen's shoulder. "Jasmine brought some news. She overheard a conversation between Colonel Gore and his staff. She cleans their headquarters." He shook his head. "Sherman has Savannah blockaded. It's a matter of time. Hardee is hopelessly out-numbered. Unless he can sneak away by some miracle, in two weeks there won't be any army left in Georgia. I don't think there is any chance of you reaching him. You should think of finding a way home."

McKenney nodded, but said nothing.

"I have friends in the mountains. They can get you from Cleveland in Tennessee to the lower part of the Shenandoah. Or, the railroad may soon be back in service. The Yankees are repairing it for their use."

"I'll think about it." Stephen looked at his folded hands resting in his lap.

"I'm afraid you must make a decision soon. Jasmine tells me that as soon as Savannah falls and Sherman moves on, the men protecting his supply lines will be free to confiscate everything. I fear we will be on the list. They are likely to come here, look for you, and steal everything. There will be many men and their search will be thorough. You'll need to make a decision in two weeks or less."

***

"Mista Stephen, is you decent?" Louise called down into the cellar. At five o'clock it was already dark, the shortest days of the year being upon them. The black girl averted her eyes to avoid any impropriety.

"Yes. Is supper ready?" Stephen asked.

"Uh-huh, but Missa Marian say they's bunches of the soldiers on the road tonight. She says to tell you she's bringin' your dinner here."

"Okay. Thanks, Louise."

"Mista Stephen." The girl lingered at the top of the stairs. It was obvious she wanted something.

"Did you need anything else, Louise?" he asked. "Well, I hates to ask, but . . . Samuel done learned to write his name an' he said yous was the one taught him. I was a wonderin—"

"I'll be happy to teach you how."

"And maybe learn some words to read like you done learned Samuel?" The girl was more excited than McKenney could believe.

"Why, sure. I'll teach you as many words as you'd like to learn."

"Oh, thank you, Mista Stephen. I gotsta tell ol' Samuel." She ran away a few steps and then ran back. "Missa Marian will be out here directly with your meal." Stephen heard her racing footsteps as she left the church.

Stephen decided against lighting a candle. Everything was becoming scarce and expensive. He could sit in darkness until Marian brought his meal. He returned to the bed and laid down. McKenney's eye lids slowly closed. The darkness was internal as well as external as he dozed off. He dreamed of his dead brother, of his home on the creek in Virginia, of his sister Maureen. Maureen and he were very close, sharing their dreams, aspirations and fantasies. Stephen fancied he could hear her calling to him.

"Stephen. Stephen . . . Stephen!" The urgency in the voice snapped him awake. The voice was Marian's.

"Yes?"

"Stay quiet! I have to close the trap door." The wooden panel closed with a thud. He heard the rug slide over the opening. Marian's footsteps raced around from place to place. Stephen recognized the sound of broom bristles brushing the floor. He heard the front door slam shut. The sweeping stopped. Stephen prayed. Time dragged on, and on, and on. He knew that it had been an hour since the door closed. Finally, the trap door eased open. Marian stood framed in the opening. "Stephen?" she called.

"I'm here, Marian."

"There were several groups of soldiers on the road. We were concerned they would stop here. They came to the door, looked in, and left."

"I understand."

"Lieutenant, things are getting worse quickly. There is more activity now. I have your supper. I'm sorry its cold, but I don't want to walk it back and forth to the kitchen because someone might see and become suspicious." She disappeared and returned in a few seconds with his supper tray. She said, "Would you light a candle?"

"Okay." Within a few seconds the candle flickered. Marian descended the stairs while casting worried glances toward the church's front. As she handed the tray to Stephen, she said, "Things are truly bad. Pray we get through this." Fear was in her voice, on her features.

Her demeanor was the final piece in Stephen's decision. "I can't stay here any longer. My presence here compounds your danger. Tell Marcus, if he can make the arrangements with the friends he discussed with me, do it. I'm ready to leave now."

Marian didn't disagree, though she showed no visible relief at his words. "I'll tell Marcus. It will take a few days. I'm sure we'll be fine until then."

Stephen nodded.

"I'll pick up the tray tomorrow." Marian ascended the stairs and closed the trap door. That act and the swish of the rug being pulled into place added its own message.

***

The sounds of the rug being moved and someone scraping at the trap door woke McKenney. As the door opened, light streaming in told him it was morning. Louise's voice said, "Mista Stephen, I's come for ta tray. Can I come down?"

"Sure, Louise." Stephen slipped on his shirt as the young woman came down the stairs.

She picked up the tray and started to leave. Stephen said, "Louise, if you get some time this morning, come back and I'll teach you to write your name."

Louise grinned broadly. "Yes, sa, I sho will!"

***

"There's one thing more, Reverend Hurley." The lieutenant pointed to the pile of sacks in one corner of the small basement. "I can't take that with me. There's no way. I'll leave it in your keeping. If, by some miracle, the Confederate cause should be able to go on, I would ask you to see the gold is returned. If not, the people of this area will need help. Use it for that purpose."

Marcus nodded solemnly. "I'll do both. You know you're leaving a legacy here. My guess is that those funds will do a great deal of good. The people here have been bled until they have very little left." He paused and smiled. "You're leaving another thing. Both Samuel and Louise are so excited about what you've taught them. I've been so blind. It never occurred to me that reading and writing are so important to them. I plan to continue to teach them after you leave. Samuel is so proud and Louise is writing her name on everything. That's all she can talk about."

Chapter 8

December 21, 1864

The Union patrols on Cotton Creek Road suddenly disappeared. In previous days, at least one group of blue uniformed soldiers varying from four to forty passed the church each morning and afternoon. Sometimes more. None appeared that day. Marcus kept one of the church family members posted to watch the road in spite of the lack of activity. By four in the afternoon, it was impossible not to sigh and relax . . . and hope. That evening, McKenney ate supper in the house for the first time in a week. After the Reverend said grace, he bubbled with enthusiasm, a condition seldom seen in the emotionally restrained pastor.

"Stephen, I have very good news. A friend of mine who lives in Madison, Father McCarthy, is traveling to Tennessee for Christmas. He's leaving on the 23rd and he's agreed to take you with him. I'll be riding with you that morning. We'll be transporting two cases of bibles to serve as a reason for the trip if we're stopped. And the best thing, Father McCarthy has arranged to get some parole papers for you. I can't tell you how, but they should get you through lines and back to your home."

"I don't know how I can ever repay you."

"You've already repaid me, Lieutenant, by promising to fight no more. I know how difficult that is for you. Your peers may judge you harshly. You may even be harsh on yourself. But when you die, it will be one less burden on your soul."

***

Landry Dawes swung out of his saddle. It was the end of a hard day of riding, but a significant one. In front of him was the Randolph County Courthouse in Wedowee, Alabama. He'd crossed the state line early in the morning—he felt he was home. Inside the courthouse, he hoped he'd find his uncle who served as Randolph County's clerk. He visualized a hot meal, warm bed, and relief from the apprehension of traveling through strange country.

As Landry walked toward the brick building, he ignored the stares of those he passed. He'd become used to them, for a young man not in uniform was an oddity in the Confederacy. Dawes sincerely hoped the areas he'd traveled through would not see the same devastation and terror that Sherman had inflicted on the land he crushed as he advanced. A time or two he'd been asked if he knew any news of the war. He would only answer with two words, "Not good."

Since he'd left the church, the Hurleys, and his friend Lieutenant McKenney, he hadn't seen a truly friendly face. The smiling man standing in the courthouse entrance changed that. His last thought before greeting his uncle were his prayers for his friends' well-being.

***

Something had a hold on his shoulder. It parted Stephen from his peaceful slumber. "Stephen, Stephen, wake up! Quickly!" He looked up groggily. Marcus Hurley's face was alarmed and concerned in the flickering light of a candle.

"What—"

Hurley cut him off. "Now. We have no time to talk. The Yankees are on the way. They know you're here. Louise told her friend about you teaching her. Somehow it got to them. Quick! Get up, we have an idea how to hide you!"

Stephen said, "Okay," as he struggled into his shirt and grabbed his crutch. Hurley practically pulled him up the stairs. They moved as fast as McKenney could hobble across the floor with Marcus' assistance. When they reached the front stoop, the Hurleys' horse stood ready with Marian's side saddle on its back. It was difficult to identify Samuel, Marian, and Louise who were clustered around the animal, the only light being from a quarter moon. Marian held a coil of rope. "We need to get you on the horse. Now!" Marcus said.

Marcus and Samuel helped lift Stephen into the side saddle while Marian held the horse steady. The side saddle allowed him to extend his leg out into space without threat of more injury. Once he was secure in the saddle, Marian led the horse toward the creek across the road. Marcus, Samuel, and Louise trailed behind. Louise stopped at the road and posted herself as a lookout. Marian plunged into the cold water of the creek, leading the horse into the thigh deep stream and out on the heavily wooded bank on the other side. She stopped at a huge oak. McKenney heard Marcus say, "Slip the loop over your head and shoulders and under your arm pits." The rope had a lasso tied to its end. Marcus threw the other end of the rope over a limb high in the tree as Stephen did as he was told. Hurley tugged on the rope, pulling it snug. McKenney felt the rope tighten across his chest and back.

Reverend Hurley said, "We're going to hoist you up in the tree with the rope. Sit on one of the limbs. When you feel secure, tie yourself to the tree." Marcus knotted the rope end to the saddle. "Are you ready, Stephen?"

"Yes," he answered.

"Okay, we'll lead the horse away; that will pull you up. You see that big limb under the one the rope's thrown over?" Marcus pointed to a ten-inch thick limb fifteen feet off the ground.

"Yes."

"Sit on it as squarely as possible. Get in as comfortable position as you can. You may be there a long time before we can get you down. Once you're set, we'll loosen the rope."

"I'm ready."

Marcus nodded to Marian who led the horse away. Immediately, the rope crushed against McKenney's flesh, pinching him, and he felt himself lifted upward out of the saddle. He looked up as the large limb inched toward him, the rope rubbing bark off of it. Stephen ducked his head forward right before he felt the limb make contact with his back. His body "scratched" its way up until he was able to place his hands on the wood and position his rear firmly on it.

"Move as close to the trunk as you can," Marcus raised his voice as much as he dared.

The lieutenant scooted his butt toward the trunk, six inches at a time. He was able to get within a few inches. He heard Hurley say, "Okay, Marian, back him up." The rope went slack as the horse retraced his steps toward the tree. Marcus quickly loosened the end from the saddle, saying, "After you tie the rope to the limb, make sure you pull up the slack. If you do that, in this dark, with the trunk between you and the church, I don't believe they'll find you. Stay quiet no matter what happens. We'll be back as soon as possible. Good luck!" Stephen watched Marcus, Marian and Samuel trot to the creek, slosh through its shallow water, and race to the rectory with Louise. He was alone.

***

After Stephen tied the rope around the limb and pulled up the end so its dangling in the breeze would not be seen, he had nothing to do, but wait. And wait. And wait. The soldiers weren't just around the bend in the road as he had supposed. The windows in the rectory went dark after what he guessed was a half-hour. He had no notion of what time it was, but reasoned it must be between nine and eleven. Moving around to get his pocket watch out was an unnecessary risk. Marcus was trying to make everything look normal, but McKenney was sure that within the dark home its inhabitants were wide awake, adrenalin coursing through their bodies as it was through his.

After relieving his initial concern that the soldiers would appear instantly, he turned his attention to making his leg as comfortable as possible. He found he could scoot around so his back rested against the trunk and he could partially support his leg and cast on the limb. That helped his comfort immeasurably. It made it more difficult to see the church and road, but he could by swiveling his head and neck around at a severe angle.

He told himself he must be reconciled to spending all night and even the next day in his perch. There was no alternative until . . . Stephen suddenly realized there was no end point. That fact sobered him. How would this end?

No grandfather clock ticked away the time as there was in the rectory. It seemed he'd already been in the tree for most of the night, but the thin sliver of moon had barely budged overhead. He tried to think of something to distract his mind from the possibilities and his leg's pain. His home in Virginia wasn't a welcome topic, for the possibilities that his parents and sister might be experiencing the same problems erased any desire to dwell on that. Thinking of his trip home fared little better. There was little doubt that opportunity was fast fleeting. It lost its luster quickly. He looked at the moon. "Maybe an hour," he mumbled to himself.

McKenney decided he'd be his own clock. He could count to 600, then start over and keep track of how many ten minute intervals passed by. He began the monotonous process; it was better to occupy his mind with something than let it wander to where it would if left unoccupied.

After he reached the end of his first count, Stephen glanced at the moon. It didn't seem to have moved at all. He sighed and resumed the charade for his mind.

***

The tedious repetition lulled his mind into a state suspended between sleep and conscious thought. A horse snorting on the road snapped him alert as surely as if he'd been struck by a whip. Stephen leaned around the tree trunk and looked down on Cotton Creek Road. Four men sat on horseback fifty feet from the church. They were motionless, apparently waiting for something. After a few moments, a metallic jingling became audible coming from the road's opposite direction. A large wagon pulled by two horses became visible in the weak moonlight. One man rode ahead of it and a number of mounted men behind. McKenney couldn't determine how many riders followed. The group stopped 150 feet from the four horsemen. The man in front of the wagon rode to them. Stephen heard him say, "Anyone leave?"

"No, sir." It was impossible to tell who answered. Straining his eyes, Stephen thought he could make out the outline of military caps on the men below. The man McKenney surmised was an officer galloped back to the wagon. He heard the order, "Dismount!" It was followed by more commands that he couldn't make out. Sounds of soldiers getting off their horses floated up to him. They quickly spread out around the church and rectory house. The officer and two other men watched until satisfied with their men's deployment. They rode to the rectory's front porch and got off their horses. After what Lieutenant McKenney guessed was one last look at his soldiers' positions, the officer, accompanied by the two men that rode with him, strode up the porch steps, across the wooden floor and beat on the front door. He heard the man shout, "This is Captain Holder of the Union Army under the command of Colonel Alfredo J. Gore, acting district military governor. Open your door and make no effort to resist or you'll be considered enemy military actives."

Seconds later, windows in the house illuminated. In less than a minute, the door opened silhouetting a man who Stephen assumed was Marcus. "Not too quickly, don't make them suspicious," Stephen murmured, hoping Hurley would receive his mental message. The men spoke briefly, then all disappeared inside the house, the door closing behind them. It wasn't long before one of the soldiers reappeared. He called for three more of the troops, who all went into the rectory.

This time the door was left open. He could hear raised voices, but he was too far away to understand any of the conversation.

Within minutes, a large group came through the lighted door. Marcus, Marian, Samuel, and Louise were accompanied by the officer and three soldiers. The men herded Stephen's friends to the front of the church. The officer yelled, "Wait here!" He said something to a man standing next to him. Within thirty seconds, a dozen soldiers rushed to the front door of the church, their rifles tipped with bayonets and held at the ready. It was evident the man the officer addressed was a sergeant. When he was sure they were ready, he gave a muffled command. He threw open the door and the men charged inside.

There was shouting and the noise of furniture crashing around. Stephen heard the sound of glass breaking and heard Marian scream, "Please, stop!" They didn't. The noises of destruction continued for what seemed an hour, but in reality was ten minutes. Anger boiled inside McKenney as he watched helplessly. After an eternity of having to listen to the destruction of the inside of the church, the sergeant appeared and said, "He ain't inside, Captain Holder."

"Shit!" The captain pointed to the helpless victims. "Get them inside. And, get the men. Have them spread out in the woods around the building. The bastard is crippled; he can't be far away."

The sergeant and one of the men used rifle butts to prod Marcus, Marian, and Louise inside. Samuel stopped and shouted, "They's not here, boss man!"

"Shut up, nigger!" Holder turned to the sergeant. "Get him inside," the captain said, and added, "Number one!" The sergeant pushed Samuel through the door and followed him inside.

Soldiers who had been searching the church boiled out the door. The captain snapped some commands at the men and they quickly headed in all directions. Three crossed the road toward the creek. One came directly at Stephen's position in the tree. The union man cautiously picked his way down the steep bank to the creek. He stopped at its edge.

After looking at the water, bending over to test the temperature, and saying, "No way," the soldier walked a few steps along the rocks at the creek's edge. He peered across the water intently, looking for movement, for an outline, for any sign of the fugitive's hiding spot. The man moved several more steps repeating the process. The trooper moved again, this time directly in front of the tree where Stephen was hiding. As he turned, one foot slipped off the rocks, plunged into the water, and the soldier cursed. He pulled his foot out and shook it then repeated, "Damn!"

Another soldier approached and said, "He ain't down there."

"He ain't here, either."

The second man said, "You think he crossed the creek?"

"Hell, no! Those rocks are real slippery. Can you see someone who cain't walk without a crutch gettin' across that?" He nodded at the creek. "He ain't here now, if he ever was. Some thieving Reb lied to get the fifty bucks." He spit in the creek.

The two men walked away from the cold water without ever once looking up.

As the soldiers crossed the road to return to the captain, screams came from the church. They were brief, but terror filled. Immediately afterward, a single shot rang out. Captain Holder yelled, "I said no shooting!"

An anonymous voice yelled back, "He was protecting his wife."

Holder cursed vociferously, dismounted and strode into the church. Within sixty seconds, he emerged and yelled, "Sergeant, confiscate everything in the house and in the church that's any possible value and load it in the wagon. Then you know what to do."

McKenney was furious; he knew what had happened in the church. He had no illusions, his friends were dead. The scavengers descended on the house carrying out sacks of material, furniture, even Marian's beloved stove. When they had taken what they saw as valuable, torches were lit, and soon the wooden home was burning furiously. It was clear that it would be reduced to cinders. The soldiers turned their attention to the church, hauling sacks from the brick building, rushing back and forth like a stream of ants. Their laughing and joking infuriated the lieutenant further. He was seething, but the truth was, he could do nothing, but get himself murdered.

The sergeant stood in the doorway and announced, "That's everything worth taking."

"Okay. I'm taking the wagon and the patrol and going back to Eatonton. Keep Hicks and Martin with you. Burn it! You know what we don't want found."

"Yes, sir."

Within five minutes, everyone was gone except for the three men charged with burning the church. The sergeant waited until wagon and riders disappeared before saying, "Light the torches."

Stephen heard one of the men yell, "What about the walls? They're brick, they ain't gonna burn."

The sergeant answered, "Let me worry about that. Just throw them onto the roof."

The firebrands were burning and within two minutes a half dozen were tossed onto the wooden shingles to do their devilish work. McKenney could not watch. He shut his eyes tight and cried softly. The fire began to roar as the flames engulfed the roof. How long he sat cocoon like, he had no idea. But when he reopened his eyes, the church roof was a huge bonfire. Having completed their task, the three soldiers stood around watching. The lieutenant closed his eyes again. Time passed without reckoning before he heard the sergeant say, "Flames are down enough to check."

Stephen looked at the two buildings. The rectory was reduced to a smoldering pile of embers, flames spasmodically erupting from them. Only a few remaining parts of the structure stood head high. However, the church still stood, its walls and steeple defiantly erect, the white cross, now smudged with smoke and ash, still gleamed in the remaining firelight. The extremely heavy timbers that framed the roof smoldered and flamed, but still held six of the eight sky lights in tact while all the rest of the roof had incinerated.

Stephen watched the sergeant walk through the open church door. After a few moments, he reappeared carrying a sack. "This is for us boys," he proclaimed. After tying the bag to his saddle, he said, "There's one more." He disappeared into the church again. The fire continued to lap at the huge rafters. As McKenney watched, one of the skylights collapsed, the stained glass crashing to the floor below. There was a hideous scream from inside the church.

The two remaining men ran into the church to see what had happened. A moment later they dragged the lifeless form of the sergeant from the building. A shard of the stained glass had fallen on him, pierced entirely through his chest, and was still smoking. They worked over the sergeant for several seconds before one shouted, "What about the bodies?"

"To hell with it. If they ain't burnt, who cares," the other man yelled.

The first man shouted, "How about Sergeant Miller's pistol and stuff?"

"Leave his revolver and shit in there. That place done killed enough tonight. I'm taking Miller back." They loaded the dead man on his horse and galloped off, leaving Stephen alone in the flickering light of the dying fires.

Chapter 9

December 22, 1864

He was sure that people would come, but they didn't. Surely, the glow from the fire would arouse someone even though the closest neighbor was almost a half mile distant. No one came. No one came. It finally occurred to him that if they did see the fire, fear would keep them away. He didn't know how much time had past—other than it was long. The light breeze which had blown away from him, toward the fires, had reversed itself. Now the acrid smell of burnt wood and light ash surrounded him.

Why didn't someone come! The people had to know what happened. They had to have enough courage to see if they could help, if only to bury the victims. Stephen was becoming irrational. Maybe he could use the rope and ease himself down. He tried to get in as stable a position as he could and then he untied the rope. It dangled on the ground, but only by a couple feet. Letting himself down using the limb as a pulley halved the ropes length. He'd have to drop some distance, maybe as much as eight feet, not a problem for a man with two good legs, but a major obstacle for one with a knee injury that was far from healed. He had to get down. How else? He looked at the creek; if he could swing out toward the water, time the release of the rope so he'd land in the water, though it was shallow, it might break his fall. "Crazy," he said out loud.

Maybe if he could lower himself as far as possible and drop, landing only on his good leg then roll. But, if he injured his good leg or did serious damage to the one already encased in a cast, it was a death sentence with no one to help him. After much thought and time, he decided and said to the night air, "Maybe that's what I deserve. I shouldn't live. If I can just look after their bodies. If I can bury . . . " The sound of a horse galloping across the church yard from the rear made him snap around so fast he almost fell from his perch.

The rider sprung out of the saddle and raced to the church entrance as soon as the horse reached the road. The person who plunged inside was small and definitely not a soldier. After a few seconds there was a scream, a woman's, and afterward he thought he could make out sobs. Soon the figure emerged from the church. The woman sat on the church steps, crying, debris strewn around her, body convulsing. She threw her head back and yelled, "No, no, no!" He recognized the voice. It was Jasmine. Stephen said to himself, "Thank God." He yelled, "Jasmine!"

She sprang up and looked around wildly.

"I'm over here, across the creek."

She ran to the road, stopped and peered into the woods on the other side of the creek.

"I'm up in a tree. It's Lieutenant McKenney. Marcus put me up here."

Jasmine began walking toward the creek, searching the tree tops as she came.

"Bring your horse," Stephen said.

Jasmine returned to her mount, grabbed the saddle's pommel, put her foot into the stirrup and swung onto the animal in a practiced, familiar manner. Within a few seconds she guided her horse into the creek.

"I'm here." Stephen waved one arm.

She gazed upward toward the sound of his voice. After a few seconds, she saw him. McKenney heard her crying. She said, "What should I do?"

"Ride over and get directly below me. You'll see a rope hanging there. Tie the very end of it to your saddle then back up until the line's taught. I'll let loose up here and just walk the horse back to me. It will let me down."

Jasmine said nothing. She positioned the horse under McKenney, tied the rope end to the pummel and backed away until Stephen was lifted upward a few inches. He hung there like a sack of flour, like the ones he brought home from the mill near his Virginia home. The rope tried to crush his chest making it uncomfortable to breathe. Jasmine asked, "Are you ready?"

"Yes," he managed in a kind of breathless whisper. He slowly descended as Jasmine walked her horse toward the spot she'd started from. Stephen's legs dangled in front of her as she got close. "Can you straddle Ellie?" Jasmine asked.

"Yes." McKenney swung his good leg over the mare, behind Jasmine. At his lowest point, he was still eighteen inches above the horse.

"I'm going to loosen the rope," she said. "Grab onto me in case the horse bolts when you drop on her. Ellie is gentle, but . . . on three . . . one . . . two . . . three." She pulled on the slip knot.

Stephen came down hard on the mare's back. The horse shifted its feet a little. Stephens leg and privates did not fare as well. He groaned.

"Are you okay?" she asked.

"Uh-huh," Stephen gasped. His arm was around her neck and shoulders and that kept him on the horse.

"You sure?"

"Yes. Are Marcus an—"

"They're all dead." She began to cry.

"Can you get my crutch? It's at the base of the tree. I'll see to them, but I need the crutch."

She nodded. Instead of getting down out of the saddle she used the reins to move the horse's head over the crutch. Jasmine said, "Ellie, pick-up." The horse grabbed the crutch shaft in its mouth, lifted it, and turned its head so Jasmine could grasp it. She handed it back to Stephen. "Hold tight," she said as she guided the mare into the creek. "I'll help, they're *my* family."

***

Lieutenant McKenney looked down at two of the corpses lying on the floor. He'd seen many more gruesome scenes. War produced grotesque carnage at every battle. But, when you knew the people, the impact was completely different. That was true of buddies killed in fighting; it was true of what he was looking at now. Louise and Samuel lay face down in pools of blood. Both had been bayoneted in the back several times. One burnt timber had fallen from the roof and landed on Samuels lifeless legs. They were killed near the front door, the most fire damaged portion of the church, but their bodies were close to the brick wall and were protected from the collapse of the roof in that section. Stephen guessed they'd been forced to stand against the wall when they were executed.

Jasmine dropped to her knees next to Samuel, placed her hand on his shoulder, sobbing with her eyes closed. Stephen looked up at the roof. The gently flaming ridge pole and a few rafters were all that remained above them. "I'm going to find Marcus and Marian. Be careful if you move. Most of the roof is down, here, but more could cave in at any time." Jasmine nodded once.

McKenney hobbled around piles of smoldering timbers. He hoped the Hurleys weren't buried under it. When he looked up to see if any particularly dangerous conditions were above him, Stephen was surprised that the roof above the rear third of the church was smoldering, damaged, but still in place for the most part. When he got close enough to see, the pulpit stood, untouched in its accustomed place. But, there was no joy in him . . . for next to the place that Reverend Hurley had delivered his sermons laid the slain minister and his wife. Marian had been bayoneted in the chest, but her body was the most violated for her head was nearly severed by a saber blow. Holder was the only one carrying a saber. Stephen growled, "The son-of-a-!" He held his tongue before uttering the last word. He was still in a church. One that seemed more holy now than it had ever seemed to him before. And eerily scary.

A few feet from Marian, Marcus was on his back, a large hole in his forehead. His eyes stared upward vacantly devoid of emotion. He'd bled profusely, dousing his beard and hair with blood and creating a puddle in which his head rested. It was too much for Stephen to bear. Samuel, Louise, Marian, Marcus. He screamed, "Ahawww!" His crutch clattered to the ground. He dropped to his hands and one good knee, broken and defeated. He moaned between sobs, "I'm sorry, Marcus. I'm sorry. I'm so sorry. Oh, God."

He felt a gentle hand on his shoulder. Jasmine's voice was urgent, "We must shelter them before the rest of the roof collapses, or the soldiers return." She helped him to his feet.

McKenney walked by the pulpit to the only slightly singed rug behind it. One small length of red embers lay a few feet from heavy woven cloth, but miraculously it remained unharmed. He used the end of his crutch to push back the rug. He pointed to a hole in the floor that served as the lifting grip used to raise the trap door to what had been his home for weeks. "If you'll get that open, I'll pull Samuel and Louise back here. Its best we put them down there. I doubt if we can dig graves and bury them quickly enough."

Jasmine nodded.

***

It was urgent, sad, hastily performed, and depressing work made super stressful by fear that the roof might collapse at any moment or that the Yankee scavengers might return and kill them. McKenney struggled to drag Samuel and Louise's bodies to the trap door. Jasmine managed to slide Marcus' body down the steps into the cellar, covering her in his blood, and stressing her psyche to its breaking point. She could not look at Marian's pitiful remains, much less touch them. Stephen struggled into the cellar, pulling Marian's body first, then Louise, then Samuel's. He laid them side by side, close to each other, and after he and Jasmine said a brief prayer and their goodbyes, Stephen placed the bed mattress over the bodies.

He and Jasmine wept as they emerged from the cellar. She closed the door reverently and pulled the rug back over it. Stephen clung to the heavy sack he'd removed from the cellar. He stepped to the pulpit.

"We have to leave." Several roof timbers fell to the floor as if to punctuate Jasmine's words.

"Jasmine, I've got to do something before we go." Lieutenant Stephen McKenney leaned on the pulpit, closed his eyes, and spoke. "Lord, four good people gave their lives here for preserving what they believed was right. Please look over their resting spot. Reward those that are good that visit here. Protect this place from evil ones that wish to do harm on this ground. Bless it for as long as they rest here." He looked up where the front portion of the roof had been and focused on the cross. It was silhouetted by the quarter moon. "Let that cross stand as a beacon for protection of the weak and reward for the virtuous." There was no amen.

Jasmine and Stephen rushed out of the church. As they cleared the front stairs, there was a rumble and a deafening crash. The whole rear of the church collapsed, burying the spot they just left in three feet of rubble and tons of brick and wood. They turned and looked at the smoking, wrecked building. Fires sparked anew. Both of them wept a last time. The threat of returning Union troops forced them to flee.

When they reached Jasmine's horse, she said, "What are your plans to get away?"

He didn't answer her. Instead he tied the top of the sack into a knot. "Take this with you. You'll need it." He held it out to her. She ignored it.

"How are you going to travel?" He said nothing.

"Get on Ellie. You're staying with me until we can figure out what to do."

"I can't."

"Yes, you can. They gave their lives for yours. You have to respect that, not just stumble around out here until you're caught and killed anyways. We don't have time to argue. Get on!"

After a couple attempts, and with Jasmine's assistance, Stephen swung into the saddle. Jasmine climbed up behind the lieutenant. She reined her horse into the woods behind the church, trying to avoid the branches that tore at the lieutenant's protruding stiff leg. Each time one raked the cast or leg he winced. Within moments Jasmine guided the horse onto two wagon ruts. McKenney would leave by the same backwoods trail he arrived by.

Chapter 10

December 27, 1864

Through his fading slumber he felt someone nudging him in the small of his back. It was cold and the blanket he slept under had worked its way down exposing his shoulder and chest to the cold air in the barn. McKenney felt Ellie's nose poke him again. In five days, Jasmine's mare and he had developed a routine. As soon as the first sun rays peeked over the eastern horizon, the horse woke him so he could let her out to get a drink in the stream next to the barn. In return, Ellie raised no objection to sharing her home with Stephen.

"Okay, okay." The lieutenant rolled onto his back in the hay that served as his bed. He felt around for his crutch. After sitting, Stephen used it to pull himself up and stand. He walked the two steps to the bale of hay that served as his lone piece of furniture. His boots were there and his shirt. The boots were all that remained of his uniform. Serving in the Confederate Army seemed like a distant memory, though it was less than two months behind him. He'd become an expert in wiggling into a boot with a stiff leg. Within a minute he was ready to open the barn door and let Ellie trot to the stream 200 feet away.

As he watched the mare drink in the cold early morning mists, he felt guilty. Guilty that he wasn't still fighting in what he knew was a lost cause. Guilty that he put Jasmine in peril by sheltering him. Guilty that he still needed help because of his slowly healing knee. And, most of all, guilty that he hadn't been able to save Marcus, Marian, Louise, and Samuel; and that he was still alive.

He looked toward the small house for signs of Jasmine stirring. McKenney was a realist. He knew there was every conceivable reason not to be attracted to the girl. That didn't keep him from increasingly marking time from each sighting to the next. The young woman's breathtaking beauty certainly was one factor, but her intelligence and kind disposition made her even more impossible to ignore.

Stephen hoped she would repeat her actions of the previous three mornings. She had visited him, bringing cornbread, fried potatoes, and hot coffee. Little else was available to the inhabitants left in the wake of Sherman's March. Indeed, Jasmine felt blessed to have ample supplies of those three items. Though monotonous, they didn't suffer from an empty belly as many of their neighbors did. As he watched, a flash of motion caught his eye 150 feet left of the "Cracker House." Jasmine emerged from the outhouse still dressed in her night clothes. She trotted to her rear door holding the night shirt tight to her throat. Before she entered, she looked over her shoulder at the barn, and waved. Stephen hoped she was smiling.

Fifteen minutes later, Jasmine reappeared carrying a tray. He hoped she would spend time with him. When she was close enough, he saw there was two of everything on the tray. That made him happy.

***

McKenney was repairing the stalls in the barn when he heard Jasmine's voice calling his name. She pulled open the barn door and spoke as she walked toward him. "I thought you'd want to know right away. Sherman took Savannah a few days before Christmas. Hardee got most of the army out, but there isn't much he can do except run." She stood in front of him, a sad look on her face. "I overheard Colonel Gore talking to an officer who was visiting from Sherman's staff. He was bragging that Sherman sent a message to Lincoln offering Savannah as a Christmas present."

"Did you hear where Hardee went?" Stephen asked. "No."

He shook his head. "If you hear, please tell me."

"Are you thinking of going back?" Jasmine sounded concerned. "You can't be of much help in a fight with your leg the way it is."

"I have something I have to do, if I can. I promised Marcus I wouldn't kill again and I won't go back to fight in the war. But, I was entrusted with the responsibility of delivering something very important to General Hardee. I mean to do that. If I can't, then it all belongs to you."

Jasmine looked at him questioningly, but said nothing. McKenney hobbled to the bale of hay and rolled it over ninety degrees. The sack he salvaged from the church lay under it. He said, "Go ahead, open it."

She bent over and picked the sack up. The metallic sounds it made opened her eyes wide. Jasmine tried to undo the knot, but her fingers weren't strong enough. She asked, "Will you?"

"Sure." Stephen took the burlap from her and pulled on the fabric until it loosened. When the sack was open he handed it back to her. He said, "Reach in and get a handful."

Jasmine's hand disappeared in the bag and came out with a handful of coins. *Gold coins!* She opened her fist and stared at the money. It was more than she'd ever held or seen at one time. She stopped counting at two hundred dollars. Her only comment was, "Oh!"

"What's in the sack is for two things. First, it's to buy the property the church is on. I'd like it to stay like it is. It's kind of a memorial to Samuel, Louise, and the Hurleys. What's left is to take care of you. There should be plenty for both."

"How much is there?"

"In the sack?"

"Yes."

McKenney did some quick math in his head. He'd been entrusted with $740,000 in gold and silver. They tried to put about the same amount in every bag. There were thirty-two bags. He said, "Between twenty-two and twenty-five thousand."

"Dollars?"

"Yes."

Jasmine's knees weakened and she sat down on the hay bale as her head swam. In the economy of that day, she could buy the church property, all 240 acres, and, by her standards, have funds left over to live like a queen.

"Will you help me get the rest back to whom it belongs?" he asked.

She nodded. Then asked, "Do you—can you stay for a while?"

***

December 28, 1864

Could we be in serious trouble?" Holder asked. Being summoned to the colonel's office made him nervous.

"There are rumors that have been transmitted to Sherman's staff." Gore sat down at his desk and opened a drawer, pulling out several papers. "The captain that was here yesterday was inquiring."

"That's not good."

"It depends." Gore placed a copy of Sherman's orders regarding foraging and confiscating goods on his desk. "We are in direct violation if we entered any dwellings *unless* the inhabitants are actively engaged in hostile acts. Of course, there must be witnesses to prosecute this." He winked at Holder. "There aren't any . . . living . . . are there?"

Holder relaxed, "None, sir."

"Read sections IV, V, and VI. Be sure anything you do is covered by the exceptions written into the orders as punitive actions for resistors. Use the same wording in your written reports. I'm sure you'll continue to find many resistors."

They both laughed.

Neither noticed the door to the next room close silently.

***

When Jasmine came home from her day's work, she didn't immediately go to visit with Stephen as she normally did. The first he realized that fact was when he heard Ellie whinny. When he looked out the barn door through the slow drizzle of the cold late December rain, he saw the mare tethered at the rear door of the house. After being sure there weren't any spying eyes, he came as close as he could to running, burdened by the need to use his crutch. He approached the house apprehensively. Stephen knocked on the door. Jasmine asked, "Who's there?" She sounded as though she'd been crying.

"It's Stephen."

She hesitated for a second before saying, "Come in." When McKenney entered her house for the first time, Jasmine stood in what was the kitchen of her small home. Her eyes were red, her cheeks stained and wet with tears, her normally neatly arranged hair straggled around her shoulders in an auburn heap. Those shoulders slumped forward dejectedly, a stark contrast to her normal proud posture. Her work dress was wet from her ride through the rain.

Stephen asked, "What's wrong?"

Anger replaced despair in the woman who stood before him. "The bastards, the lousy bastards. They killed Marcus, Marian, Samuel and Louise so they couldn't be witnesses to their stealing. I overheard Gore and Holder talking . . . they're killing all the people they're stealing from because Sherman's orders don't allow them to do what they're doing. Not the way they're doing it."

"I figured even Sherman couldn't be that much of a Devil. He is enough like Satan without—" McKenney left the rest unsaid.

"If they knew you . . . and I . . ." Jasmine looked at him—suddenly a slight smile crept on to her face. "You look like a drowned rat."

They both shared a brief, sad laugh. The realization they needed some relief overcame them simultaneously.

"You look like you took your bath in your clothes, too." Stephen grinned and Jasmine blushed.

"You can't go back to the barn until you get dry." Jasmine pointed to an opening and said, "There's a stove in there. I started a fire when I got in. You can sit by it. I'll see what I can find for us to eat."

"That's kind of you." Stephen limped across the floor and into what proved to be Jasmine's living room, the third and last room being her bedroom.

Flames flickered through the open grate that served as a door to the potbellied stove. A supply of kindling was neatly stacked next to the cast iron device whose vent pipe extended into the ceiling. A discolored ring on the boards that the stove pipe disappeared into told Stephen there was a leak that needed fixing. Several hooks were screwed into the ceiling directly above the stove, whose raised letters proclaimed, *Made by The Brewton Foundry*. Warmth streaming from the fire inside felt very good as he approached. He looked around for a chair to pull close to the stove. When he surveyed the room, he was surprised. The room had a large comfortable looking stuffed sofa, two high-backed chairs, and two wooden tables that had a more luxurious look than the normally homemade furniture in most of the homes inhabited by the region's poor. There were three other plain wooden chairs close to the stove. Stephen guessed they were there to be used for that exact purpose—to allow Jasmine and her guests to warm themselves on cold nights.

"I think it's going to turn cold tonight." Jasmine stood in the opening to the kitchen. "I'll give you two more blankets. You'll need them. Go into the bedroom. The blankets are on the shelves next to the window."

McKenney nodded. He went into the bedroom and was as surprised to find a huge four poster bed in it as he had been by the furniture in Jasmine's living room. It would have looked more in place in one of the surrounding plantation houses. There was a large ornate chest of drawers on the wall next to the bed. A narrow rack with a straw mattress was in the opposite corner of the room. Her dressing chair was made of wooden slats and sat next to the "sleeping pallet."

The blankets were where Jasmine had described. He picked the two that looked the most worn, pulled them from the stack, and realigned the remainder so they were as neat as when he found them. Jasmine stood in the doorway as he turned to leave.

She smiled weakly, moved to let him pass, and said, "There's coffee on the stove. I'm going to change. Please, stay by the fire." When he passed her, she entered her bedroom and slid the curtain closed that served as a door.

Stephen looked at the stove. She had placed a couple pots on the top and pulled two chairs up close to the warmth radiating from its fire. The lieutenant obediently sat in one of the chairs, keeping his eyes fixed on the black cast iron stove in front. It seemed a very long time until she walked up behind him.

Her hand touched his wet jacket. "Those won't dry with you wearing them. Not before you have to go to the barn. I laid out a pair of men's pants on my bed. They should fit. Strip your wet clothes off and we'll dry them. You can wrap another one of the blankets around you to keep warm." She wore the blue dress that he had first seen her in. Jasmine picked up a long pole and used it to hang her wet clothes on a couple of the hooks over the stove, explaining that mystery. He knew his clothes would soon be beside hers.

He nodded and rose to go to the bedroom.

"I'm counting on you being a proper gentleman," she said. "You can be assured none other will appear."

***

McKenney stood in the rear doorway in his recently dried clothes, the two blankets folded over his arm. "Would you put Ellie's blanket on her?" Jasmine asked.

"Certainly."

Jasmine touched his shoulder. "Oh, I almost forgot. I sent word to Father McCarthy. He's returned from Tennessee by now, I'm sure. I inquired about the parole papers you said Marcus talked to you about. Would that help?"

Stephen nodded and said, "That sure would help—a lot. I wouldn't have to worry every second . . . about being seen."

She reached out and grabbed his arm as he started to leave for the barn. "I worry about them. When it's possible, can we go out and check on . . . ." She began to choke up.

"Certainly."

✝✝✝

December 29, 1864

"It's so cold this morning. Come eat breakfast in the house," Jasmine spoke to Stephen through the open barn door.

"That's very kind of you." He looked across the 150 feet of open pasture, past the house, at the country lane in front of Jasmine's house. "What if someone comes by? Will that cause you trouble?"

She laughed bitterly. "If you mean, will my reputation suffer, I can assure you that when you're someone like me, it doesn't matter. I don't have any neighbors living close.

Besides, very few folks use the road. The Yankees haven't shown desire to be out this early. No one will see or care."

He nodded and walked next to her. She adjusted her pace to the speed he could muster using his crutch. "Were you warm enough last night?" she asked.

"Yes, ma'am. Warm as toast." He was shivering as he spoke.

"You're a very poor liar, Lieutenant McKenney."

He laughed. "I guess if I'm going to be poor at something, that's as good an item to be poor at as there is."

They both laughed.

The only sound was the one made by their feet as they walked across the frost crusted brown grass and weeds of the pasture. Both watched the road, but as Jasmine predicted, no one appeared. When they were several feet from the door, Stephen asked, "Do you think you can get me some paper and pen and ink? I want to write to my family."

"I have everything you need in the house."

A trace of surprise flitted across Stephen's face.

"I *can* read and write." Jasmine's tone left no doubt that she was indignant.

"I'm sorry. I just thought since Samuel and Louise didn't know . . ." He didn't finish. After another two steps he added, "Jasmine, I'm really sorry."

She stopped at the door and squared around to face him. "My mother taught me. When you're the master's play toy you get some advantages. Nicer clothes, better food, separate living quarters, and even a little learning. It makes the man feel less soiled if his mistress isn't a dirty illiterate animal, even if he is."

Stephen bent over and looked at his feet. He had no idea what to say. They stood at the back door completely still, one embarrassed, the other angry. McKenney spoke his thoughts, "I don't know what to tell you. I didn't mean to insult you. I would never do that. I like you too much."

A strange look appeared on Jasmine's face. She remained silent and motionless for a full minute, one that seemed like an hour. Eventually she said, "I had no right to attack you. You didn't do anything to me. And, I've been guilty of . . . ." She paused. "But, I won't apologize." She smiled faintly as she opened the door. "We need to eat before breakfast gets colder. Then, I'll get what you asked for."

***

Lieutenant Stephen McKenney took stock of his life as he prepared to write three letters. One would be to his parents; that was obligatory—that was first. The second would be to Maureen, his beloved sister. There was no one closer to him in the world than his sibling. They shared the chores that growing up on a farm required. Mark, Stephen's younger brother, was a sickly youth often incapable of working alongside his brother and sister. Though no animosity existed between them, Mark and Stephen weren't close. Mark was close to death several times, it strengthened Stephen and Maureen's bond. They milked cows, weeded gardens, cleaned stalls, chopped tobacco, and brought in the hay crop as a team. They were each other's closest friend.

The third letter was one he hoped he wouldn't need to use. With all that had transpired and what might follow, it was obvious that Jasmine's situation could become precarious. While Marcus had said the young woman was well liked, he wondered what would happen without the reverend to buffer the racial reaction. She was vulnerable at best. If it should become known that she was aware of what happened at the church and knew the Hurleys were murdered, her life was likely to evaporate as quickly as a drop of water on the pot-bellied stove. That letter would be a vehicle to see to her safety, *if he couldn't.*

He sat at the kitchen table. Jasmine had encouraged him to stay in the house to write, assuring him that no one would call and it would be warmer. She said, "Besides, if you keep a fire in the stove it will be comfortable when I get home." It was a weak excuse, but one he appreciated as he dipped his pen in the ink bottle.

He wrote:

Dear Mother and Father,

As I write this letter much has happened since my last message to you. As you are sure to know, Atlanta fell and the army evacuated. I was chosen to be detached under Colonel Garren's command and sent with critical supplies and information to join with General Hardee. As we moved toward joining Hardee at Savannah, our rear guard collapsed at Lovejoy Station. A Union cavalry unit attacked our supply wagons and the battle resulted in the virtual annihilation of both groups. Colonel Garren was mortally wounded and what was left of the command fell to me. We became trapped behind the enemy advance, our ranks further decimated, and during our attempt to escape I became injured, NOT wounded. Because the injury was a serious leg problem I was forced to order the few soldiers who remained that could move with dispatch to leave me. I was sheltered for a month by some of the finest people I've had the occasion to know, a minister and his flock. This came to an unfortunate end which I will not detail. I have passed into the shelter of another and I have hope that I'll see our farm again. If fate decrees that I should not, know that I have loved you with each breath. And, if I return, it may be with someone who has become very dear to me. I believe the prayers I know you say for me will help keep me safe and my prayers for you will do the same.

With my greatest love,

Stephen.

He folded the letter, addressed an envelope, and slid the letter inside. It was the easiest he would write. McKenney sighed, looked out the window at Ellie, who stood in the lee of the barn while cold December winds wrapped around the structure. Stephen rose from his chair and stretched. When he sat down again, he knew what he would have to put on paper would be terribly difficult.

My Dearest Maureen,
I write this letter with the strong conviction it will be my last opportunity to communicate with you. Honesty has
always marked our relationship and I must maintain that with you. I beg you not to share this with mother and father since I have not told them the severity of my situation. After the loss of Atlanta, I was detached from Hood's Army and

sent with important material to join Hardee under Colonel Garren's command. A Union cavalry unit fell on us killing all but 21 of the 60 men in Heath's group. Seven were wounded past being able to continue. Among those killed was Garren and I was forced into command. I will only say I failed. At current I am far to the rear of the enemy's lines and am in some jeopardy. I've brought major misfortune upon those who helped me. Four lives were forfeited though not entirely though my dereliction. I pray for forgiveness. My dear sister, you know me to not be of faint heart. I shall do all I can to return, but I must be honest with myself as well as you. My left leg is ruined. I'll never run again and probably not walk without a crutch or cane. This makes for many more problems in my current situation. If I do return, I hope it will be with someone. I have found a woman that I believe I will want to share my life with; one that I believe you will heartily approve; but one that comes with difficulties. I'll not speak of these here. It is about her, Jasmine Jones, that I must beg the greatest favor. I will instruct her to seek you out and for you to see her established in our county if we are separated or I am dead. She will not be a burden. Jasmine is smart, beautiful, all the things you are. There are reasons she cannot stay here, in large part because of the help she's given me. Dear sister, I implore you to do this for me. Know this, I will think of you with my last breath.

With my greatest love,
Stephen

McKenney read and reread the letter. He considered saying more; he considered saying less. At the end, he folded the letter as it was and inserted it into the envelope he'd addressed. He reached for another piece of paper, inked his pen, and started to write.

Dearest Jasmine,
I address you this way for in the brief period of our acquaintance I have become most fond of you. If the occasion arises for you to read this letter, it is probably true that I am dead. This letter is to express my feelings for you if I'm denied the opportunity to do so by fate. I am in love with you though our time together has been so brief. The four people that will be in my last thoughts will be of you, my parents, and my sister Maureen. My greatest regret is I'll be denied the favor of sharing life with you. Since your kindness shown to me may be an instrument of doom for you, it is necessary that I provide you a path to happiness. If we are parted, go to my home in Virginia. I will leave you to use your own best devices to reach Harrisonburg in the Shenandoah Valley. A map and instructions are enclosed with this letter for getting from that town to my home. Seek out my sister, Maureen. She will expect your coming. You can trust she will be your new sister. What you will tell of your past I leave to you. They know nothing. I ask you to pursue the purchase of the church and its surroundings. Take the rest of what we share and escape to my home where you will be welcomed, be safe and be happy.
　With my greatest love,
　Stephen

The Lieutenant stared at his last letter for a long time before folding it and placing it in its envelope. He took another piece of paper and wrote on its top, "Directions from Harrisonburg to my home." He began penning the map. Stephen felt he had turned over an hourglass for the final time.

Chapter 11

November 26, 1954

Landry Dawes and his son slid into their car looking into the sun which had risen to fifteen degrees above the tree line. Skies were clear, cool, and crisp. Both men were quiet, each with their own thoughts.

Landry Junior was wondering about the waitress, Julie. How old was she? How could he see her again? He would be a freshman at Georgia Tech next year. The drive wasn't bad from Atlanta to Eatonton, maybe three hours. He wondered if she was dating anybody steady. How would he find out the answers to his questions? When his father pulled the car onto the side road, he read its sign, *Cotton Creek Road,* and he knew. The young man snapped his head around and said, "Can we come back here to eat lunch?"

His father appeared to ignore him. Turning onto the asphalt seemed to deafen the man. The boy watched his father stare down the road in a trance, gazing at a world that young Landry didn't see. He spoke louder. "Hey! Dad!"

Mr. Dawes' head jerked backwards slightly and he said, "What you need, son."

"I just asked if we could come back here for lunch. You okay? You seem like you're out somewhere else."

"Sorry, Landry."

"Well?"

"Well, what?"

"Can we come back to the restaurant for lunch? That's the third time I asked." He got snarky, "You losing your hearing?"

"I'm sorry, Landry. Look, I've got lots on my mind. Yes, we'll go back to Flora and Fanny's for lunch." He shook his head and grinned. "Why do you want to go back?"

"I like their food."

"Oh. I guessed wrong. I thought you might have wanted another look at the waitress we had."

"Ohhh, shit, Dad!" The boy looked out the window, shrugged his shoulders and locked his jaw.

"Sorry . . . again . . . I guessed wrong." Dawes Sr., smiled, realizing that he wasn't mistaken. His son would be silent as he assuaged his pride. No one wanted to be seen as that transparent, unless they purposefully allowed themselves to be read for an ulterior motive. He knew his boy would stew silently until some thought wisped through his youthful mind and allowed it to move onward.

It was just as well, for he had his own thoughts to wrestle with and they were formidable opponents. They were ones he couldn't share. They'd become more difficult since their morning stop for breakfast. When his boy had casually mentioned selling the property they were just about to reach, his son had no way of knowing that his father was considering that very course of action. A neighboring land owner had offered a very attractive sum for the property. The one catch, the one that Landry Dawes had trouble accepting, was that it must be all the property—that included the church site—and the cross.

The money offered was a sum that would insure the Dawes family would live in comfort, not splendor, but comfort for a few generations. It would allow him to modernize his Alabama farm's milking operation without going into debt. He could replace an aging tractor and other equipment as well, and still have a significant sum to bank. Logic told him that was the wise move. His heart rebelled with fervor.

The cross, the steeple it stood on, the ruins of the church behind it, they were the blood from which the Dawes drew their strength. He fought with the ghosts of his ancestors; their faces coming to life from the photos that adorned his farm house mantle. Now there were more voices he'd have to hear. It was clear the cross was a revered spot for the local population. What stories related by locals would be added to the one Julie told when they made their promised visits? How much would the weight of guilt derived from the possibility of selling the property that was already resting on him increase? Then there was the envelope.

They passed a mélange of dwellings that ranged from ramshackle mobile homes to immaculate brick structures sparsely spread along the road. Cotton Creek appeared from the woods and became the roads mirrored companion. After two curves, the pavement ended and became graded red clay. Dawes knew the end of the pavement marked the beginning of the church property. He slowed to a stop.

His son looked at him questioningly. "Something wrong with the car?"

"No. I thought you'd be interested. This is where our property starts. Right back there at the end of the paved road.

It runs back up into those rolling hills and goes to the creek. I've walked the property line a couple times. If we have time we'll do that. It's a pretty piece of land."

"Neat." That was his son's response to anything that pleased him.

Mr. Dawes looked at the rolling woods which was one of the area's remaining properties undisturbed by agriculture or housing. The lumber in the pines and oaks were valuable and the man offering to purchase the land made it clear he was going to timber it. The tall stately trees' intertwining limbs made naked by winter's winds seemed to be folded together in interlocking prayer positions asking that they be left alone. Dawes thought, *Damn, Landry you're getting soft in the head.*

"Well?" His son tossed his hands upward in disgust. "We gonna sit here all day?"

Youth was so impatient. "Your wish . . .," Dawes said, and let up on the clutch.

***

"Untie the ladders first." Dawes Sr. stretched as he stood next to his open car door. "You need help lifting them off the car?"

Landry Jr. looked disgusted, "Noooo."

"I'm going to look around a bit. Just move the ladders and all the stuff in the trunk over to the steeple." Dawes took a few steps toward the church ruins.

His son looked up at the cross. "That's way up there. Will these ladders get us high enough?"

"Yes."

"Damn, it's a big sucker."

"It's seven feet tall." Landry Senior walked around the portion of the front church wall that still stood. It looked like it did the first time his father had brought him to help, as he was introducing his son to their family obligation—no, tradition was what his father had called it.

The church's dimensions were originally forty feet wide by a hundred feet deep. An unusual occurrence was that the walls all collapsed inwardly. Dawes assumed there was a scientific reason for this. It couldn't be attributed to the fire for the raiders only set the roof ablaze and for some unexplainable reason most of the floor charred lightly, but didn't succumb to the flames. The construction was such that the doubled brick wall partially rested on the wooden flooring. As the wood deteriorated over the decades, the weight of the walls pulled in, eventually claiming section after section of the building. The result was a huge pile of bricks and some other items that time and termites had little effect upon. A few spots toward the front of the church remained uncovered by bricks.

The only parts of the structure still erect were the steeple and a part of the front wall. The steeple was a four foot by four foot solid object constructed entirely of bricks, anything short of a bomb hit would not even shake it. The remaining portion of the wall was tied into the steeple on one side. It was fourteen feet high to the point where the gable had been built over it and that wooden construction had long disappeared. The rear wall had been built differently, the gable also having been built of bricks and having been a four-brick thick structure. Its original height had been twenty-two feet at the ridge pole. The result was that the biggest pile of material lay toward the rear of what had been the old structure. Its collapse the night of the fire undoubtedly aided in shielding the oak floor.

When Dawes Sr. visited the first time with his father, the other half of the front wall and a portion of one side wall still stood. They both succumbed over the years, though the site was the same as it had been just five years before. Small spots of the old oak floors were exposed with little or no clutter on them. The slight charring actually acted as a preservative. Some of these areas would support weight; others would collapse with capricious unpredictability. The danger associated with falling through a section of the floor undoubtedly accounted for the reticence that locals had about disturbing the site. Though most steadfastly avoided treading over the ruins, a very few overcame their fears to carefully trespass.

The huge number of stories about the old church and the mysterious things that transpired there were so staunchly believed by the areas residents, they viewed the ruins as having supernatural power. It was widely held that several ghosts frequented the site. Though there were many tales of positive occurrences caused by visiting there, enough dire happenings, including murders and unexplained deaths, transpired on the site that local folks had valid reasons to choose avoiding even passing the old church. Landry wondered what he might learn of its history if the individuals Mrs. Autry promised would visit came to talk to him. He wondered . . .

"Damn, Dad, what a junk pile." His son stood by his side, shaking his head as he stared at the rubble. "We don't have to sift through that, do we?"

"Nope. We want to stay off the rubble. Walking on that floor isn't safe."

"All the painting stuff is up by the steeple." "Good."

The boy looked up. "You sure those ladders we have are long enough? That sure looks like a long way up to the top of the cross."

"It's thirty-one feet. Height of the steeple is twenty-four. Luckily the steeple's flat on top. You can stand on it and do most of the painting." Mr. Dawes smiled at the doubt on his boy's face. "You'll see. It isn't all *that bad*. You're taller than me; that will make it easier."

"I'm gonna paint it?" Landry Junior looked shocked.

"You didn't think I brought you here to observe, did you?"

His son said nothing for several seconds, shrugged his shoulders. Then asked, "Is it safe?"

"You brought up the ropes and pulleys?"

"Yes. There's enough of those to climb Everest."

"The stool?"

"Yes."

"I can promise, you won't break your neck. Once we get a rope around the cross and around us, we won't be in any danger of falling to the ground."

The boy didn't look convinced. "How's that thing attached to the top?"

"The bottom of the cross extends down into the solid mass of brick by eight feet. Believe me, unless you do a bad job of knot tying, you'll not be doing a swan dive from up there."

Landry Jr. looked at the cross, frowned, and shook his head. He wasn't reassured in the least. "I guess we should get started," he said.

***

Landry Dawes, Sr. watched Landry Dawes, Jr. gingerly stand on the top of the steeple for the first time. Young Dawes looked down at the extension ladders resting against the brick structure to the ground below. Twenty-four feet looked more like 240 feet. The rope tied around his waist and around the cross made it impossible for him to plunge off the steeple. He wasn't worried about the eight inch I-beam failing after seeing it up close. The steel bar could bear the weight of their car without bending.

"You sure you don't want me to get up there with you?" Dawes Sr. was still on one of the ladders. He held the gallon of paint that it would take to apply two coats on the cross. Brushes were stuck in his carpenter's belt pouch.

"I'm okay. I'll get used to it." The boy was trying to convince himself, not his father. He carefully side stepped around the flat surface, circling the iron structure, ducking under the cross-member while being careful not to trip on the ropes securing the ladders to the I-beam's base. "I think it will be better if we don't both try standing on this at the same time." One of his hands gripped the painted steel with vise-like fingers. "Okay," he said, "I'm ready. What do I do first?"

"You need to look for any sign of rust. You know, just like I taught you when you're checking a piece of farm equipment."

"Okay." The young man began the careful systematic inspection of the steel starting at the base and slowly working upward. He took his thumbnail and scratched at a spot. The blemish was flicked off easily by his effort. "Why are we worried about a little rust? This thing would last forever if you didn't do a thing to it."

"Nothing lasts forever. Everything has its time to come and go. All we can do is to try to preserve it the best we can for as long as it serves a purpose."

Young Landry said nothing. He continued examining the cross. The boy rubbed another spot; it proved to be nothing. "If I do find a spot, what do I do?"

"I've got the wire brush and the pint can of rust inhibitor with me." He patted the carpenter's belt. "You brush it until all the rust is off. Slap some anti-rust paint on it. Let it dry. That's it."

Landry Junior shrugged his shoulders and continued his inspection, finishing one side, and moving around to the other. As he became more absorbed by his task and spent more time on his precarious perch, he became more at ease. He rubbed and scratched several spots; all passed the test, but one. A small reddish stain where the cross member was attached proved to be rust. Young Dawes said, "I need the wire brush, Dad. There's a spot at the weld." He knelt down as his father handed him the brush. When he stood up, he grasped the cross with one hand and leaned against the rope, purposely testing it. It pulled tight, but held securely. His safety *assured*, he did his best to, in turn, assure the cross' survival.

***

"Can you reach the top?" Mr. Dawes asked his son.

The boy reached up and easily touched the upper edge of the cross. "No problem," he answered. "You're not that much shorter than me. How come you can't reach the top?"

"You remember when I rolled the tractor over on me? Well, both my rotator cuffs were injured. I can't hold my hands above my head long. That's the reason I brought the stool. I'm glad you don't need it."

Landry whistled. "You were up here last time standing on that thing we lugged from home? By yourself? Dad, that's stu . . . that's not wise."

"Yep, you're right. That was stupid."

"Why in the world did you do that?"

Dawes Sr. took a deep breath. "Some things you just have to do. Is the rust preventative dry?"

Landry tapped the red paint with his index finger. "Uh-huh." He looked at his father and said, "Let's get this done."

"Let's do it," his dad agreed. He removed the can of white paint from the ladder hook on one of the top rungs. Dawes hefted it onto the top of the steeple, pried the top off and handed his son the paint brush he removed from his belt.

The young man bent over, dipped the brush in the paint, straightened and began painting from the top down. He repeated the process like a robot . . . something that his youth allowed . . . something his father envied. Landry Junior was very careful, being sure everything was thoroughly coated. His father took quiet pride in his son's show of responsibility.

Occasionally, a car or truck would drive past, slowing or briefly stopping as they stared at the curiosity before them. One person waved, but most just drove on. The vehicles were very few, not totaling a half dozen.

It took under an hour to put the first coat of paint on. After making the last stroke, Landry said, "That's it except where the rope is tied around. How do you do that?"

"When everything else dries, you move it, paint where it was and you're done."

"Daaaaa. I should have known. You don't need to be a nuclear scientist to figure that one." He surveyed his work. "How long will it take to dry?"

"That stuff dries real quick. It's one of the reasons I buy that particular paint. We should be able to put the second coat on in three . . . four hours." Mr. Dawes looked at his pocket watch. It was a few minutes before eleven. "We ought to go to lunch, take our time, get back around two, then start painting at say . . . two-thirty."

"I'm used to it up here. I'd rather stay, but that sure would be a long wait."

"I thought you wanted to go to Flora and Fanny's for lunch." Mr. Dawes' smile was wicked.

"Yeh, I forgot." Young Landry tried not to smile. He shuffled toward one of the ladders, but stopped abruptly. The boy turned his head toward the road. A car was driving over the red clay slowly until it reached the point that Dawes had parked. The auto turned off the road and stopped next to their Ford. "Looks like we have our first company," Landry said.

Dawes Sr. watched the doors open on the Nash Ambassador. The driver was a tall, slender, middle-aged man and was the first one out of the car. An old man emerged from the passenger side and a middle-aged lady came out of one of the rear doors at the same time. The fourth and final individual to get out was a familiar one; her red hair shining in the sun. Julie carried a large paper sack. She looked up, smiled, and yelled, "Hi guys, I brought you something to eat."

***

"What else? Fried chicken." She'd trotted ahead of her companions and answered Landry Junior's question. When she arrived, Julie looked up at Landry the way the young man hoped that she would. Her older airs were left at the restaurant.

"Sounds great to me," he said.

"You gonna introduce us, Julie?" the old man asked. He used a cane to steady himself as he advanced. The middle-aged couple, who'd hung back a bit, held hands as they walked up to the Dawes.

"Sorry." Julie blushed. "They're both named Landry Dawes, but I forgot the numbers."

"I'm four," Dawes Sr. said, "He's five." The father pointed at his son.

"I'm Irv McCall." The old man didn't wait for Julie's introduction. He thrust his hand toward Mr. Dawes. They shook hands and McCall repeated his actions with the boy. All repeated the ritualistic, "Pleased to meet you."

"These are my parents, Adam Smith and Arlene," Julie said. There was another round of handshakes and *pleased to meet yous*. Then an awkward silence ensued. Finally, Julie asked, "Where would you like to eat?"

Mr. Dawes scratched his temple. "Ahhh, I don't know. Never thought we'd get such a fine treat. I didn't bring any chairs." He looked at McCall. Sitting on the ground might be a problem for the old man. McCall appeared to be in his late seventies or more. "We could eat in my car, but getting all six in there would be a tight fit."

"Landry number five and I can find someplace," Julie volunteered. She looked toward Cotton Creek. "How about by the creek? There's a couple trees that have fallen over we can sit on." Her wide-eyed expression completed her transformation from worldly waitress to innocent country girl.

"Fine." The young man required no arm twisting, while Julie's mother smiled and her father frowned.

***

Mrs. Smith opened one of the four remaining brown sacks of the six bags of food Julie had assembled at Fanny's. Each contained chicken, a breast and a thigh, two small paper cups containing mashed potatoes and white gravy, each covered by waxed paper and a rubber band, and a handful of napkins. She handed one to Mr. Dawes, one to Irv McCall and one to her husband. Dawes and her husband sat in the front seat of the Ford; McCall and Mrs. Smith sat in the rear. "Now, I can tell you that this chicken is among the very best that will ever make your fingers greasy, but you won't believe it until you eat it. The recipe is a Flora and Fanny family secret." When she looked in her bag, she murmured, "Oh, all the silverware is in here." She smiled and nodded once, "If Julie and your boy need forks, they can come get them."

"I've been a lookin' forward to a meetin' you for years and years." Irv McCall leaned forward; he was anxious to speak. "I always reckoned I needed to thank someone about this here spot and what it did for me. You're the right person, I'd be a guessin'." He showed no interest in opening the paper sack. "This here place and that there cross done saved my life."

"Really? How'd that happen?" Dawes asked.

"It was twenty-two years ago. Ya'all know'd what it was like then. It was the Depression. Hard times. *Hard Times*. I was still a good hunter back then. At fifty-six, I could shoot and scramble around these woods with the best of them. Huntin' was the way we got a good share of the meat we put on the table. It was good huntin' then. Still is. Less quail, though. Anyways, I was out here one Saturday a huntin'. I'd spied me a big ol' white tail buck. Not a hundred feet away. It were the spring, so there was leaves and weeds a growin'. Heavy cover. I hunkered down and raised my shotgun. The deer moved and I moved some. Just as I was about to squeeze the trigger, Bam! I felt this burnin'. It felt like someone done hit me with a two by four. My left shoulder, neck, back all just turned red. I yelled out as I rolled down to the ground."

"Did somebody shoot you?" Dawes asked.

"Sure as rain in the spring." McCall shook his head. "I must a passed out for a few seconds. Next thing I know'd, there is this face above me lookin' down, scared as hell. When I opened my eyes, he just run off. I yelled, 'help!' Then some other things. Not too nice, I'm afraid. I kinda figured he was going for help, so I just laid there for a spell. Pretty soon I figured out he wasn't comin' back. I'd done walked two miles to get here and I was damned sure I wasn't gonna make that. It was then I looked up and saw the cross. There it was, all white and gleaming in the sunlight. Something told me if'n I could get to it, I'd be okay."

"What did you do?" Mrs. Smith asked.

"Walked. At first, I walked. I was as dizzy as I done ever been on a Friday night drunk. I kept fallin' down. Getting' up. Fallin' down. Eventually, I couldn't get up no more. They say I kept losin' blood. I crawled the last two hundred feet. When I finally got there, to the base at the steeple, I looked up at the cross, said a little prayer, and passed out. Right as the lights was goin' out, this bald eagle flies up and lands on the cross. Last thing I thought was I ain't ever seen one here, and that's an omen. When I woke I was in the Milledgeville hospital. First thing Doc said to me was, *Damn, man, are you lucky to be alive! You ought to be dead twice and some to spare. It's a real miracle*. They said I was close to not a havin' any blood left. But, you see I'm here, kickin'. The sheriff saw that eagle when he was driving over on 16 and followed it here. Walked right up to me. Now, you tell me! I know it was this here place what done it. Oh, occasionally, one of those buck shots need takin' out, but other than that . . . I'm right spry, yet."

"That's really a great story, Mr. McCall." Dawes noticed some scarring on the old man's neck for the first time.

"Call me Irv."

***

"I do believe that chicken is the finest I ever tasted."

Landry rubbed his stomach and wished the foot of space separating him from Julie was erased. "It sure was good you had those forks stuck in your pocket." Subconsciously, he adjusted his rear's position on the tree trunk they shared as a "lunch room."

Julie laughed. "That's an occupational hazard. I've carried enough forks and spoons and knives home to start my own restaurant. That is, if I hadn't carried them back."

They looked at each other. In their eyes was the look that happens infrequently and is, oh, so valuable. Landry asked, "How long you been working at Flora and Fanny's?"

"Year and a half. Started there right out of high school. I studied typing and such. My dad's brother works over at the mental hospital in Milledgeville. He's going to get me a good one. Job, I mean. But, working at the restaurant isn't that bad. Other than some men that takes slapping."

"How did you get off to come here?"

"Oh, Mrs. Autry was all for it. She even said the lunches are free."

"Wow. That's nice."

"Yes, that's something. She usually squeezes a nickel until the Indian is riding the buffalo."

They both chuckled at the old bromide.

Julie made a face. "Ouch. I'm sitting on something sharp. Mind if I move a little?" She closed the gap between them to an inch.

"No, not at all."

Julie smiled and nodded, but said nothing.

"How old are you?" Landry asked.

"Nineteen."

Landry lied. "Me, too."

"What do you do?"

"I work on the farm right now, but I start college at Georgia Tech in January. Dad's hired man quit us right before harvest and I stayed home to help."

"Oh. That was very sweet of you." Julie smiled.

"You know, it's not too far from Atlanta down to here." Landry looked for a reaction.

"Not far at all." Julie practically purred.

"Would you like to go out sometime?"

"Yes, I would. I never dated a college *man* before."

"We should write."

"That's a wonderful idea! My order pad and pencil are in the car. We can exchange addresses when we go back."

***

"It's not that complicated of a story." Adam Smith stuck his napkin inside before he wadded up his brown sack. He handed his fork to his wife. After a few seconds of indecision he gave the remnants of the gravy saturated bag to Mrs. Smith for safe handling. "It was an act of frustration, I guess."

"Frustration and your parents nagging us for grandchildren," Arlene added. She gathered the empty bags from everyone and carefully condensed them into one for the garbage. "Well, I have to admit, I wanted babies, too."

"Wanted? Hell, Arlene, toward the end we spent as much time going to doctors as we did in bed."

Arlene leaned forward and punched her husband lightly on his arm, but said nothing.

"That's where we were coming from when . . . well, we'd been to this specialist in Atlanta. He'd done tests and more tests. Other doctors had already told us we weren't going to have kids. Doc Sheldon was our last hope. When we got there, he sat us down, went over the test results like we were Emory medical school graduates. Hell, I didn't understand one word of it, but I could guess it wasn't good by his expression.

Finally, I just asked—are we going to have kids or not? I won't ever forget his answer. He says, 'There is absolutely zero chance of your wife becoming pregnant.' It was a blow 'cause he'd been positive the first time we went to him. We'd done all the things he'd told us. Some of them were—"

"Please, no details, Adam." Mrs. Smith interrupted her husband.

He nodded and continued. "We were pretty low and a little angry. It was going on ten years. Arlene was pushing thirty and . . ."

A look from Mrs. Smith silenced that thought and he began a new one. "Okay. Anyway, we were driving back from Atlanta. We always used Cotton Creek Road to get to our place. When we got right in front of here, Arlene yells, 'Stop!' I did, but I didn't know the slightest reason why I was. All of a sudden, she jumps out of the car, starts running to the steeple, and she's stripping as she's going. Hell, it was two in the afternoon. Granted it was Tuesday, but she was determined. She started yelling at me to 'Come here!' and I did. I said, 'Arlene have you gone crazy.' She said . . . ."

"No details."

"Okay. I went to strip down and suggested we go find a spot that didn't allow anybody happening by to see a lurid show. She said, no it had to be right there under the cross. Well, I got her to—"

"NO DETAILS!" Mrs. Smith's face was red, but no anger showed on it.

"All right! I guess that isn't important. When we finished and that was after a while, we were walking back to the car, she says just as calm as can be, 'Adam, I'm pregnant.' And, damned if she wasn't. Nine months later, Julie came along. Forrest, Robert, and Agnes followed. Sometimes when you get what you ask for . . . well, you know."

"What changed?" Dawes asked.

"A prayer and this place," Arlene said.

"And what a lot of good people did to make this place that way," McCall added.

Chapter 12

December 29, 1864

Steel gray skies and harsh cold winds hovered over the landscape McKenney watched as he waited for Jasmine's return from working. The weather was as wretched as it appeared. Poor Ellie had shivered in the pasture and even after having sought the shelter provided by using the barn as a windbreak, she still looked miserable. He'd gone out, hobbled across the pasture, let her in the barn and covered her with her blanket. The mare still shivered for a while. When Stephen checked the water buckets, thick ice had formed in each one. He broke the slick gray coating and removed the pieces, but knew it would only last minutes. By the time he finished and returned to the house, his teeth chattered and his body shook. Sleeping in the barn the coming night would be challenging.

The heat provided by the valiant wood stove in the living room did help moderate the house temperature some, but the only room that couldn't be described as uncomfortably cold was where the stove radiated its heat while it fought a losing battle against nature's vast resource. Even in the living room, the only truly comfortable place was in a twenty-foot radius of the cast iron. The lieutenant fed the beast faithfully, adjusted the damper to maximize its heat output, but wasn't sure he was maintaining the temperature level in the little house.

The large stack of kindling was dwindling and he wondered if it would last the night for Jasmine. He carefully scanned the lane, looking for any traffic traveling the frigid road and found nothing. Stephen was soon swinging the axe he found sticking in the sawn oak logs, reducing them to stove sized kindling. It took several minutes to adjust to the weakened knee, but something he'd done since the age of ten came easy. The pile of stove wood grew rapidly.

"Please, don't hurt yourself." Jasmine's voice came from a few feet behind him. She tried to hold her dark brown cape around her as tightly as she could with one hand. Her cheeks were pink from the cold. Behind her, she pulled a two-wheeled cart with several items stacked on it. "Oh, you've cut a lot of wood. I'll carry it in, you go inside." She motioned for him to follow her into the house.

Jasmine positioned her cart next to the kitchen table. She said, "The people I work for were in a generous mood today. The Finns gave me eggs; Mrs. Ellis gave me a sack of flour and a sack of corn meal. She warned me they'd have some bugs in them, but that's fine. And old Mr. MacMasters gave me a whole smoked ham. A big one. He said to have a happy New Year, but to be careful. Food is getting harder to come by."

"I think that's good advice. That's true of anything." Stephen started to the door. "I need to carry the wood in."

"No, you don't. The hardest thing for you to do is to bend over to pick it up off the ground. I can do that just fine." She pointed at a cupboard. "There's a sieve in that. You can get the weevils out of the flour and corn meal while I'm getting in the wood."

Stephen just nodded.

***

Long after their meal of limited portions of corn bread and ham, they sat chatting, their chairs pulled as close to the stove as they could while wearing their coats. The December winds had increased to an even higher velocity and howled around the frame house. Talking about what was happening around them was too bitter to dwell upon. They chose subjects from the past and the future by silent agreement.

"I'll never complain about cleaning the fireplaces out at home again. Either my sister or I always had that job. Maureen always managed to avoid it, somehow. That . . . and cleaning the outhouse."

Jasmine giggled and said, "She sounds like a smart girl."

"Oh, she is. You remind me a lot of her."

Jasmine looked at the stove to shield the look in her eyes. "Is that a good or bad thing?"

"Good. Very good. Besides being smart, she's strong, independent, but warm and kind. I see all that in you. I want you two to meet. Maureen will like you. I bet you become like sisters." Stephen nodded his head slowly and grinned. "Yep, my whole family would like you."

"They live a long way off." She continued to stare at the stove.

"Have you ever considered leaving here?"

"Yes."

"Why haven't you?"

"Because it isn't easy for a woman to do that. Everyone I know and can depend on is here." She took a deep breath and looked down. "Was here." Slowly, she raised her eyes and looked into Stephen's; a glint of defiance shown in them telling him she was more aware of the gulf between them than he was. "It's particularly hard if you're someone like me."

McKenney's face turned serious. He cocked his head to one side as he reached out and touched one of her hands. He said, "May I?"

She nodded, but the defiance was still there.

He gently grasped her wrist with one hand and positioned her palm upward. With his other hand he lightly brushed her fingers so they extended outward with his hand, palm up, resting on top. "I don't see the difference, do you? Neither have claws or hooves."

"If I were as dark as Louise, would you feel the same?" Her eyes, voice, and expression were cynical.

Stephen remained silent for several seconds. "You're Jasmine, not Louise, but if you were as dark as she was it wouldn't make a difference in the way I feel toward you. Does it make it easier? Yes, I'd be lying if I said anything else."

"Feel toward me? What did you have in mind? A special spot in the quarters? Or the furniture your wife doesn't want any more? You've seen my souvenirs. Don't tell me you didn't wonder where a poor nigger got a nice sofa and bed and such. Well, I'm not Howard Waltham's bitch, no more. Reverend Hurley convinced me that was wrong and I'm done with that!" Jasmine's eyes flashed.

"That's not what I had in mind."

"What did you have in mind? You going to take me to your parents and say, mom and dad, I want to marry this ex-slave girl." The anger was lessened, but still there.

"If our affection continues to grow, yes, that's exactly what I have in mind."

Jasmine looked at him skeptically, yet behind the surface, Stephen could see veiled emotion. Jasmine wanted to believe him. He said, "I thought there was the start of something between us. I don't believe I was wrong or I wouldn't be so bold. I have never been anything but a gentleman to you. That won't change. I am an honorable man."

Jasmine's look changed to one of hope, "I wish I could believe that."

The lieutenant answered simply, "You can." He rose, went to the kitchen and returned with the letter he had written to her. He said, "Please don't open this unless we're parted or if something happens to me."

***

The hour grew late and the time for Stephen to go to the barn arrived. Jasmine walked to the back door with McKenney when he prepared to leave. As he opened the door, Jasmine reached out and grabbed his arm. She said, "It's too cold for you to stay in the barn. Please go out and check on Ellie and see she's all right. Bring the blankets back in. You can sleep on the floor by the stove."

"Are you sure that's okay?"

"Yes. Hurry on before I change my mind."

When he returned, the mattress from the pallet in her bedroom was on the floor in front of the stove.

***

December 30, 1864

"Howard Waltham is waiting." The corporal stood in front of Colonel Gore's desk.

The frown on Gore's face told it all. "What does he want now?" The obsequious little plantation owner was a constant visitor to the Colonel's office. "Move the chairs away from my desk. Move them away. I don't want that little sneak near me."

"Yes, sir." The corporal pulled the chairs ten feet from Gore's desk. "Anything else?"

"What did he say he wanted?"

"He says he has some information for you."

"Send the little puke in."

The corporal exited the office and mumbled, "Pot calling the kettle," after the door closed behind him. He walked over to a balding man dressed in a plum colored coat who stood in the middle of the room. A faked smile was plastered over the visiting man's face that had an eerie look that suggested a mouse's countenance.

"Colonel Gore will see you now. I think you should know he's real busy. I'd get in and out as fast as you can."

"Thank you. Thank you." Waltham entered the Colonel's office, carrying his top hat and a cane in his hand.

"Good morning, Colonel," he said, the smile still in place.

"What do you want this morning, Waltham? Make it damn quick. I got lots to do." Gore's scowl was intense.

"I'm sorry, so sorry. I was wondering if you found those rebels that were staying with the Hurleys? The ones I reported to you?"

"What you're asking is if you're going to get paid your bounty for reporting them. NO! There weren't any Confederates there."

"There had to be one. He couldn't ride. I think he had a broken leg. His name was Stephen, I've been advised. One of our servants told us he was there in the church that morning." Waltham implored his master, "Please believe me, he was there. Someone told me they saw a stranger, a tall thin man, who was walking with a crutch sneaking through a pasture. It must have been him. He probably hid when your men came. I wouldn't doubt he probably was watching the raid. But then he may have *went away* with Marcus." Waltham paused to be sure his message was delivered. "We haven't seen the Hurleys since—"

"You aren't going to see the Hurleys. After we burned down that den of rebels, the reverend took his people and left for Charleston that very night. I doubt you'll ever see him around here again. I'll go farther, I know you won't. That's what happens to that kind. They disappear." It was the colonel's turn to pause and deliver a message. "Now, stop wasting my time and get out of here." Gore motioned to the door. "And when you leave, tell the corporal out there I want to see him right away."

"I certainly will, sir. Sorry to have bothered you. I'll get the corporal for you." He smiled broader. "May I wish the Colonel a Happy New Year?"

"Yeah. Happy New Year. Now, get out!"

Waltham scurried from the room and within a few seconds the corporal entered and asked, "You wanted to see me, sir?"

"Yes. You go find out where Holder is and get him in here, *now!*" The Colonel slammed his fist down on his desk. "I think he has loose ends to tie up."

***

Stephen watched the man drive a carriage very slowly along the lane in front of Jasmine's home. He first noticed the horse and buggy as he started to emerge from the outhouse and quickly ducked back into it. The man's full attention was focused on the house; it was obvious that he was looking for someone, probably Jasmine—or McKenney.

The carriage stopped and the man jumped down and tied the horse's reins to a tree in the yard. He cautiously approached the house. McKenney lost sight of him, his vision blocked by the structure. After a couple moments, he reappeared walking stealthily around the house. He stopped and peered in every window. When he reached the rear door, the man opened it, stuck his head inside, and called out, "Jasmine. Jasmine, you here?" When he received no answer he entered for a moment, but quickly exited. The man walked toward the barn. Ellie ran to intercept him and did not look happy with his presence. He stopped when the mare blocked his path. He yelled, "Jasmine. Jasmine, you here?" When the horse snorted, the man turned and ran, his purple coat streaming behind and his top hat in his hand. The horse took a few steps after him, but quickly decided he wasn't worth the effort.

Stephen continued peeking from the outhouse as the man untied his horse, climbed into the buggy, and drove off. McKenney fancied he heard the man curse as he did.

***

"How many bodies were there? Answer the damned question!" Colonel Gore's face was red and his tone furious. He realized the corporal in the next room could hear. Gore got up from his desk, walked to the door and said, "Corporal

Hodges, I want you outside our front entrance. I don't want anybody entering this building, do you understand?"

A muffled voice responded, "Yes, sir," as the Colonel closed the office door.

"You told me there were four you buried." Gore pounded on his desk as he returned. "Is that right?"

"Not exactly. I told you four were killed. There wasn't anybody strange there. Just the Hurleys and their two niggers."

"I don't understand!"

"Well, sir, when we went back the next day, there weren't any bodies. The walls had collapsed over where they were laying. We left them." Captain Holder knew he'd been caught in a lie.

"So you think they're all lying out there under the rubble? Well, they'd better be! I just told the Waltham man the Hurleys were in South Carolina. You're going to make that lie true. Get organized today, get everything you need lined up, and tomorrow you do it. You understand what I'm saying. You by yourself. I don't want any witnesses. Not one."

***

"It's going to be very cold again tonight," Jasmine said. She placed four pieces of kindling in the stove and poked at the coals causing the flames to flare up around the newly added wood. "I think you should stay in here again tonight, Stephen."

"What about the man I saw here today? Is it possible he might come back looking for you?"

"He won't be back tonight. It's too late."

"It's not nearly so cold, I can sleep in the barn," McKenney said.

"No. Just see to Ellie and come back, you hear?" Jasmine backed away from the stove and started for her bed-room. "Keep the fire up, it gets cold in my room if you don't. It will keep me from having to get up to feed the stove during the night. The mattress will be out for you when you get back."

Stephen made the trip to the barn, putting the blanket on the mare and checking her water. There was no ice in the bucket.

When he returned, the mattress was in place right in front of the stove. Three folded blankets were stacked on top.

He decided he wouldn't need to wear his jacket so he removed it and his boots, tossed them aside, and leaned his crutch against one of the chairs. His dependence on the "third leg" was lessening, but still required. He eased down and spread the blankets out before lying on the mattress and pulling the covers over him. After a few minutes, his body warmth, plus the heat from the stove, made him very comfortable. His eyes closed and sleep crept over him.

Dreams enveloped Stephen . . . or so he supposed, for a few seconds. Someone lifted the blankets and lay down close to him. When a soft arm reached around him, he realized he was not asleep. Jasmine was there. When he rolled over, her arms wrapped around his neck, eyes shining into his. He put his arms around her. At his touch, her body pressed against his hard and her leg reached over and around him. Jasmine's lips sought . . . .

Chapter 13

December 31, 1864

"I think this is our best opportunity, Jasmine. Most of the soldiers will be celebrating. Those left on guard won't be that keen on doing anything past the minimum. They have to do their duty. We have a good chance to make it after the sun goes down. It'll be dangerous until we get to Madison. When I get those parole papers from Father McCarthy, the chances of a problem are a lot less." Stephen paused, gently touching the blankets covering the woman lying next to him. "Are you okay with leaving, with betting everything on me?"

"Yes, Stephen." Jasmine looked up at the stove then at the first light as it penetrated her home's windows on the east side. Leaving wasn't a difficult decision. All those who had meant the most to her—were dead. True, her house and property would remain, but they were *something,* not *someone* to cling to. She would go. Ellie would accompany them to Madison where the mare would find a good home with the priest. There was only one thing she felt compelled to do. She hesitated to ask.

McKenney said, "You know the priest. Do you think he would be willing to marry us? After last night, I believe it would be best." He pushed back the blankets from his body, the cast being its only covering. He groped for his pants, then started to dress.

Jasmine lay on her back under the blankets with only her head exposed, her long dark auburn hair framing her face on the white mattress. "I honestly don't think so, but I don't know."

"I guess we'll find out." He used a chair to pull himself up on, hobbled to his crutch and picked up his shirt. Stephen froze for a second, dropped his shirt back on a chair, and went over to Jasmine. He said, "Let me help you." He extended his hand and turned his head away, mindful of Jasmine's privacy. Her hand touched his, but little weight was pulled against it. She used the assist to maintain her balance. When he was sure she was on her feet and heard the swish of a blanket, he looked back at her. She stood next to him. One hand held the blanket together in front of her, the other reached for Stephen's face. Jasmine closed her eyes and rose on her toes, inviting a kiss. McKenney responded with gentleness. The kiss was soft, but prolonged.

"I'll dress now," she said.

As she walked toward the bedroom, Stephen said, "Pick what clothes you want to take with you. We don't have much time."

She stopped. "Do we have time to visit—"

"Yes. I want to go, too. They deserve that respect."

***

"Oh, I hope this isn't terribly bad news for you my darling, but I do believe I'm pregnant." Melissa Waltham certainly picked a time for her announcement that precluded that the possibility didn't exist. She lay naked in the bed next to Heinrich Holder, their perspiration intermingled from the love making they'd just finished. "I'm over a week late and I'm never late. And, I'm nauseated in the morning."

Holder tried, but was unsuccessful at holding back his snarl. "Shit," his muffled expletive, though unintended, was audible. It was his second piece of horrible news in two days.

The woman immediately began sniffling. Holder knew he'd marry her. Her family had extensive land holdings in the area, their cooperation with the Union authorities insured they do well in the future, she was pretty, and Melissa performed like a champion between the sheets. Besides, he had no real reason to return to New York after the war's conclusion. He quickly spoke to allay her fears. "Melissa, please believe me it's strictly the timing that upsets me. I have every intention of marrying you. I hereby promise that. But, there is the problem I spoke to you about that I have to resolve, dearest."

"Really?" A smile appeared under the tears.

"Yes, really. As I told you earlier, that's why I have to leave you, now. I must do this thing if we're to have a good future."

"I am *so happy* to hear that!" She scooted over close to him.

"Good. When I've finished this most repugnant duty, I'll return to you. Tomorrow we can celebrate." Holder tried to sit up and swing out of bed, but the young woman's arm circled over his shoulder, restraining him, and pulling him back downward to the mattress.

She murmured, "Can't it wait for just a little longer?" Melissa positioned her head in the middle of his chest and began to kiss it. Holder slowly relaxed.

***

"It isn't in very good condition. The seats are all torn up, but the man said the wheels are in good shape and the axles are sound. The man admitted that he'd salvaged it out of the Tillman Plantation's ruins. I did like you said. I bought it for less than you thought I'd have to pay." Jasmine looked for a way to get down out of the wagon. "The step is torn off, I guess."

"It will work just fine. We're not going to a church social. It's a cargo wagon and it will hold together better than about anything else you could have bought." McKenney checked each wheel, pulling, pushing, and examining the axle. "Actually, for what we want it for, it's perfect."

"You think we'll make it all the way to Virginia in that?"

"I can see us pulling up the gravel road to my father's farm, sitting in that seat. Let me help you down." He reached his hand to her. She jumped down the three feet from wagon to the ground.

"It's bigger than anything Ellie's pulled before. Will she be okay?" Jasmine looked at her horse with concern.

"Ellie didn't have the least bit of trouble pulling it home, did she?" Stephen looked over the leather work attaching the horse to the wagon. He nodded his approval.

"No problem that I could see." She didn't sound relieved.

"Ellie will hardly know we're behind her, Jasmine." Stephen pointed to a large carpet bag and a burlap sack. "You said that's all you have to take. We may add some weight during our visit to the church. I won't know about that until I see if we can get to the cellar. I have the clothes on my back and little else. She'll be fine, Jasmine. And we'll take our time to take it easy on her."

Jasmine nodded. "I want to make a last check in the house." She hurried off to go inside, but there were no tears.

***

"I understand how you feel, father. It pains me not to go back. I feel like a coward." Landry Dawes sat on the edge of the creek he and his father had used as a conference table since his earliest years. "But, father, I gave my word. I gave it to a preacher. He saved me from capture and probably saved my life. I can't quit an obligation to which I've voluntarily taken an oath. I hope you understand. After all, it was right here you instilled in me that a man's word and his ability and willingness to keep it, is the way a man's worth is evaluated."

His father sat silently. He swished a long stick in the slowly running waters of the stream. "Knowing that . . .this is difficult for you. It puts you between loyalty to your country and loyalty to your word and, as I see it, God, if you gave your word to this Hurley fellow. It's a decision you have to make. I won't fault either way you decide . . . now that I know the total story."

"Well, you don't know the whole story. I asked Reverend Hurley what I could do for him. He's in his sixties, couldn't get on the church roof and needed the cross on top of the steeple painted. When I asked what I could do for him, that's what he answered. So it's this way . . . I promised him that I'd return and paint that cross every five years for as long as it stands there. Not only that, I promised my son would carry on with the task and it would pass on down through our family."

His father swished the stick in the creek, making violent circles, creating wavelets. He said, "When you go, I'll go with you. I'll help hold the ladder, or what's needed. After several seconds delay, he tossed the stick into the water. "Landry, at times you make me *very* proud of you." He placed a hand on his son's shoulder. "Let's hope that when tomorrow brings us a new year, it reverses our Confederacy's fortune and brings an end to this war."

"I hope *both* your wishes come true, father. Of one thing I'm sure, the war will end this coming year. How it ends, from what I've seen, will not end well for us."

***

The only humans Stephen and Jasmine passed on their circuitous trip to the church were two families in a carriage that wished them Happy New Year, two drunken Union soldiers who'd cursed them, and a man on a horse who nodded to them, but said nothing. They covered the three miles from Jasmine's house to the church in less than thirty minutes. Part of the route was the wagon track that McKenney had utilized in his attempt to protect the information and materials he'd assumed command over, the one he'd seen end his attempt to get to General Hardee.

When they passed the overturned wagon with its detached wheel, he wondered if Corporal Evans made it through the enemy's lines. A short distance past that wreck, the cross was visible above and through the leafless trees. The sun was only a couple degrees above the horizon and its fading rays illuminated the white steel. Coming darkness would aid them in making the trip to Madison after they'd finished their goodbyes.

"Stephen, I think it would be a good idea for us to stop along here. I'm afraid someone might be there. If it were the wrong person . . . . I can cross the hill and check while you stay in the wagon. It'll only take a few minutes." Jasmine reached out and touched Stephen's arm. "Let me do this."

"Whoa, Ellie." Stephen reined the horse to a stop. "Okay. But, I want you to be very careful. If you see *anybody*, don't let them see you and *come back immediately.*"

She nodded as she jumped down from the wagon.

***

Jasmine picked her way through the familiar woods where she'd finished her adolescence, playing with the older Louise. The last ten years of her twenty-two had been good ones except for the eighteen months she'd fallen back into the control of Howard Waltham and became his whore. She'd regained her path, thanks to Marcus Hurley's efforts. Ascending the small hill that shielded the wagon from anyone's vision that happened to be at the church site was so familiar that she paid little attention to her activities until a horse whinnied ahead of her. Someone was at the church ruins. She immediately tensed and changed her approach to be as stealthy as she was capable.

Jasmine approached the top of the hill. She bent over from the waist, going from large tree trunk to large tree trunk to stay out of the vision of whoever was at the burned and partially collapsed building. Standing behind a huge oak tree located slightly past the crest, she peeked around the trunk. A large covered wagon with two horses in harness stood close to the steeple. She couldn't see anyone in the open. However, the front church wall, one entire side, and part of the other remained intact, so the owners of the wagon could be hidden behind them. She watched for what seemed to be an eternity. There was no movement, nothing visible that would indicate there were humans present. Jasmine was just as sure the horses and wagon were not runaways.

"Shit!" A loud male voice cursed. It was clearly audible and came from the ruins. A man walked from behind the wall to the rear of the covered wagon. She only got a fleeting glance, one that only disclosed he was of average size and build . . . and did not wear a uniform. The sun was already slipping behind the low hills and trees, making the lighting opaque and blurring what it shone upon. When the man reemerged from behind the wagon, he had put a great coat on and a white bandage was wrapped around one hand. He quickly disappeared behind the remaining walls.

Jasmine didn't take long to decide what the man's business was. He was looking for things to scavenge from the church. The thought angered and alarmed her. Would he find the hidden trap door? Would he disturb their bodies? Jasmine did not think further, she acted. Quickly moving from tree to tree, she reached the last large oak that could hide her at the clearing's edge. From her vantage point, she could see the area where the rear wall had collapsed over the pulpit, rug and the door that the rug covered. It did not appear to be disturbed. Most of the inside floor area was hidden by walls that remained standing.

The sun had dropped below the horizon. It would be dark soon and . . . the sound of bricks crashing around and more curses made her more apprehensive. If the man was moving everything around, he might find the trap door. She raced from the tree to the cover the wall provided. Her breath was coming in hurried gulps and her hands shook as she eased in position to look around the wall.

The man was hunkered down in the gloom made by the disappearing sun and the shadow of the steeple and the front wall. His back was to her as he picked up bricks and set them down randomly. Jasmine was puzzled until she remembered the place he was fumbling through was the place near where Samuel and Louise's bodies had been! Who was he? She had to know!

As silently and as fast as she could move, Jasmine ran around to the front of the building, stopping as she reached the steeple which extended outward four feet. Flattening out against the brick structure, she moved her head to the corner and eased it out until she could see.

Jasmine could see the wagon and horses, but she would have to move to the outside surface of the steeple, the one in plain sight of the road, to be in position to peer through the church's front door opening. She eased around to the front of the steeple, staying in contact with the bricks. Her head moved past the corner of the structure, just far enough to allow her to observe the man. He was on one knee, his head down, completely absorbed in whatever task he was performing. She couldn't see his face, but there was something about his outline . . . she moved to get a better vision angle. The noise of horses moving and wagon sounds drew her attention. Before she could turn to look, the man evidently heard the noise for his face came up to see what was happening. She recognized Captain Holder immediately. And . . . he . . . her! For just a second, both froze, not knowing their next move.

The man reacted first, lunging to his feet, reaching for something under his coat and screaming, "What are you doing here?"

Holder could see half of Jasmine's body exposed from behind the sheltering steeple. The captain pulled a revolver from beneath his coat and raised it, pointing it at her. She jerked back just as Holder fired. Jasmine heard the zing of the bullet as it passed the bricks. Before she could run, Holder appeared around the edge of the steeple. His gun moved toward her. The scowl on his face matched his savage command. "Don't move!"

He was only three feet away and could not miss her if he shot, but she knew she must scream her accusation, "Murderer!"

As he started to raise the gun to point at her forehead, a blur of motion came from one side. McKenney lunged for the gun and Holder's arm. He grabbed it, deflecting the captain's aim, the bullet hitting the bricks and ricocheting off into the gray dusk. The two men struggled for control of the weapon, both tumbling to the ground and rolling around. Another wild shot was discharged into space, harming no one. Stephen managed to roll over on top of the captain and tried to wrench the revolver from his hand, the gun disappearing between them. The gun went off again, and immediately, Stephen tossed the weapon toward Jasmine, yelling, "Get it!"

Jasmine pounced on the revolver and cocked it in one motion. When she looked up, Holder was rushing at her. She fired. The bullet tore into his right shoulder. He stopped and dropped to his knees. His right arm drooped limply next to his body and he clutched his right shoulder with his left hand. Slowly, he fell to one side, groaning in agony as he hit the ground.

But, Jasmine had no interest in Holder. She ran to Lieutenant McKenney, to her man Stephen. He lay face down on the ground at the base of the steeple. She rolled him over and the darkening stain in the middle of his chest told her everything. His eyes were open and he said, "Go to Virginia. My sister will expect you . . . . Did you kill him?"

"I shot him. I don't know."

"If you didn't . . . don't. I want the chance to see you again someday."

"Don't talk that way!" Jasmine sounded desperate.

The sound of the wagon moving behind her made Jasmine spin around. She pointed the gun at Holder, who had gotten up, staggered to the wagon, and had somehow pulled himself into the seat.

She screamed, "You bastard!"

He said in a low pained voice, "What did you do with them?"

It took several seconds to grasp what the Yankee captain meant. She sneered as she answered, "They're buried in a place you'll never find if you look for them a thousand years."

The captain said, "Shoot me if you will," snapped the traces and slowly maneuvered the wagon out of the church yard, leaving on Cotton Creek Road. She would have liked to have shot him, but Stephen was her concern. Ellie and the wagon were standing thirty feet away. Her mare's ears were alert: the horse was nervous, but didn't bolt despite the gunfire.

Jasmine knew she had little time. Stephen had to get to a doctor quickly to have any chance to survive. Tossing the gun to the ground, she grabbed Ellie's halter and quickly led the animal and wagon next to the lieutenant. Jasmine ran back around to him. He was looking up at the cross as she leaned over him. Stephen smiled and said, "I love you, my beautiful Jasmine."

"Quiet. I have to get you in the wagon and to the doctor." She bent over and got her hands under his armpits and lifted him as Stephen struggled to help as much as he could. Jasmine leaned him against the wagon's rear. "Can you hold on until I get up in the wagon?" she asked.

Stephen managed to say, "Okay."

Jasmine quickly pulled herself into the wagon. Again grabbing Stephen under his arms, she dragged him into the bed, pulling his head as close to the seat as she could. He reached up and grabbed her arm. "Do you have the revolver?" he asked.

"No."

"Get it."

Jasmine jumped down, ran over to the gun, picked it up, and sprinted back to the wagon. She scrambled into the seat, grabbed the reins and clucked for Ellie to go. As the horse headed for the road, Jasmine looked back and down at Stephen. She said, "Hold on, Dear." His eyes looked past her. She knew. She cried. She left for Madison. "I will take you to Virginia, Stephen. I promise . . . we'll both rest in the Shenandoah like you said we would, my only love."

Chapter 14

January 2, 1865

"They have done as well as the art will allow, my child." Father McCarthy seated himself in the pew in front of where Jasmine sat at the rear of Saint Michaels. The church was one of several spared by the marauding Union soldiers in their orgy of destruction.

"Thank you, Father," Jasmine said.

"My dear girl, are you quite sure you want to carry through with this? Even by train, the war makes this a most difficult trip for an able-bodied man. And, that's without transporting a departed loved one with you." The priest's concern was riveted on his countenance.

"I'm quite sure."

"I wish you would reconsider."

Jasmine shook her head, "I'm sorry, but I must do this."

"If you must," the priest shook his head, "I've arranged for a servant to accompany you to Chattanooga. I've written a request for safe passage for you and have an endorsement letter from the military governor here in Madison. He's a more reasonable man than your Colonel Gore. I believe it will get you through the lines. Go directly to the highest authority you can find, my dear. That paperwork and the fact that you're transporting a body of a Confederate officer should serve as ready passage through our lines."

"Thank you, Father." Jasmine looked at the wooden box that housed the coffin Stephen McKenney's remains would repose in forever. "His body was prepared as good as it possibly can be?" She repeated a question asked and answered several times.

"Oh, yes. Mr. Gilroy is a fine undertaker." Patiently, the priest tried to reassure her. "And with the funds you provided, he tells me that beside the normal precautions, the whole body was wrapped in white linen, the void in the coffin was filled with salt, and the coffin itself is sealed. He told me all that could be humanly done to preserve . . ." The priest hesitated seeing the distress in Jasmine's face. "Barring an unforeseen circumstance, you should be fine."

She nodded.

"May I ask you a question? You have such a strong commitment to Lieutenant McKenney. How did it arise?"

A suggestion of resentment flitted over the young woman's face, but so quickly Father McCarthy didn't see it or chose to ignore it. She took a deep breath and said, "Lieutenant McKenney and I had fallen in love and we intended to marry. Now, may I ask you a question? Would you have married us?"

The priest stiffened. His hesitation was lengthy. He finally answered. "If you came to me and I didn't have certain knowledge that I have, I wouldn't have hesitated to marry the two of you. But, since I know about your lineage, the law prevents me from doing so. I believe that is wrong, but I would not have had a *legal* option."

Tears formed in her eyes as she looked away. She stared into space, despair closing over her. She shook her head as moisture tracked downward over her cheeks.

"And, the Lieutenant wanted this as badly as you?"

Jasmine nodded.

McCarthy suddenly brightened. He said, "Come with me," before he led her into his office. "My child, I can tell you what would have happened. There would have been a ceremony, of course, and afterward, I'm legally commanded to fill out a paper—a marriage certificate. It would be like a rebirth for you. You would no longer be Jasmine Jones. You would be Jasmine McKenney and your life would start new from that point."

"Why are you telling—?"

The priest held his index finger to his mouth requesting her patience and silence. He walked across his office to a desk, opened the drawer, and removed some papers after shuffling through several. From the desk top he removed an ink well and pen. He walked to a table near Jasmine and laid them on its top. He dipped the pen in the ink and wrote something on the bottom. He said, "I would have signed it, just like I have this blank one. It would have made it much easier to explain your transit to Virginia. It would change many things for you. You would be Mrs. McKenney to the whole world." He placed a blank piece of paper next to the document and laid the pen on it. The priest cocked his head to one side and said, "I think I hear someone calling for me." It was absolutely silent. "I'll be gone several minutes, maybe a half-hour. I'll close and lock the door so you're alone and you won't be disturbed in your grief."

Jasmine said nothing, but she asked her question with her eyes. The priest's head dropped in what one could have interpreted as a nod and this coincided with his faintly discernible smile. He went back to the desk, carried an envelope he'd removed from its surface, and dropped it on the table next to the marriage certificate before he left. Jasmine watched the door close behind him and heard the key click in the lock, before she rushed to the table.

***

January 9, 1865

"You will take good care of her, won't you, Father McCarthy? I know she's only a horse, but she's important to me." Jasmine stroked Ellie's forehead with soft, loving strokes. "I promise I'll be back for her. As soon as the war ends, I'll be back. Did I give you enough to pay her keep?"

"Yes, too much."

The priest looked at her critically. "Jasmine, I'll not be asking you how you came by your funds, but, I will give some advice. Tell no one that you are carrying money. Seemingly, you have a significant sum. I can assure you, that things being as they are, any number of men would slit even a pretty throat like yours for a smaller sum than you possess. In fact, I would request assistance frequently, enough to instill the thought that you are destitute."

"That is certainly good advice and I'll be sure that I do that." She hesitated a few seconds then blurted out, "I'll ease your mind, Father. Stephen gave me the money. Let me show you something." Jasmine opened her carpet bag and removed Stephen's letter from it and handed it to McCarthy. He read the letter then took a deep breath. When he returned the paper to Jasmine, he looked vindicated and said, "Thank you," as the letter touched her hand. She quickly returned it to her bag.

One of the priest's servants stuck her head in the stable door. "Fatha McCarthy, the carriage be ready." She left as soon as McCarthy said, "We'll be right there."

Jasmine put her hands on either side of Ellie's head and said in a choked voice, "Good-bye, Ellie. I'll be back for you. I do love you." The horse snorted as if to acknowledge her understanding.

"You have the safe conduct papers, the colonel's letter, and every other important document in place for safekeeping?"

"Oh, yes! And, thank you so much, Father." Jasmine's gratitude was sincere.

"If you'd like, I'll keep track of any events concerning the Hurley's property for you. I'll send a post to you at the address you gave me."

"Yes, that would be wonderful."

"Father Causey went into Atlanta a few days ago. He's made all the arrangements." The priest removed a small pink purse from beneath his raiment. "Tickets and bills of lading for the coffin are in this. Keep it close. He was able to get you through to Port Royal. That's if raiders don't disrupt the rails. The railroad is in Union hands most of the way. General Stoneman seized most of East Tennessee and is moving into Western Virginia according to my source at the military governor's office. One of my people will go with you as far as Chattanooga to help protect you. His name is Leviticus. He is trustworthy and very capable of defending you, but remember, your trust *must* have limitations."

The priest put his hand on her arm and led her through the stable door into the cold January air. The carriage and a wagon bearing McKenney's coffin stood waiting. Black men sat in the driver's seats of the two vehicles. Father Causey waited in the carriage. A third black, one of the largest men she'd ever seen, stood next to the carriage. He was well over six feet, she guessed by five or six inches. Huge shoulders and gigantic biceps were outlined by the coat he wore. The Priest spoke to him. "Leviticus, this is the lady I've asked you to see reaches the state line at Chattanooga. She has a ticket for your return. Check on her at each stop. Father Causey will be waiting for you when you return."

He smiled and nodded. "Cain I help da lady in da carriage?"

Jasmine had never seen such a large hand as the one that was extended toward her to help her maintain her balance as she stepped up into the carriage. Leviticus immediately trotted to the wagon and vaulted into the seat next to the driver.

"It's a full six hour trip to the station. You must leave now." Father McCarthy waved as the drivers started.

"Good-bye, Father McCarthy," Jasmine shouted. "Good luck and good-bye, *Mrs. McKenney*."

The words shocked her; it was the first time she heard what was to be her new name spoken aloud. She also wondered at the meaning of McCarthy's instructions to Leviticus. Why had the priest instructed Leviticus to check on her at each stop? Finally, she realized what his words explained. Jasmine would *not* be traveling in the colored only car; Leviticus would. She felt very guilty . . . and very free for the first time in her life.

***

January 11, 1865

Jasmine awoke from uneasy sleep as the train rocked to a halt in Dalton, Georgia. The stops, scheduled and unscheduled, were frequent and the cold passenger car was an inhospitable place. Cinders blew in through windows left open, despite the cold, she guessed because the frigid air was considered a better alternative by those sitting near windows than breathing squalid vapors emitted by unwashed bodies, festering wounds and stale vomit.

Many of her fellow passengers were soldiers, most recovering from wounds, returning from war. They were short legs, arms, and many sported large white bandages on all parts of their bodies. Some were sick, constantly coughing, hacking, spitting and blowing their noses. Most were Union troops. The few Confederates traveling under parole were treated with great suspicion and rudeness. All the southern soldiers had serious injuries or they would have been sure to have ended up in a prisoner of war camp. Their papers were checked at each stop, they were hassled, and in two cases removed from the train. Any pretense of gallantry that existed in the war's beginning, was long since abandoned. Sherman had driven the last nail in that coffin.

Three of the five other women in the car sat close to her. She supposed it was an unspoken pact for mutual protection. The two remaining women were accompanied by men, or rather, traveling with a man. One sat next to a man obviously blinded in battle. Bandages covered both eyes. The second attended a man with one leg and a hand removed. He groaned each time the car lurched on the hastily rebuilt and poorly maintained tracks that had been repaired infrequently after both armies had wrecked them.

A porter announced, "Dalton. Dalton. Thirty minutes. Dalton. Dalton. Thirty minutes," and repeated that as he walked down the aisle.

"Are you going to get off for a few minutes, dear?" An older lady, whose name was Matilda, stood next to her. Jasmine had learned that the woman, a Georgia native, was married to a Union officer. She was returning north after her sister's funeral.

"Yes. I don't want to miss an opportunity to get out of here for fresh air."

The two women climbed down out of the passenger car. When they did, Leviticus was waiting for Jasmine. He asked, "Missa McKenney, is you all right?"

"I'm fine."

"You don't be needin' nuttin'?" He looked as though he felt he was failing in his duty.

"No. Not a thing." Jasmine noticed he looked disappointed.

"Oh-oh, here comes a Yankee." Leviticus positioned himself between the young lieutenant and the women.

Jasmine said softly, "It's okay, Leviticus." He stepped aside.

"Begging your pardon, ladies. The conductor tells me you're both going north past Chattanooga. Is that correct?"

Matilda said, "Yes," and Jasmine nodded.

"Well, a bridge has been destroyed between here and there. It will take five or six days to repair it. However, if you wish, we intend to transfer a car and take a track that bypasses the problem. If you want to go, I'm sorry, but we'll have to leave in ten minutes."

"I'm traveling with my husband's body. I can't make the change unless his casket can go, too," Jasmine said.

"Oh. You could be the one. Is your name Jasmine?"

"Yes." She felt very uneasy.

"You'll have to see Captain Ford about that." The lieutenant gave her a strange look. "You sure don't . . . well, you go see Captain Ford. He's in the station house."

***

The Captain looked up from the table that was serving as a desk at the young, beautiful woman in front of him. He smiled. "What can I do for you today, Miss?"

"The officer outside said I should see you about getting my husband's body transferred to the train bypassing the damaged bridge and Chattanooga." Jasmine smiled, but felt very apprehensive.

"I believe I can help you. What's your name?"

"Jasmine McKenney."

The Captain's head jerked back a tiny amount and starred at her incredulously before saying, "Jasmine?"

"Yes?"

"Just a second." He picked up a stack of papers and began thumbing through them. After glancing though a dozen sheets, he pulled out a handwritten note on telegraph stationery and read through it. When he finished, he relaxed and smiled. "It's just a coincidence. I have a notice here to stop a Jasmine Jones traveling with a man listed as armed and dangerous." He chuckled. "Jasmine Jones is a nigger. She's accused of the attempted murder of a Union officer. I'm very sorry about the mistake and apologize for adding to your grief."

He read the distress in her face, immediately went to the door, and shouted instructions to the lieutenant. Ford returned saying, "Everything will be taken care of. I would advise you to be careful toward the end of the trip. After you cross into Virginia, you'll be in an area where Mosby is active. He is particularly fond of attacking the railroad. There is a rumor he was wounded, but you can believe his men will be around. Be careful and stay on the train as much as possible. Mrs. McKenney, you have my sympathy, and I pray you have a peaceful trip with your beloved."

Jasmine nodded and left with a serious countenance realizing she'd had a close call . . . and had been very lucky.

***

"Thank you for watching over me, Leviticus. Having you with me has been most comforting." Jasmine found his ticket in her purse and handed it to him.

He looked at it and shook his head. "I jus' don't know. I jus' don't know."

"What's wrong?" She asked.

"I'm gonna be honest, Missa McKenney. I was strong thinkin' a not goin' back. I knows I ain't no slave no more. But, I ain't never been treated bad like this. Father McCarthy, he jus' take me in a few weeks ago. He's been good ta me. I'm big and I cain work hard. Do most anything. I was a goin' a go north; not goin' back. But, I don't know, I jus' don't know."

"Are you afraid someone will hurt you?"

"Naw sum. I ain't feared of dat. But, comin' up here, I ain't never been treated so poorly. Dem Union soldiers treated me like a dog. A stupid dog. In dat train car, dey was talking about us like we was trash, like some of a the bad plantation folks does. I don't wants a go from a spot ain't good for me to one dats worse."

"Jasmine, they're getting ready to leave, dear." Matilda, her fellow passenger, called to her. "They've already moved the coffin for you. And, they just made the last boarding call." The woman stood on the train car's boarding steps and was waving her arm.

"I'm coming," Jasmine shouted back.

Jasmine reached up and touched Leviticus on the shoulder, "I've got to go. You have to make your own decision. Do what you want." She left him staring at the ticket. Jasmine heard him say, "I ain't never hadda make no decision. I jus' don't know. I jus' don't know," as she stepped on the train.

Chapter 15

November 24, 1869

Landry Dawes was very uncomfortable, uncertain, uneasy, and *undeterred*. He was uncomfortable because of the cold Georgia drizzle that drenched his face and clothes uncertain because his numerous attempts to contact the Hurleys had been unsuccessful . . . uneasy because of the perceived hostility of the people that stared at him each day since he'd traveled from his Alabama home. Landry was undeterred because his commitment to paint the cross was as strong and fresh as the day he'd made it. It would be good to see the Hurleys again.

Landry left what had previously been the family farm after the fall harvest. It was now much different than its prewar status. Never a grandiose plantation, the Dawes farm had been a family operation depending on its members, hired labor, and a family of black slaves. Reconstruction and the Freedman's Bureau changed that. A combination of taxes, a punitive military administrator and changes in the economy forced the division of the forty-six acres into plots of varying sizes that became part of share-crop farming; a system that pushed whites and blacks into a feudal arrangement that bred poverty.

The Radical Republicans gained control of the US Congress after the 1866 elections. Unlike Lincoln and his vision for reforming the Union, Thaddeus Stevens and his compatriots were more interested in punishing the former Confederacy than reuniting with it. Bitterness, spawned by these policies, swept the South like wildfire. The unfortunate blacks were the pawns in this tragedy. Suddenly, "free," they were anything but that. The unscrupulous from both North and South descended on them, victimizing, demeaning and exploiting the black population.

Resentment toward blacks filled the old Confederacy where whites saw the "Negro" as a cudgel used by northern politicians to inflict pain and suffering on them. Worse, as blacks tried moving to Union states, they found no welcoming population. They were reviled by northern whites with as much vitriolic disdain as they experienced in their previous home. Many northern communities, counties and states passed legislation varying from eliminating black voting rights to the outright prohibition of their living in a location.

Hated more than the blacks were "carpetbaggers" and "scalawags," names given to northerners who came south to participate in the exploitation of its people and southerners who joined in the dismantling of the society they themselves had been a part. Any stranger passing through, or stopping in a community, was eyed suspiciously for the real possibility existed that the individual could be a carpetbagger or a scalawag. The rise of the Ku Klux Klan and Red Shirt societies was a lawless and vicious reaction that many southerners saw as a necessary balance to Union oppression. History was to write the sad tale that Landry Dawes was living.

During the six days since he left his home near Troy, Alabama, the hostility bordering the trails and roads for most of the 240 miles to Eatonton was nerve-racking. He became used to challenging questions, hateful looks and disparaging comments. If there was a reason for a prolonged conversation with these local residents and he could establish himself as one of them, the reaction was reversed. He was looked upon as a fellow sufferer, to be welcomed and assisted.

The evening of his third day of travel was representative of his experience. The weather was cool, but dry. Landry had crossed the Georgia state line and found himself far enough from the next town as the sun set that he decided to camp in a grove of trees, thirty yards off the road. He used a piece of canvas to make a crude lean-to, ate a few strips of jerky, and after securely tethering his horse, laid down for a night's rest.

"Hey, you! Wake up!" woke Landry from a deep sleep. He felt cold steel pressing against his cheek. His eyes opened to the sight of three men dressed in white robes and hoods standing over him. One held a shotgun, with the barrel pushing against his face's flesh. He blinked, realizing he was viewing the eerie individuals in torch light. "What cha doin' here, boy?" the man holding the torch asked.

"Trying to get a little rest. I'm traveling." Landry remained frozen, being careful not to give the shotgun owner any excuse to pull the trigger.

"Where you going?" The torch bearer was unfriendly sounding.

"Eatonton, up near Milledgeville."

"What's your name, boy?"

"Landry Dawes."

"Where you from?"

"Near Troy, over in Pike County, Alabama." Landry moved his head slightly, but the twin barrels followed him. He asked, "Mind pointing that scatter gun somewheres else? I ain't done a damn thing wrong. If you want me to move on, I'll be right happy to."

The man holding the torch eyed him for a moment before he said, "You just stay real still, fellow." He looked at the man holding the shotgun. "Move it off'n him, Jed." He turned back to Landry as the gun swung away and said, "What's your business?"

"I'm just passing through."

Landry's answer seemed to anger the man. He snarled in a gruff voice, "Damn it, I mean over to Eatonton."

"I'm going over to repay a favor for a preacher-man that patched me up and helped me after I got wounded in the war."

"Who'd you fight for?" the voice demanded.

"I was with General Wheeler. I got shot at Lovejoy's Station."

The eye holes in the starched sheets that comprised the hoods exchanged glances. The shotgun pointed skyward. "You can stay and welcome." The tone had changed completely. "If you want some breakfast, and don't mind lots a corn bread and not much else, my place is up this road six or so miles. They's two cow skulls hanging on the gate."

"I might take you up on that." Landry sat up, pulling his knees to his chest, and wrapping his arms around them.

"We been having more than the usual number of skirmishes with the damn Yankee carpetbaggers and renegade scalawags. Just so's you know."

"That the reason you're decked out? You figured I was one of them?"

The robed figures laughed collectively. The one holding the shotgun said, "Not hardly. One of our friend's place got confiscated by the Freedman's Bureau and them damn Yankees done gave parts of it to some nigger families. We just convinced them they'd best not stay."

When the men rode off, Landry didn't sleep well, nor did he accept the invitation his night visitor had extended. The violence served with the cornpone would make it taste too bitter.

He turned his horse's head down the road, noting that the wooden sign declaring he was going to be riding on Cotton Creek Road was the same as one that was there when he'd left stealthily, five years before. It was in bad need of repair and relettering. His uncertainty pressed to the front of his mind as he neared where he hoped he'd find the church. The chaos that followed the end of the war explained the lack of response from the preacher for a period of time. Communications, including mail service, was a hit or miss thing for over a year after Appomattox. Even after the spring of 1866, things were slow to return to "normal"—the damage done was deep and the resources needed to recover simply didn't exist.

He'd been busy helping his father struggle to save what they could of their holdings. Contacting his benefactors was no less important, but the priority was low when the family's survival was in the balance. The letters sent were swallowed by a system that struggled to make the most basic of deliveries and couldn't be burdened with returns. A year before the trip he knew he must make, he tried to inquire about the Hurleys through the military governor's office. The answer was a curt rebuke, stating they didn't have time for such activities. A letter addressed to the mayor of Eatonton was never answered. Landry didn't know if his failures were due to the postal service or, as was more probable, the Hurleys had moved.

What he'd do if a new pastor ran the church, he wasn't sure. Dawes decided that he'd ask the new preacher if he could fulfill his vow at least one time. Past that . . .

The creek appeared from the woods and seemed to act as a barrier to the red clay road, keeping it above its banks. That told him he was approaching his destination. He looked above the tree line for the cross in the late afternoon gloom the overcast created. After a few seconds, he spied the white top. Some pines and the high density of the deciduous trees on which a few withered leaves remained blocked any possibility of seeing the structure. He breathed a sigh of relief. Landry looked back at the canvas covering a can of paint, two long lengths of rope, and saddle bags carrying brushes, scrapers, food, personal effects, and changes of clothes. He was relieved he'd not have to use the canvas to set up a lean-to on this wet, cool night. The Hurleys were sure to invite him for a good supper and to spend the night inside their warm comfortable home.

Landry's sigh of relief changed to a groan of despair when his horse rounded a bend and he could see what remained of Hurley's church. The gray outline of the steepleand the remnants of the walls stood forlorn, but defiant. Marian and Marcus' rectory was a knee-high pile of rubble. "My God!" Landry reined his horse to a halt on the edge of the weed covered church yard. Tears came to his eyes. He exclaimed, "Marcus, I'm sorry. I should have stayed." Guilt poured over him. Emotions raced through Landry. Guilt, continued at first.

Then, dejection. Confusion. Anger. And, finally, rededication. He couldn't face the night alone, depressed, lying sleepless on the wet ground. Landry decided that he'd spend some of the meager amount of money he had for a room. He turned his horse toward Eatonton. Besides, someone there would know what happened to his friends.

***

Landry signed the hotel register. He was dripping wet, but hoped the walk from the livery stable hadn't drenched his clothes and other effects in one of the saddle bags he carried on his shoulder.

The clerk looked at his name. "Mr. Dawes, that's one dollar fer the room fer two nights. We don't got no one night rate. You get breakfast fer that. If'n you want a hot bath, that's a dime more. Rules ain't many, but we hold 'em high. Nobody than what's registered can sleep in the room. If'n you're drunk, puke in the slop-pot. Don't let anyone else use your key to the outhouse and no whores in your room. If'n you want that kinda thing, go down to Holder's place."

"Sounds fair." Landry put the pen back in its holder. "You been around here long?"

"Most all my life."

"Did you know the Hurleys?"

The clerk immediately became suspicious. "Yes."

"I was at the church today. What's left of it. Do you know what happened to them?"

"Why tell?"

"During the war they took me in for a while and helped me get back home. I promised Reverend Hurley I'd come back and do something for him. That's what I'm here to do. I want to keep my promise."

"I can tell you what I know, cain't tell you what I don't know, *fer sure*." The clerk straightened up, threw his head back, and looked down his nose. "Most everybody here about was real fond of the Reverend and his Missus. When the Yankees raided out there and burned the church, they claimed that Marcus and his folks skedaddled, right then. The captain that run the raid said Marcus told him he was a going to Charleston. Folks here been trying fer five years to contact them. Ain't had one bit of luck. When Bill Partin was up in Charleston, he tried to look fer 'em. Couldn't find a hair. No bodies, though. But, that don't mean a whole lot. So's, you figure it out."

Landry frowned and tapped his fingers on the desk. "Who was the Yankee officer?"

"Same guy that owns the other hotel and the whore house, Heinrich Holder." The clerk frowned and spit tobacco juice into a spittoon behind his desk.

There was a glint in Landry's eye. He was glad he'd brought some weapons along. He thought for a moment then asked, "Who owns the property? I'd like to talk to them."

"Some folks named McKenney. But, if'n you want to talk to them, you got a long ride. They live in Virginia. But, wait a minute." The clerk spun the register around and turned back a page. "Yep, lookee there." He pointed to a name. It read *Maureen McKenney*. The clerk looked over his shoulder. "She's in room 21. Not there now, though. I remember her real well. She went out some time ago. Now, that woman's a real looker."

***

Landry had an argument with himself the entire distance between the hotel and the ruins of the church. The portion of his mind defending his decision to proceed with painting the cross, won. As he swung down from his saddle, he said to the abandoned ruins, "Well, I tried."

He had. Before he left Eatonton, he knocked on the McKenney woman's hotel room door, asked about her at the desk, and even checked a couple nearby restaurants, but no one knew who she was nor had seen a strange woman that morning. Without more of a description for the lady, spending more time was fruitless. Landry headed to the Hurley's property without a clear course of action planned. He didn't have one until he'd arrived. If the McKenney woman didn't want the cross painted, he couldn't think of a good reason why she wouldn't, it meant she'd just have to remove two more coats.

How he was going to get up on the top of the steeple to do the job—that was another thing. He'd used Marcus' ladders and there was a roof to work from last time. That's what he'd planned to do again. The roof and the ladders were now charred and weathered cinders scattered somewhere in the piles of rubble. The top of the steeple was flat; working after you got up wasn't a problem. Getting up, was.

Landry examined the shear brick walls on the three steeple surfaces to which he had easy access. "A squirrel couldn't climb the son-of-a-bitch," he mumbled. He thought about looking for a ladder lying somewhere the fire would have missed it, but said to himself, "That would take too much luck. Besides, like be they'd have rotted by now." The nearest farm he could borrow one from was over a mile away. He shrugged his shoulders . . . maybe that was the best way. Before he climbed back into the saddle, Landry saw the lengths of rope tied to its rear that he'd brought with him. An eighteen-hundred's farm boy knew rope was one of the most useful things a man could keep around. He removed a hundred foot coil of five-eighths hemp from his saddle.

Within ten minutes he tied a brick on one end of rope, tossed it over the steeple twice so that it formed a "U" around the base of the cross. He secured one end to his horse's saddle, with the horse standing close to the bricks. Lucky, his chestnut gelding, and he loaded hay bales into the barn using a similar method. Landry tested the rope by pulling on it to see if it would slip. It felt like it would work. Long, hard hours of farm work prepared him for what he would attempt. He tied the paint can and a bag with brushes and other needs to the end of the second rope that he could pull up. Then Landry tied a loop under his arms with the first length of hemp . . . and with Lucky pulling slowly at his command . . . he walked the steeple wall, the only difficult part being right at the top. At the end of another fifteen minutes, Dawes was brushing paint on the cross, whistling as the slow cool breeze kept him comfortable in the bright sunlit, cloudless sky.

***

Landry sat on the edge of the steeple, being careful to keep his body positioned in a manner so he'd neither lean against the paint and ruin his work, nor tumble off the high, twenty plus foot structure. He'd almost done both. His decision to stay on top was one he regretted, but going up and down was, by far, the hardest part of the task. Stubborn, like his father, Landry had invested a couple hours of sitting time before he realized he'd have been better off on the ground waiting for the paint to dry. It wasn't in his nature to give in or up.

As he sat, waiting, he wished his father's health had been good enough to accompany and help him. A stroke had left him limited use of his limbs. Landry hoped, but doubted, his father would ever fully recover.

He tested the paint with his finger. It had a "skin" on it, but wouldn't take the brush yet. Landry shook his head in disgust. "Damn it!"

"Mister, can I ask what you're doing?" A voice answered his curse.

Landry looked around and saw two women sitting in a carriage driven by a huge black man and pulled by two matched gray horses. The carriage pulled into the church yard and approached the steeple. Lucky snorted and the horse's ears elevated. "Easy, Lucky!" Landry yelled. The carriage driver pulled up, realizing that it might spook the horse. "Thank you," Dawes yelled. "I'm tied to the rope that's tied to my horse and I don't want him to pull me off this thing." One of the women was elderly, the other younger, he guessed close to his age. Under the bonnets they wore it was difficult to tell much about what they looked like except the colors of their hair, gray and blonde respectively.

"You appear to be painting the cross, sir. May I inquire why?" the younger woman asked. There was sharpness in her voice that rankled Landry.

"I made a promise to the preacher whose church this was that I'd see to the painting of this here cross. No matter what. I aim to keep my word. You appear to be powerful nosey about what's happenin' here. *May I inquire why?*" He borrowed the sharpness in her voice and made it more acute.

"You may. My family owns this property." The blonde woman turned her head to an angle where Landry could see her features. He sucked in his breath. The hotel clerk was right, she was a looker. She asked, "May I ask whom I'm addressing?"

"Landry Dawes, at your service." His attitude adjustment was rapid and complete. A combination of her assertion of ownership and her beauty accomplished that. "Would you be Mrs. McKenney?"

"*Miss* McKenney. Maureen McKenney. How did you know?" The lady remained defensive.

"I was asking about who owned the property after . . . well . . . I saw this had happened." Landry pointed at the ruins. "The hotel man said you did and he said you was staying there. I tried getting your approval before doing this, painting, but I couldn't find you this morning."

The older woman said, "He must be the one, Maureen."

"I don't have any objection to your painting the cross, Mr. Dawes. I would ask that you not disturb the rest of the grounds. My sister-in-law wishes it to stay as it is. It is actually her property."

"Thank you. I'll certainly observe your sister-in-law's wishes." Landry paused then asked, "Might you be kin to Lieutenant Stephen McKenney, of the CSA?"

The young woman's demeanor, even her posture changed. "Yes, he was my brother." Her assertiveness and aggressive tone fled.

"*Was?*"

"Yes, my brother was killed here during the war."

"No! I'm sorry. I didn't know. He was a friend of mine.

We were together in this church. The reverend here took us in. I left before all this. I didn't know nothing about . . . ."

Landry looked up at the sky.

"It's all right. We've had time to get over our grief."

"Begging your pardon, I didn't know that your brother was married."

Landry's comment caused a stir in the carriage. The older woman's head swiveled toward Maureen and Maureen quickly said, "I'm sure there are quite a few things we could learn from each other, Mr. Dawes. I'd certainly like to discuss your time spent with Stephen. May I be so bold as to suggest we dine together tonight? That is, if you have no other plans."

The older woman said, "I'm afraid I won't be able—"

Maureen interrupted. "Mr. Dawes seems a complete gentleman. I have Leviticus to see me to and from the restaurant we choose. It will be okay." She looked up at Landry. "What time would be convenient?" She assumed his assent.

"I gotta finish this. Two, maybe three hours by the time I get down. I need to clean up. Ma'am, I don't have any fancy duds with me. You sure . . . ?"

"Please, don't let that deter you. Wilson's restaurant is appropriate. Would seven be too difficult for you? That's five hours from now."

Landry nodded, "That's all right, Miss McKenney."

***

Landry looked at the prices on the menu and visualized how little money remained in his pocket. Wilson's Restaurant was more elegant than his life-style and funds were comfortable patronizing. He felt everyone in the room was looking at him. Being the only man in the dining room not wearing tailored shirt and pants . . . and not wearing a jacket and tie . . . made him feel conspicuous. Maybe he felt like everyone was watching him . . . because they were.

"They serve good food here, Mr. Dawes." Maureen was oblivious of the stares that were divided equally between Landry and her.

The waiter approached to take their order, his expression indicating he smelled something unpleasant. "What would the lady and gentleman have?"

"I'd like a glass of wine before we order. Do you still serve the Elderberry?" Maureen asked.

"The mademoiselle is most discriminating. Yes, we do. May I pour one for the gentleman?" The waiter looked at Landry.

"I think I'll just have coffee. I'm feeling poorly," Dawes said, frowning as he did.

The waiter rolled his eyes and walked away.

Maureen looked guilty as she peered across the table at Landry. She said, "I fear I may have done you a disservice, Mr. Dawes. I assure you that is anything but my intent. My apologies."

"No apologies are needed ma'am. I'll live through it. Besides, I don't get the chance to eat with a woman as pretty as you down in Troy, Alabama."

Maureen blushed. "That's where you're from?"

"Yes, ma'am."

"Please, call me Maureen."

"Yes, ma'am, if you'll call me Landry."

Landry subconsciously felt the coins in his pocket. It would be a lean trip home.

***

The meal was interwoven in the tales they told each other. Landry recounted how Stephen happened on the church, the Hurleys and Samuel's nursing of his injury, the development of their friendship, and the constant threat posed by the Union scavenging parties. Maureen told Landry Jasmine's story of the destruction of the church, the Hurleys, Samuel and Louise's murders, the love affair and marriage of Jasmine and Stephen, of her brother's death, and of Jasmine's fleeing to Virginia with Stephen's body.

The conversation went on and on despite the disgusted looks of waiters and the owner. Maureen continued with that part which she knew from her personal experience. She said, "After I received Stephen's letter, his tone told me he didn't expect to survive. I didn't receive it until a few days before Jasmine arrived, such being the problems in getting posts exchanged. I knew it was her when I saw the carriage come up the road to our house. My parents welcomed her as a daughter through their grief. It was soon after that, she shared that she carried Stephen's child. She had twins, a girl and a boy. Their names are Stephanie and Stephen. Both are healthy toddlers and one of the reasons she does not travel to here. And, there are other complications."

"I'm happy to hear Stephen has children. He was a fine man." Landry hesitated. "Do you know where he met Jasmine?" He wished to shield Maureen from any unknown unpleasantness.

Maureen looked at him, coldly at first, but regaining her warmth as she gauged his intent. "Jasmine is my sister in all things, Landry. We could not be closer than if we came from the same womb. I think you *know* how they met. You and I are two of the three people still alive that know about them. The other is a priest whose silence can be counted upon. I would entreat you to preserve that confidence."

"Be assured that I will."

"Her parentage is one of the reasons she doesn't return here. There are too many bitter memories. And, though it is entirely false, she is wanted for attempted murder. The man who killed the Hurleys and killed Stephen was shot by her in self-defense."

"Who was that?"

Maureen's voice lowered. "A Union officer named Holder."

"The same one who owns the . . . ."

She waved her hand and cut him off. "He's become an important and powerful man here." She leaned toward him. "Remember, there are many ears in this room."

"So you come here to take care of her business?" Landry made a silent commitment to himself in regards to Holder.

"Yes. I purchased the church and its lands. I pay the taxes. I see that the priest that is Jasmine's friend is provided for. I check on the ruins and try to protect them as well as I can by hiring a lawyer and a keeper to see after them. The lawyer does his job, but judging from the height of the weeds in the yard the other man doesn't." She hesitated and said in a whisper, "And, I see if I can find a way to destroy Holder."

Landry picked up a halffilled glass of port resting on the table in front of him. "I'm not real good at this kind of stuff, but I'll drink a toast to that if you'll drink to my assistance."

"Most certainly."

"Lady." The waiter approached Maureen and stood next to her. "Your nigger wants me to tell you it's getting close to curfew. And, he is right. They'll throw his ass into jail if he's outside a minute after ten. You'd best be leaving. Will the gentleman be paying?" He leered at his two guests.

"Yes," Landry snapped. After counting out the required sum, he slapped it on the table. He had less than two dollars to spend on his return home. Landry considered that no sacrifice after his evening with Maureen.

"Thank you. It was most chivalrous of you, but not necessary." Maureen said as they walked to the front door.

The huge black man stood outside. "I's sorry, Missa Maureen, but I be in a heap a trouble if'n I don't get in. The carriage be in the back." He ran off to get it.

Maureen watched the huge black man disappear around the side of the building. She said, "Leviticus and Ellie, Jasmine's horse, were the reasons I came here on my first visit. I came for the mare and I ended up taking that big fellow back to Virginia, too. Jasmine had asked me to see how he was doing, which wasn't very well. He's become foreman on our farm, the most valuable person there." The carriage rattled around the side of the building. "Would you accept a ride back to the hotel?"

"Ma'am, I would, just to talk to you, but it wouldn't be proper. I'll walk."

"I wanted to talk to you about doing something for me at the church. I'd pay you. Maybe, at breakfast, at the hotel?"

"I'll be happy to do your work, but I won't take no money, ma'am."

"Please, call me Maureen. Landry, I do hope I see you before you leave."

Dawes couldn't see her features clearly enough to see what he hoped was in her eyes. He said, "Miss Maureen, we'll see each other at breakfast. I was planning on leaving for Troy tomorrow. Early. But, I can delay that. I'll do what you want. And, Maureen, I hope to see you many more times."

Chapter 16

November 26, 1954

The two Landrys watched the Smith's car and their four visitors disappear around the bend in the road, reducing the vehicle to flashes of color glimpsed through spaces between trees. Mr. Dawes removed his pocket watch, a family heirloom as sacred as the cross painting tradition. "It's 12:30. We've got two hours to kill before that paint's dry enough for us to finish. Do you want to walk part of the property lines? We don't have time to make it all the way around, but we could see some of the nicer parts."

"That would be fine, but I think we're about to kill some of that time. Look coming up the road." Dawes' son pointed to a black Packard slowing on the road in front of the church. It came to a complete stop. Two men sat in the car's front seat having what appeared a very animated conversation; they stared at the church ruins, then at Landry and his father. They backed up several feet and positioned the car's wheels so they could drive over the same weeds crushed by the Smith's vehicle. The Packard inched its way over the church yard to within several yards of the Dawes. "Dad, what do we have here?" Landry asked as he watched the newcomers exit the car.

The two men that had just arrived were dressed for a business luncheon rather than a trip to Georgia farm country. Both wore expensive tailored suits, ties, uncomfortable looking starched shirts and highly polished shoes. One man was bald, but had a full beard and mustache, and looked to be in his fifties. The other was short and sported short brown hair cut in a flat top. A large three ring notebook was tucked under his arm. He was young; Mr. Dawes guessed the man wasn't a great deal older than his son. They picked their feet up as they walked through the weeds like kittens strolling over a dew-covered lawn. Though they looked nothing alike, both wore black rimmed glasses and Mr. Dawes detected a clone quality about them.

"To whom do I have the pleasure of addressing?" the older man asked.

"I'm Landry Dawes Senior and this is my son Landry Junior."

"Let me introduce myself and my associate." His tone was self-important and he swelled up like a toad as he delivered his prologue. "I'm Doctor Arthur MacMillan Vale, Professor of Historical Studies at the University of Georgia, specializing in late 19th Century Events, particularly the Civil War, Reconstruction, and The Spanish American War. My PhDs are in both history and anthropology. This is my assistant, Jim Willis." The younger man smiled, nodded, and half-bowed, obsequiously. Doctor Arthur MacMillan Vale continued, "I'm here to consult with you regarding what facts you might add to my knowledge of this location. I've had conversations with Mrs. Autry on past occasions and she was intelligent enough to contact me when she learned of your presence here. We've dropped everything to come down to ask you some questions." He paused as if waiting for his small audience to fall to their knees in adoration.

Mr. Dawes did his best to conceal his contempt, his face and tone staying bland as he replied, "I'm flattered." His son made no attempt to hide his similar feelings, but remained silent.

"Fine, fine. Would you be able to answer some questions now?" the professor asked.

"I guess so." With a peculiar glint in his eye, Landry Senior smiled at the man.

Vale looked at his assistant and ordered, "Jim, be prepared to take notes and to locate the records I request to see."

Willis nodded, removed a pen from his pocket, opened the three ring binder to an empty page and stood there like a dog waiting for a scrap from his master's table.

Vale nodded his approval and returned his attention to the elder Dawes. "I'd like to verify I have the right person with whom to discuss this property." He glanced at his protégé, activating the robot, who quickly found the needed information. The professor didn't wait for an acknowledgement from Landry, but instead immediately asked, "Are you Landry Davis Dawes who resides in Eufaula, Alabama, Post Office Box 4917?"

"Actually, no. I've found it way too cramped inside that box. In fact, even the largest one available in the local station isn't large enough." Dawes face was dead-pan, emotionless.

Landry Junior laughed and Willis cracked a fast disappearing smile.

"If you correct your statement to ask if I receive my mail there, Yes, I do." Dawes had made his point. The ivory tower was reduced several stories.

***

"No, that isn't correct. Jasmine McKenney didn't inherit the land. And, the McKenney family wasn't related by blood to the Hurleys, not in the least. What is true? Marcus and Marian Hurley didn't survive the war. The McKenneys purchased the land from the Reverend's family who lived in Charleston, South Carolina. I'm sure record keeping during that period was an inexact science. The war, all the reconstruction era politics, and the subterfuge that was rampant in land dealings at the time made paperwork better suited for use in the outhouse than proof of ownership and transition. That's probably why the records show no sale in the old Milledgeville records. The sale was made in another state; just the deed was recorded there. When my great grandfather bought the place, the owner previous to the McKenneys didn't show in the records."

Dr. Vale looked confused. "If the records are so incomplete, how did you learn so much regarding the property's history?"

"Because, the McKenneys *are* related to the Dawes. Landry Davis Dawes, the first, married Maureen McKenney in 1871. Years later, when Jasmine decided against leaving the property to her children, she decided to sell the place to my family and let her children have the money instead."

"Why did she do that? Did she think her kids would destroy the church ruins?" Vale asked.

"No."

"Then?"

"She didn't want her children relocating here." Mr. Dawes tried showing his displeasure with his look and tone of voice, but the professor was slow in identifying the signal. Vale asked, "Why was that?"

"Because, she didn't want them living here."

"You don't know, or won't tell me?" The professor was piqued.

"I won't tell you." Landry Senior's tone said, *that's final*.

The professor realized he'd made some tactical errors. He decided to use a different approach and open a different topic of interest. "I see I'll have to reexamine my facts regarding the property's ownership time line. But, there are some important historical events and some items I've heard about that aroused my curiosity. I'd like your help with some of the reported happenings that are said to have occurred here. If I tell you what I've found out so far, would you comment on its authenticity and tell me anything additional you might know?"

"Okay." Mr. Dawes folded his arms in a defensive manner.

"I guess I'll start with the first written information I have. It's based on an old newspaper article back in November of 1874. According to the report I have, a man named Heinrich Holder committed suicide out here. His wife found a note that was interpreted as his, which was included in the article announcing his demise." Vale motioned to his assistant. "Jim, will you find the article and read the part pertaining to the note?"

"Yes, sir." Willis thumbed through some pages and found what he was looking for. He cleared his throat and read from the article, *"County Sheriff Flarity was quoted as saying, "We believe Holder hung himself based on the brief note written to his wife. This note read, My Dear Melissa, I fear I must attend to a problem that has weighed heavily upon me for many years and I am the only person who can perform what must be done. When I have completed what I must do I will live a new unfettered life without fear. Heinrich'*

Rumors have circulated for years that Holder was somehow involved with the disappearance of Marcus Hurley and his family during the War Between the States. Since the location chosen was an oak on the grounds behind the ruins of Hurley's church, the sheriff believes they are related. Holder served in the Union Army and held the rank of captain. Flarity said the marks on the body were inflicted by tree branches as Holder's corpse was swayed violently as a result of his racing his horse forward to commit the act. His family—"

"That's enough, Jim," Vale said. "That was the official explanation for the man's death. But, rumors have persisted that he was murdered. The popular tale is that ghosts that frequent the ruins did the deed. We know that isn't true, but do you know anything more?"

Landry grinned, "I can tell you two things that are fact. First, ghosts didn't hang him. Second, he didn't hang himself."

"Who did?"

Dawes grinned wider, "You'll have to figure that out for yourself."

"Well, that's most helpful, Mr. Dawes." The professor forced a smile. "Could you tell me what you know about an event called the *Thanksgiving Massacre?*"

"That was in 1884. Not much got passed down to me about that. Tell me what you know about it. If I know something you don't, I'll fill you in."

"Let me have the book, Jim." The professor took the binder and thumbed through it. When he located what he wanted he removed two pieces of paper. One was a flyer offering a reward for information leading to the arrest of the persons killing five men, all of whose names appeared in print and were from the surrounding county. The second was an old photo. It showed five white robed figures lying at the base of what was clearly recognizable as the steeple's bottom. A rope hung down from the cross above. Discolored irregular blotches stained three of the white sheets. One head was at an impossible position in relationship to the body. All were obviously dead.

Landry looked at the picture. "I've never seen this." He nodded. "What's the story that goes with this one?"

"There isn't one. At the time this transpired, the KKK was extremely strong. It enjoyed support by most of the whites. There was a major effort to find the people responsible for the killings by local officials. Union administrators were less zealous. The reward poster brought in some leads, but nothing came of them. Talk surrounding the murders pointed a finger at a group of Union troops who caught the Klan members on the road. There never even was an explanation of why the five were at the church. It didn't make sense. No blacks lived anywhere near. In fact, no one did."

"I can't help you with this one; I don't know any more than you do."

The professor looked disappointed.

Jim Willis said, "Doctor Vale, you might ask about the reports of hauntings."

"I can tell you some stories about those," Landry volunteered.

Vale perked up, "There are many reports of strange lights, noises, of appearances of ghosts, and some situations where people claim to have had conversations with a spirit. Are there any of those you are comfortable in repeating?" Behind the question, Dawes detected a veiled bit of sarcasm and skepticism exuding from the professor.

Landry grinned, "Have you heard about the choir?"

"Yes. You know about that? What can you tell me?" The professor became alert, but guarded.

"My great-great-grandfather told a tale about meeting a man who claims he saw it. He met the guy on a trip down here to paint the cross. The man said he was fishing in the creek one summer evening when he heard singing. The man couldn't tell for sure, but he thought the sounds came from the ruins or behind them. It was faint, but he was sure he heard hymns. The man walked across the road to look for who was singing in such an odd place. At that time, more of the walls still stood. He swore he walked around the church, could hear the singing, but couldn't see a thing. Then the singing stopped. The fellow came back around to the steeple and stood by it for a few seconds. He told great-great-grandfather that there was a cold breeze in his face and he said he happened to look at the front door. Two white figures came floating out of the door. The fisherman said you could see them clear as day; one was an old man and the other a woman of the same age. He said it was real strange—you could see through them and there was no color, just a white shadow. Two more followed. The man skedaddled. He'd had enough.

It was on a Sunday and he said he never came here to fish . . . on Sundays . . . ever again."

"That's like what I've heard. Two of Mrs. Autry's friends told me something very similar." Vale paused and stared at Landry Senior with intense scrutiny. "Have you ever seen the choir?"

"Honestly, no. There has been one occasion, the last time I was here, I believed I could hear singing. It was a Sunday. I never could be sure whether it was wind through the pines or something else, but I swear I heard the words to *Rock of Ages*. By the time—"

"That's the same hymn one of the other people I've spoken to swears she heard." The professor was entranced, temporarily dismissing his doubts.

"Well, I never saw the choir, but I did see one thing I couldn't explain and had one thing happen to me here that makes you think about ghosts or spirits."

"What were they?" The professor, his assistant, and Landry Junior moved a little closer.

"The first one is pretty simple. It wasn't the least bit scary . . . well, maybe a little. This goes back ten years. Dad had lost his arm in a car wreck, so it was up to me to meet our obligation. I was here by myself. I'd finished painting the cross. There are some big walnut trees up in the woods back there." Mr. Dawes pointed to the trees behind the ruins. "I took a sack and headed up there to pick up a bunch of nuts. I got fairly far up the hill when I happened to look back. There was this black girl carrying an old wooden bucket. She was headed across the church yard toward the creek. Her dress went down to her ankles; it wasn't something you'd see worn today. I watched her cross the road and go get water from the creek. She walked back like you would with a full bucket of water. You know, one arm extended to balance the weight. When she approached the church, I yelled, "Hello, there!" She either ignored me or didn't hear me. I went down to see what was going on. There wasn't anybody there. I looked all over. No car. No people, nothing, except . . . a bucket of water."

"Extraordinary!" The professor said. Jim Willis' eyes increased two sizes. Landry Junior added, "Damn Dad, that's creepy."

"I never could tell for sure if it was a person who got scared or was . . . something I couldn't explain."

"Amazing. Anything else?" Vale asked. His skepticism and sarcasm oozed.

"No. I looked around for an hour trying to find the girl or some trace of her. Not a thing. But, my Dad and I had a really strange thing happen to us the first time I came with him. It was a nice day, maybe a little cloudy. We parked his old flatbed truck and started unloading the ladders, paint, and stuff. When we finished that, it was still real early in the morning and dew covered everything, so we walked over to the creek to give things time to dry out. Fished a little. I guess we were there an hour, maybe more. When we went back, everything was gone. No ladders, no ropes, no paint, no brushes, none of the stuff we'd placed next to the steeple was there. We hadn't seen a vehicle or anybody on horseback the full time we were by the creek. Dad was upset. He was sure somebody stole everything or was playing a joke that wasn't funny. We split up and combed the church yard, the woods, walked the road, but didn't find a thing. I was walking toward the main road when I heard my father call, "Landry! Landry! Get back here, quick!" I hadn't noticed, but it had gotten very windy, fast. When I looked at the sky, the western horizon was boiling with blue and black clouds. It was a hell of a storm and it was racing toward us. I didn't quite make it to the truck when the real winds hit. They knocked me over once before I got in the cab. The whole truck wobbled in the gusts that hit. It rained in sheets, blew like a banshee, and there was some hail, but in fifteen minutes it was gone, the skies turned blue and it was fine. But, the weirdest thing was when we finally got out of the truck. The ladders, paint, everything were stacked back on the flat bed. It was just like we'd never unloaded them. Now that's *strange.*"

"Looks like we're getting more company," Landry Junior said. An olive drab Willys Jeep bounced across the church yard leaving the road as soon as it cleared the woods. It tossed its three occupants around like rag dolls. Close behind was a Studebaker that required a much more careful approach. It gingerly traced the tracks made by the previous visitors coming to a stop behind the Packard. By the time two women opened the car doors, two young men that the Dawes recognized as being in Flora and Fanny's and a third older man had all already exited the jeep and were a few steps from them.

"Which one a you is the Cross painter?" The older man from the Jeep moved his eyes from one man to the next traveling from Vale to Dawes and back.

"It's the tall one in the sweat shirt, Pa." One of the young men from the restaurant pointed at Mr. Dawes. "That there one is his son." He motioned at Landry Junior.

"I want to shake your hand, fellow." The man's angular arms, weathered features, and solid build marked him as a man who probably earned his living the same way Landry Dawes did: he farmed. "My name's Cecil Hancock." He extended a hard calloused hand which Landry accepted in his equally hard, equally calloused palm. "These here are my boys. The big one is Wes. The one that does the talkin' is Chester."

"Landry Dawes, and that's my son, Landry Junior." Dawes nodded his head in the young man's direction. "These other gentlemen are Professor Vale and his assistant Mr. Willis. They're from the University up in Athens."

Hancock glanced at the other two men, said, "Pleased to meet you," and return his entire attention to the elder Dawes. Vale and Willis' return salutations might as well been unsaid for all the notice Hancock gave them. He refused to drop Landry's hand, pumping it as if it would produce water after a while. "You can't imagine how long I've been a-wantin' to meet you. I believe what you do keep's this spot a blessed place. I know it, and the angel that comes here saved my life." Hancock finally released Landry's hand.

Vale and Willis became interested onlookers. Willis removed a pen and opened the notebook.

"I think you're giving me more credit than I deserve. I just—"

Cecil cut off Landry. "Oh, we know the story 'bout your people and how it got started. At least, parts of it. What we don't often get is a chance to thank you. So, thank you!"

Dawes shook his head. "What happened?"

"All this took place twenty-four years ago. You're old enough to remember how times was back then. I was a young fellow, just married, and my pap up and died. He left the farm to me and a pile of bills and debt. It weren't his fault. Hell, wasn't nobody had no money then. That farm was what was left of the land my ancestors got when Georgia was still a colony. Their grant was from Oglethorpe hisself in 1740. My great whatever was some kind a officer when Oglethorpe fought against the Spanish and that's what got him our place. The damned Yankees done took over half the place after the War Between the States. My great-grandparents struggled to keep what was left of the land and pass it down. All of a sudden, I was in the place to lose it all. My wife come up sick with tuberculosis. The price of cotton went to hell. I lost half my help 'cause I couldn't pay 'em. I worked my ass off and everything I did seemed to make it worse. The day I come here, I got turned down by the bank for another extension on my loan. Losing my family's land and dishonoring them, I couldn't take that. I come out here to commit suicide."

"Why come here?" young Landry asked.

"Well, to my way of thinking . . . committing suicide was bad . . . against God. I didn't want to go to Hell. So, I thought if I come here, get under the cross right at the steeple, and I prayed for forgiveness, I might end up *not* going down."

"What changed your mind?" Mr. Dawes asked.

"Not what, who. An angel, that's who," Hancock said.

An obviously skeptical Doctor Vale half asked and half scoffed, "Did this angel fly down and sit on the cross? How did you know it was an angel? Did it have wings or a halo? Or, did it just tell you?"

Hancock looked at Vale coldly. He said, "Fellow, you don't know Jack shit." Cecil shook his head in disgust. "No, he didn't have no wings, or halo, or say a thing. And no, he didn't float down or appear in a flash of flame or smoke like he was coming from Oz. I didn't see where he come from. I was facing the steeple, leaning against it with one hand, concentrating on getting the courage to pull the trigger with the other. All of a sudden, I hear this voice say, 'Is dat gonna help you or who's loves you boss man?' I turned around and there stood an old black man, smiling kinda sad-like.

"I remember saying, 'I'm not worth a damn thing to them,' and him saying, "Don't you's think dey oughta be judgin' dat?' Those words made me think how what I was doing would affect others for the first time. He said, 'Boss man, why don't yous put dat der gun down so's we can talk.' I did. We sat down on the ground, leaned back against the steeple, shoulder to shoulder, and just talked. He convinced me what I was doing was a lot worse than losing the property, *if* I failed. I ended up saying, 'Samuel,' that's what he said his name was, 'what can I do, what's my answer?' He said, 'I'll think on it. You's come here tomorrow. If'n I think a somethin', I'll either be here or I'll leave the answer under a pile of bricks right where you is sittin'. You go on, but leaves dat der gun here.' Nothing had changed, but somehow I just knew it would be all right. And, it was. I left him standing there. When I got on the road where it goes into the woods, I turned to wave good-bye. He was gone. I ain't never seen him again."

"Is that it? What caused things to change for you?" Vale asked.

"I came back the next day. The old man wasn't no where 'round. But, there was a pile of bricks right where he said they'd be. And, under that pile, was an old burlap sack, mostly falling apart. In that sack was $5000 and a piece a paper with the words, *keeep beeleevin . . . Samuel*. I carried it straight to the bank, paid what I had to and had enough to get me through the next year. But, there was one other thing that made me keep believing."

"What was that?" Dawes asked.

Hancock took a deep breath. "I was real careful to keep that note from Samuel. I folded it up real neat and stuck it in my pocket. When I got home, I took it out to look at it. The words were still there. I showed it to my wife, she looked at it, turned it over and over, then said it was just a piece a blank paper. She looked at me like I were crazy. I still have it. It don't have words others can read, but I can."

"Oh, my!" said one of the women who'd arrived in the Studebaker and silently joined them. She was the younger of the two, a matronly looking fifty. The other lady was silver haired, with ramrod straight posture, patrician features and a serious demeanor.

The silver haired lady shook her head, cleared her throat and said, "Angel? Angel? Not hardly. Cecil Hancock, angels don't come out of heaven for every ripstitch. Did this Samuel have wings?"

Hancock folded his arms, looked angry and stared at the old woman before answering, "No."

"Did you feel his presence . . . did your body tingle when you were sitting shoulder to shoulder?" She was insistent.

"No."

"Was he bigger than a normal man or was there a glow coming from him?"

"No."

"Cecil, I ain't doubting you saw something. I don't doubt what you say happened. I know you to be an honest man. You stand away from the moonshine jug farther than most. A spirit of some kind, a ghost, maybe. But, an angel . . . no you didn't see an angel."

Hancock snorted. "What makes you an expert? You ever seen one, Glenda?"

The elderly woman stiffened to her full height and a knowing, superior smile covered her features. "What you saw weren't an angel. A spirit probably."

Vale rolled his eyes, but tried to mask his disdain. Willis was busy writing. Both of the Dawes were caught in another form of disbelief, but aimed at Vale's disrespect, not Cecil or the old woman. Hancock said, "You may be right, Miss Glenda. You may be right. But I know what I believe."

He and his sons stood awaiting any other reaction from Cecil's tale. All were silent except for the women. Finally, the elderly lady spoke again. "This place saved my life, but in a much different manner, so I believe anything Cecil or any of you'd say regarding the things that happen here."

"Please, Miss Glenda, don't go getting yourself upset," the younger woman said. "Your heart."

"Oh, Annabelle, don't get your girdle twisted. I'll outlive *you.*" The older woman looked at the men. "She's my nurse and is way too fussy. Sometimes, I swear she does it just to frustrate me. Annabelle just can't accept that I'm a cantankerous, bitchy old biddy, and I'm not about to change."

She cocked her head to the side, held it back, and looked at them through round glasses that made her eyes look owlish. "I'm Glenda Pearl Perkins. I'm the richest, meanest woman who lives from here to Milledgeville. Cecil Hancock, you don't add a thing to that." The Hancocks all smiled, but remained *very* quiet. She continued, "Don't waste time shaking hands with me because part of my temperament might rub off on you . . . and . . . don't waste time shaking hands with Annabelle, because, frankly my dears, she don't give a damn. And, frankly, my dears, the one of you I want to know is the one who paints the cross. And the rest of you—well, you know." She raised her arm so it extended straight at Landry Dawes, turned her hand up so her index finger pointed skyward and slowly brought it down to aim straight at him. "You're the one, correct?"

"Guilty, ma'am."

"Good, I wanted to meet you and see what you inflicted on this whole part of Georgia. *Me.* Thank you. I'm sure that if you and your ancestors hadn't kept the tradition and sacrifice you observe, this old church and that cross wouldn't maintain the strong power it has."

"Pardon me for asking, but how did this place save your life?" Vale said.

"I'm not about to pardon you . . . or tell you," she looked at Mr. Dawes, "unless you want to know."

"Yes, ma'am, I'd very much like to know." Landry Senior grinned at the old lady's voracity.

"Okay. The good Lord was kind to me in most every way, but one. I was born rich and have gotten richer. When I was young, I was a real head turner. I'd sashay by and all the boys would come to attention." She winked at Landry, who laughed. Annabelle blushed and held her hand in front of her mouth. Glenda looked disgusted,

"Damn Annabelle, they all know what their equipment is for." Everyone laughed except for the more deeply blushing Annabelle.

"I had the fastest horse, the best sense of humor, the first automobile, still have the biggest house in town and so on. But, what I didn't get was taste in men. I've picked what turned out to be three of the most worthless critters to stand on two legs each time I decided to marry.

"The first was the worst. His name was Edgar Waltham. We both came from old money. For my part, I'd had enough of him before the honeymoon finished. I was for an annulment or a divorce. Anyway, the feeling was mutual, but Edgar figured a way to get rid of me without the divorce. He took me for a ride out to here one day, talked me into walking into the church, and then he whacked me on the head with a brick just as hard as he could. Luckily, he wasn't that strong and my head is hard. He knocked me silly.

"When I half woke up, he'd pulled me next to one of the old crumbling walls. I could hear him grunting and pushing on the outside. It wouldn't collapse. Edgar came around inside of the church to see what the problem was, walked up close to the wall ten feet away from me, pushed against it once, and, *kathump,* that section caved in on him. Just so happened, one of the old steel lantern hangers was attached there. Skewered him like a hog.

"The only reason the rest of that wall didn't come down on me was the power of this place. Providence. Providence. I was put here to make the rest of this area suffer more than Sherman did."

"Was it windy that day?" Vale asked.

"No," Glenda answered. Her voice was sharp when she added. "There weren't any earthquakes or volcanoes either."

"Or little green men." The smug look on the professor's face stated his feelings, but he added, "I'm a man of science, so ghosts, angels, and intelligent falling walls are difficult for me to accept. I guess I'd have to see one of those strange happenings to believe."

"Hey, Dad," Landry said as he pointed to his wrist watch.

Mr. Dawes nodded. "You folks will have to excuse my son and me. We have to finish what we came here to do." He pointed up at the cross. "Second coat."

"Come on, Annabelle, these folks need to get back to work and we're done here." Glenda was already walking to the car. She said, "Bye," which was quickly echoed by Annabelle.

Cecil Hancock said in a voice low enough he thought Perkins couldn't hear, "She's got the biggest mouth and heart in four counties. There goes one wild and wonderful old war-wagon."

Glenda shot him a bird, drawing chuckles from the group. She stopped at Doctor Vale's Packard, walked completely around it, examined the car from top to bottom, the ground it sat on, looked back at the little knot of men, and yelled, "Professor Whatever . . . . You were talking about needing to see strange things happen. Do four flat tires on your car qualify, when they were just fine and full of air when I pulled up here?"

Chapter 17

November 20, 1874

Landry Dawes leaned against his wagon as he watched two men on Cotton Creek Road. They guided their horses off the red clay onto the church yard. One was a heavy set fellow who looked like he'd been dumped in the saddle with a sugar scoop. The second man was thin and wore a full, unkempt beard. The only thing common in their appearance was the way they slouched in their saddles and the gray, broad brimmed hats they wore.

The heavy one was a scruffily dressed rascal. His jacket was open forming an inverted "V" framing a shirt that strained its buttons as a copious stomach tried to push its way out. Stains streaked the shirt's butternut colored front which was only partially tucked into his pants made of dark gray denim. The pant legs disappeared into Wellington styled boots that looked as though they lacked a shine since they came from the box. The man hadn't stood close to a razor in three or four days.

His fellow horseman was lean to the point of being emaciated. The man wore blue coveralls, a faded red shirt and a tan jacket that featured many holes, the cloth covering only a slightly larger area than the voids. His bare feet stuck in the stirrups showed a thickness of clay and darker dirt coating them indicating they'd not been bathed in days.

As they approached the wagon, Landry noticed that the fat one wore a holstered gun and a star was pinned to his shirt. His full round face made the hat look small perched atop his cranium. Tobacco juice escaped the corner of his mouth and left a track to his chin. He had a smile on his face. Landry nodded to them when they were within a few yards.

"Hey there," the fat man said.

"Hey," Landry answered.

"Haven't seen you around these parts, stranger. I'm Rufus Flarity, the sheriff of this here county. Reckon I don't intend to sound unfriendly, but I'm bound to tell you we have some strict vagrancy laws hereabouts. Mind if'n I ask who you are and what's your business here?" The smile remained, but the words were serious.

"Not at all. My name is Landry Dawes. I'm here to paint the cross on top of that steeple. And, before you need to ask, my wife's family owns this property."

The sheriff struggled to get his hand into his pants pocket, but eventually pulled out a folded piece of paper. He opened it, glanced at it, then asked, "Mind telling me her name?"

"Maureen McKenney."

"That ain't the name on the deed for this place. Least, not the first one. Who might that be?" The smile continued.

"Jasmine McKenney."

The sheriff took a deep breath, folded the paper and returned it to his pocket. "Okay. If you see that lady, tell her we're earning the ten dollars she pays to post this here place."

"I'll see she knows," Landry acknowledged. He peeked at the thin fellow who showed no interest in what was being discussed. His dark eyes stared into space from their deep sockets set above the beard that shrouded the man's features. He was a mute, expressionless manikin straddling his horse.

The sheriff's smile continued. "Mind if I ask why you come here to paint that thing? I hear tell, you do it 'cause of the Reverend Hurley and his wife. That right?"

"Yes, and Samuel and Louise."

"Who's they?"

"They were Marcus and Marian's servants."

"Oh, the niggers."

"The servants," Landry repeated.

"The *niggers*," the sheriff emphasized. His smile faded for the first time.

"Sheriff, Marcus considered them part of his family, so, I do, too," Dawes held his ground, but without rancor.

The sheriff's smile returned. "You can't hardly argue with that. The Hurleys was loved hereabouts."

"They were fine people."

The sheriff rolled his large head to one side. "Mind if I ask if'n you know anything about what happened to them? They disappeared during the war. They ain't never been heard from again, 'round here."

Landry looked the sheriff in the eyes. He hoped he'd be able to detect some message, but the smile was an effective camouflage. "I wasn't here when they . . . *disappeared*." His pause was calculated to get a response from Flarity.

It did. Flarity's head bobbed a little and he said, "You said you wasn't *here* when what happened, happened. Ya'all didn't say you *didn't know* what happened." The smile was constant.

Landry remained silent.

"I know you didn't do no wrong to the Hurleys. You wouldn't be here painting that thing if'n you did. You probably loved them same as me and the rest of the folk here. Now, if'n I was to say my interest in finding out what you know about what happened here . . . it was to confirm what I already think happened . . . and if'n I was to tell you what I believe . . . would you say if it were closer to what you know . . . or not?"

Dawes looked at Flarity; he decided he believed him.

Landry said, "If it was close to what I heard, I would."

"All right. It ain't complicated. I believe a Yankee captain led a raid out here and killed them. That's as simple as it gets."

"That's closer."

The sheriff smiled broader. "And, if'n I was to say that the captain is now a big shot in Eatonton, would I be close?"

Landry nodded. "If you said he owned a hotel and a house of ill repute, you'd be real close."

The sheriff's grin reached Cheshire proportions. "I just betcha they're so close, they might be the same. And, I thank you."

"What do you intend to do?" Landry asked.

"Oh, way things are now . . . it'd be tough in court. But, you never know." The sheriff looked at his man. "Harkness, we need to head back to town." The skinny man reined his horse toward Cotton Creek Road. As the sheriff followed, he looked over his shoulder and called back to Landry, "There's like to be some happenings out here tonight. If'n you come, well, that's up to you." After the horse plodded another ten yards, Flarity pulled his mount to a halt. He didn't look back as he asked, "Is Jasmine McKenney a sister or a sister-in-law to your wife?"

"Sister-in-law."

"If'n her name was Jasmine Jones before she got married, she'd best not be here with you. That's for her benefit, hear? Those Yankees running things have long memories. Her name wasn't Jones, was it?" He swiveled around in the saddle.

Landry answered honestly, "Jasmine's not here," and then he lied, "and her name wasn't Jones."

The sheriff faced front and started his horse. "Didn't think so."

***

"Hey, Holder."

The voice was one he knew well, despised, and one to which he didn't have time to listen. He pretended he didn't hear Rufus Flarity yell at him. Heinrich hated the fat, slovenly man who was the first to break the hold on local government held by his Union supported friends. Several more had followed. It was the damned KKK. Their attempts to repress the black vote were increasingly successful, thanks, in part, to men like Sheriff Flarity. He continued walking on Eatonton's Main Street sidewalk.

"Holder, wait up!" The sheriff yelled loud enough so that neither Heinrich nor the half dozen passers-by could ignore the command.

Holder spun on his heel to face the obese man waddling toward him. Heinrich smiled a contemptuous, derisive smile. "What do you want, *Sheriff*?" He made Rufus walk to him. Neither man offered their hand. The sheriff's customary smile was pasted on his face.

"Oh, I just wanted to see what your plans are for the next day or two." Even on the cool November day, perspiration ran down the fat-faced, man-pigs countenance. The sheriff's smile remained, but hate burned in his eyes.

"I'll be here. Why?"

"Well, looks like we're 'bout ready to solve one of the old mysteries we've had around here. Yep, looks like we're gonna finally find out what happened to the Hurleys. I got someone who knows the whole story. Run into him out to the old church ruins. He's staying out there, doing some work around about the place. And, he knows where there's an eye witness. Since you were the last person to admit to seein' them before they, how did you put it, run like rats to *Charleston*, I'd like you available when I talk to them. Seems they may be our last chance to solve this thing. I'm sure . . . *real sure* . . . you'd want to be there. So, you *be sure* to be here day after tomorrow. Understand?" Rufus' smile disappeared for an instant, then it snapped back like a rubber band.

Holder tried to disguise his shock and fear, but realized he hadn't been able. He asked, "Why not today? Or tomorrow?"

"I have to go to Atlanta. I'm leaving in an hour. Won't be back until too late for tomorrow. So's I can't. But come the next day, then . . . I'll see you." Rufus smiled broader, turned and walked away, leaving Holder stewing in his thoughts.

***

Holder was completely dressed in black when he left Eatonton that same evening. The moonless night made Holder's form blend into the darkness, causing those who heard the clop, clop, clop, of Heinrich's horse's hooves strain their eyes to see the semi-visible rider. His old military revolver was strapped to his side, a new Henry repeating rifle was in a scabbard behind his saddle, and a Bowie knife was stuck in his boot. He was ready to kill.

***

Landry pulled out his pocket watch, opened the cover and strained to read the hands in the flickering light of the campfire. When the sheriff left the steeple that afternoon, Dawes had a good idea of what Flarity had in mind. He expected the forms of the sheriff, Holder and some number of local citizens to materialize out of the gloom into the dancing campfire glow. Landry knew the sheriff's type. He'd do what he thought he had to, regardless of what or who the Federal authorities attempted to protect.

However, it was now 10:12 and there was no sign of anyone. He snapped the watch closed and returned it to his pocket. It was past when he expected their arrival. Dawes decided to wait until eleven. If they didn't make an appearance by then, he'd go back to his hotel for some rest before starting his trip back to Alabama. The flames needed more wood so he took the few steps he needed to reach the abundant fallen limbs and branches that littered the ground in the woods near where he'd chosen to build his campfire. Landry had chosen the location behind where the wrecked and charred timbers of the rectory still covered the ground because it was near the old outhouse, now deteriorated, but serviceable.

As he gathered wood, he heard night sounds—crickets, frogs, owls hooting, whippoorwills calling—all things one would expect to hear on a mild November night in the Georgia woods. Wind whistling through the pine needles created a soothing symphony that Landry had listened to his whole life. It told him everything was okay. His eyes had adjusted to the dark and he could see branches and limbs on the ground and he loaded his one arm with piece after piece. It brought back memories of fetching kindling for Marian Hurley's stove. They were bitter thoughts. It hurt . . . so he quickly dismissed them and looked at his armload of firewood. Yes, he told himself, that should be plenty to last for the three-quarters of an hour he intended to stay.

But, there was something wrong. He could *feel* it. Dawes straightened up, froze, and listened to . . . only the wind in the pines. He had company. A chill climbed his spine. The animals had sent their silent warning. It was up to him to use that alert to his advantage. His guns were in his saddle bag and the scabbard tied to his horse. He carefully examined the area around him before stealthily taking a route to his horse through the densest cover available and in full recognition that cover that hid him could also hide an assailant.

***

Landry reached his horse. He hid his rifle in the armful of wood he carried, dropping some of the load to make room for something more potent to defend him from whoever, or whatever, he felt sure lurked in the woods. He threw the saddlebag containing his revolver over his shoulder. Nonchalantly, he walked over to the campfire, putting the wood on the ground a few feet away from the flames. He sandwiched his rifle between two limbs and carried them to a spot next to a large fallen tree where he hunkered down, trying to present as poor of a target as possible for anyone thinking of shooting him. All he could do was wait. After long minutes, the night sounds returned one band section at a time. Dawes wondered if the stalker had thought better of his intent and had abandoned the hunt. Though he wondered if he was alone, he *knew* leaving now involved too much risk.

If he had to, he'd wait all night. He didn't want to play the mouse for someone's cat in pitch black darkness; a cat who knew the terrain better and might have the advantage in numbers. Adrenalin pumped through him and he was super alert. Landry opened his saddle bag and removed his revolver. The gun was fully loaded with six cartridges and the rifle lying next to him had four shells in it. That was ten chances to stay alive.

The woods became silent again, this time even the pines refused to sing. Dawes lay down with his back against the log, propped his body up on his left elbow, and clutched his pistol with his right hand. How many would there be? Landry didn't want to believe it, but he must have guessed wrong about the sheriff. He must be in league with Holder and the Union officials. After a few suspenseful moments, the hoot of an owl restarted nature's noises. Dawes relaxed.

He placed his gun on the ground, fished out his pocket watch, but it was so dark he couldn't read the hands. The fire was dying and produced less and less light. That was good and bad. The watch went back to his pocket and the gun back in his hand. He waited. Though the evening was cool, perspiration formed on his temples and ran down the small of his back. He knew how the rabbits he hunted felt. A slight tremor developed in his hand because of the death grip he had on the gun butt he clutched.

The owl hooted again and another answered. Within thirty seconds, the tree frogs, chirping crickets, and night birds lost their voices. Landry became tense, sensing things were rushing to a conclusion. It became very quiet. His finger tightened on the trigger.

The metallic *click* of a hammer being cocked told him what he needed to know. As he flattened himself against the ground, the sharp snap of a rifle sounded and he felt something hot slice over one shoulder blade. He raised his pistol and fired wildly at the spot he thought the shot came from, but even before the firing pin in his gun did its work, a scream came from the darkness near where he guessed his attacker was. A man dressed all in black took a couple steps forward into the fire light and fell, face first, on the ground.

"Put that damned gun down, Dawes. You're liked to shoot somebody you damned well shouldn't."

Landry thought he recognized the sheriff's voice. "Let me see who you are!"

"It's Flarity. Now, put that damned thing down or we'll have to shoot you." The fat sheriff walked out of the shadows. The gun dropped from Landry's hand.

The sheriff put a hand to his mouth, cupped it, and made a "hoot." The owl Dawes was listening to had been a very large one, indeed. "Harkness and Boyle, you come on over and get control of this piece of shit. He's started to wake up." Flarity nudged the man lying on the ground with one dirty boot.

The gaunt man who'd been with Flarity that afternoon and a muscular looking man came into the campfire's glow and stood over the figure on the ground.

"Damn, Harkness, I figured if'n you hit him hard enough, we wouldn't have to go through no more. You miss his head?"

Harkness nodded.

"You okay, Dawes?"

"His bullet just grazed my back. Who is that?" Landry scrambled to his feet. As he did, two additional men walked into the light. One of them said, "Quentin is watching the road, Sheriff."

"Good," Flarity answered. He looked at Landry with his perpetual smile on his face. "Why, you know who he is. You might not know what he looks like." The sheriff reached down, grabbed the man's hair, and lifted so Landry could see the man's face. "Mr. Dawes, meet Mr. Heinrich Holder, late a captain in the Union Army. He's a real butcher, he is." Flarity dropped Holder's head. "A couple of you boys get this piece of shit on his feet."

The men snatched Holder off the ground and supported him until he regained enough consciousness to stand. Eventually, Holder said, "Get your hands off me."

Everyone, but Landry and Holder, laughed.

"No, that ain't gonna happen," the sheriff said. "You just tried to kill this here gentleman. That's attempted murder. And, I got five men here to prove it. Now, attempted murder wouldn't get you hung. So's, I need to know why you wanted this Dawes fellow dead? He know something you don't want me to know?" Flarity turned to Landry. "You know something about this . . . *man?*" The sheriff pronounced his last word as sarcastic as he could.

"I know what I was told."

"What's that?"

"That he killed the Hurleys. He actual—"

"Quiet boy. Least, for now. I need to know how he killed them and then see if'n what you know agrees. If it does . . . well . . . ." The sheriff looked at the surly Holder. "This man just accused you of murder. I believe him. Now, you can make it a might easier if you tell me how and who you killed."

"Go to hell, Flarity!" The defiance shown in Heinrich's eyes.

"I reckon I will . . . but you're gonna beat me there."

"Go to hell, Flarity!" Holder repeated.

"I offered you the easy way, but I see that ain't gonna happen." Flarity growled, but maintained his smile. "Shorty, Boyle, get his pants down and get him on his knees. Bend him over."

"No!" Holder screamed, but the four men had him stripped and on the ground as ordered.

Flarity walked around to look in the man's face. He said, "This *is* your last chance. Who did you kill and how did you do it?"

"I didn't kill anyone, you bastard." Holder continued to struggle in vain.

"All right." The sheriff walked over to the fire and removed a four foot long limb. One of its ends glowed cherry red.

"What are you going to do?" Landry cried in an alarmed voice.

"Shut up!" the sheriff barked, the smile leaving his face for a second. He walked up behind Holder and said, "Heinrich, you always said I was a pain in the ass. Well you're about to see how much." Flarity thrust the glowing embers into Holder's rectum.

A blood curdling scream came from Holder, followed by sobbing.

The sheriff, still smiling, walked around in front of Holder and said, "Now, you can tell me what I want to know, or there are more parts of you I can ruin. Who did you kill and how did you kill them?"

Holder babbled some incoherent sounds.

"I didn't understand. Let me get another limb."

"No!" Holder shrieked. "I killed the Hurleys with my saber."

"I want to understand. You run them both through with your sword, right?"

"Yes."

"That agree with what you know, Dawes?"

"Yes, but—"

"Buts don't matter none." Flarity's smile was still there. "We got us a guilty man what just confessed. That's all we need." Then his smile faded and his eyes glinted in the firelight. "You gather up anything that's yours, get on your horse and leave, we don't need you here no more. Don't you go thinking of telling about what's about to happen here. That sister-in-law of yours would hang sure as this son-of-a-bitch is about to. Best if you forget we saw each other here tonight. You understand me?"

Landry did. He said, "Yes." The pain from the wound across his back underlined the sheriff's words. Flarity had been perfectly willing for Holder to have killed Landry in order to have the justification required for lynching Holder.

Dawes gathered his belongings, got on his horse and left the men standing around the campfire. Flarity called after him, "Go get your wagon back in town, rest up, and get out of here tomorrow. Stay real quiet and you'll be welcome back in five years."

Landry said nothing as he rode away, nor did he turn when groans and shouts came from behind him. He didn't have to look to know.

Chapter 18

May 17, 1886

Maureen Dawes stood on the railroad station platform in Atlanta. She hadn't seen her sister-in-law for eight years and wondered whether she'd recognize the woman. Though they maintained regular correspondence and had promised to exchange one of the new George Eastman photographs, that hadn't happened. Maybe it was because those eight years had produced unwanted changes to her appearance, and she assumed the same was probably true for Jasmine. Even between friends that had become closer than blood sisters, there was a line that personal pride held sacrosanct. Her body wasn't the lithe, slender, fluid moving vehicle it once was and lines in her face told their story as surely as a clock told time. Five children, hard work as a farmer's wife, the time period God had seen fit to have her live her life, all were ingredients that aged her.

Last time she'd seen Jasmine was when Maureen had returned home for her mother's funeral and to help straighten out her parents' affairs. When Maureen made the final decision to marry Landry Dawes, after a year and a half of frequent visits and daily letters, the burden of running the McKenney's Virginia farm passed to Jasmine. Since both her brothers were killed in the war and since both her sisters were victims of deadly childhood diseases, there was no other heir. In that year and a half of living with Jasmine, Maureen realized that her parents could not have been in better protection than that of her sister-in-law. Her parents and

Stephen's beloved adopted each other in a loving relationship that is seldom achieved. The McKenneys, mother and father, became the family identity that Jasmine had so unfairly been denied. She accepted her role and immersed her whole self into being the loving replacement for parents whose children were wrenched from them by war and fate.

For their part, Ma and Pa McKenney loved and idolized the beautiful woman who had so briefly been their son's "wife." It was because, not in spite of, the brevity of Jasmine and Stephen's union that the elder McKenneys cherished their twin grandchildren. Both grandparents fervently believed Stephanie and Stephen Junior were heaven-sent to replace their son. They lavished their love on Stephen's off-spring and did everything they could to see to their well-being and happiness. The McKennys had been *almost* completely happy. *Almost.*

"No, Stephanie, you can't invite Ellsa. She has her church, just like we have our church. Nigras have their place and we have ours. You must remember that." Maureen watched as her mother denied her granddaughter's request to take a black playmate, the stepdaughter of one of the farm hands, to a church function in front of Jasmine. The pain in Jasmine's face was difficult for Maureen to withstand, though she knew the real pain was Jasmine's. To compound the situation, Ellsa was a mulatto.

Only Maureen shared Jasmine's secret. Though not as fervently racists as most whites of the time, her parents were and would remain staunch in their convictions that the races should be separate. Casual comments in daily conversations often sent Jasmine to seek seclusion in her room to weep or fume in anger at their prejudices. It was an insoluble problem, unless Jasmine decided to unveil her heritage. Seeing the plight of Negroes all around her was a constant deterrent, particularly in light of the impact on her children.

The cruelest cut of all came from comments made by her children as they grew older and adopted the vocabulary, ideals, and prejudices held by their grandparents, a strident Jasmine could only partially rebuff.

"The train is running twenty minutes late." Landry joined his wife standing at the station platform. "I stowed our bags down at the Mobile & Girard office. The clerk is a relative of Uncle Herman's from over in Wedowee. He'll take good care of them until I can make arrangements for a carriage."

"I didn't know you had any relatives working for the railroad," Maureen said.

"I didn't know either until he saw my name on my pick-up ticket. It was one of those, are you kin to, conversations. Turns out he's a second cousin. You know us Dawes, we're everywhere."

Maureen laughed, "Yes, we are."

Landry looked at his wife for several seconds, shook his head and said, "Aren't you gonna tell me what this is all about?"

"I really don't know." Maureen looked at him with that unique expression she'd maintained from the time they'd met . . . when she was drawing a line he wasn't to cross. "That's the truth. But, even if I knew . . . if Jasmine wanted to keep a secret . . . I wouldn't tell you."

He shrugged his shoulders. "It's just damned strange. After all this time, practically not wanting to leave

Woodstock, or, at least, that part of Virginia, I don't understand it. We've begged her to come to our place more times than a cat has kittens. It's always *no*. I mean . . . a firm *NO*! Now, to just up and tell us to meet her in Atlanta, and for her to say she wants to go to Eatonton. Hell, it's hard to even talk to her about Georgia much less her home town. You don't think that's mighty strange?"

"I've never known Jasmine to do strange things, Landry. She's one of the most practical people we know."

"I guess we'll find out soon enough." Landry pointed down the track. "That's her train."

***

They looked at each other as they sat side by side in the carriage while it rolled through East Atlanta. Jasmine's once vibrant auburn hair was mostly gray as was Maureen's blonde, though the difference was less discernible in hers. Jasmine carried her extra twenty pounds better than Maureen who'd added thirty-five. They held each other's hand as they had often: at Stephen's burial, in the last traumatic days of the war, at the birth of seven children between them, and at the funerals of the elder McKenneys. Though their appearances changed, the timeless nature of their relationship did not.

Landry whistled to himself as he guided the horses through the city's outskirts. He paid no attention to what he considered women's prattle and instead silently lamented time spent away from the creek that ran through their farm during the best fishing season.

As the conversation progressed, it centered on their children, an almost universal trait mothers share. "Let's see, you know Landry Junior is finishing his first year at the

Agricultural and Mechanical College in Auburn. He loves the school and he's doing well. Larinda is courting and we believe she'll be engaged by the fall. Marina is just finishing school, and of all things, wants to be a school teacher. Henry is in the middle of high school and is falling in love with a different girl daily. And, Marcella, heaven help us and the young men around Troy, is starting high school this fall. She's a tornado looking for a place to land." Maureen's face as well as her comments disclosed she was in a constant state of prideful exasperation caused by her youngest. "That girl is likely to be first in her class academically and last in manners and gentility." Maureen shook her head, "She's still more comfortable climbing trees and wrestling with her brothers than pursuing any lady-like activities."

"Oh, Maureen, Marcella sounds a lot like you when you were young from what I've heard. You've done wonderfully well," Jasmine said.

"Well, I wish they had a more serious bent like your Stephanie and Stephen do. You must be so proud of them. Both will graduate from college this year, won't they? And Stephen. Imagine, a career army officer. His father would be so proud! Are you going to West Point to see him graduate?"

"Yes, it's one of the reasons I won't spend much time here." Jasmine looked out the carriage window at a black family walking the road, their belongings packed on a mule, their bodies and clothes caked with dust. As the carriage passed, she kept her eyes on their forlorn, hopeless faces.

"What is Stephanie going to do? What is the name of her college? I can never seem to remember it." Maureen tried to return Jasmine's mind from where she knew it had traveled.

Jasmine faced Maureen. "Smith College. What's next, I'm not sure. She has two men pursuing her, but she claims she doesn't want to marry, at least for a while. She's talked about medicine. That's difficult, if not impossible for a woman, but the girl is hard-headed enough that she might actually get into medical school." Jasmine paused, "She's been reading about some woman named Blackwell who is a doctor. She wants to go to Michigan. There's a university with a medical school that will admit women located in that state. I wish she'd stay in Northhampton, that's the little town in Massachusetts where her college is at. One of the men who wishes to marry her is the son of the largest industrialist in that state. But, she has these crazy ideas." Jasmine turned and placed both her hands on top of her sister-in-law's. She leaned close, her eyes imploring Maureen's help. "Dear, I need you to do something for me."

"What's wrong, Jasmine?" Maureen's deep concern was evident in her tone and countenance.

"Stephanie has always been curious about my past. She's wanted to know about my parents. She knows I'm from this place and that I own land here. I lied about it. She believes that my parents owned the property. I've told her they were killed in the war. But, Stephanie keeps asking more and more about who my relatives are, why they never contact us, why we never see them. She knows something is wrong, but not what it is. I don't want her to know. Most importantly, I don't want her to have to live the lie I've had to. It's so unfair. Their lives, the ones they've known, end if . . . If people were to find out . . . Stephen's life . . . her life . . . they'd both change in ways they can't comprehend."

Maureen looked at her sister-in-law whose tears flowed freely. The desperation in Jasmine poured out of her mouth and into Maureen's heart. She knew she would do anything to alleviate Jasmine's pain. She said, "What do you want me to do?"

"I need to cut all ties with my past. In order to do that, I need to be able to answer Stephanie's questions with things she'll believe. I have to remove any reason she would have to come here. If she did, there's a chance—" Jasmine shook her head violently. "That can't happen."

"But, what can I do?" Maureen repeated.

"Two things. They both will be difficult for you . . . and for Landry." Jasmine took a couple of breaths. "I want you and Landry to take title to the church property and I want you to promise to keep it in your family. You don't know how hard this is. Stephen trusted me to safe-guard the place where the Hurleys rest. My uncle and half-sister are there. It's sacred to both of us. But, Maureen, I can't risk my children . . . Stephanie is always wanting to come down here to see the property. That would be one less thing. She's so . . . so . . . nosey. If I sell the property to you and can show her the papers, she won't have reason to come here. I'd give you the money back." She waited for a response from Maureen.

Maureen sat silently for several moments. She knew her husband was interested in buying land, but in south-east Alabama, not Georgia. Even so, she also knew how Landry felt about the Hurleys. "I can ask Landry. I can't promise, but I believe he will, but only if it's a real sale. I'm sure he wouldn't take your money back. One thing I know, we would have to pay you some now and the rest later. The farm is just now starting to do well. Reconstruction has been very hard on our area. As far as the promise not to sell the property, I'm sure he wouldn't have a problem with that." She gripped Jasmine's fingers and squeezed. "We'll see. You said there were two things."

"This is hard." Jasmine looked down at her lap.

"I can't do what you want if I don't know what it is."

Jasmine sat silently summoning courage she honestly wasn't sure she possessed. After several minutes she said, "I wouldn't ask, but . . . well . . . you're one of the few people in this world Stephanie looks up to. If you tell her something . . . she'll listen . . . she'll take it to heart. Besides you and I, there is a professor at Smith she really believes in, but I can't possibly approach that woman. And, on this, she'll have doubts about what I tell her. Stephanie instinctively knows something is . . ." Jasmine fell silent.

"What are you asking, Jasmine?" Maureen was becoming increasingly uncomfortable.

"I want for you and me to make up a story of what happened to my parents . . . one that she'll believe. One that will keep her from digging into my past. One so traumatic that she'll leave it alone."

"You want me to help you make up a lie, and then present it to Stephanie? You want me to lie for you?"

Jasmine sat silently for a few moments then silently nodded. When Maureen didn't respond, she said, "Yes, I'm begging you. I know how horrible it sounds. I cringe at the thought of even asking. But, I just—" She began sobbing.

It was Maureen's time to struggle with a major and difficult decision. After several moments of soul search and misapprehensions, she rolled her hands over the top of Jasmine's. She asked, "Jasmine, do you trust me? I mean, really trust me?"

"Oh, yes!"

"Okay. I'll do what I can. I'll write to her, and if necessary, I'll even travel to visit her. But, what I have to do, I will only do on my own. You can't be part of it. Do you trust me that much?"

It was quiet. Finally, Jasmine said, "Yes." Her head shook, "Please don't—"

"I promise, I won't tell her that."

"It's not that I'm ashamed of what I am. I'm just as good as you or anyone else that's white. So were Samuel and Louise." The anger and bitterness spewed out of Jasmine.

"You're right. I know that, but not many people here would agree with me. Maybe up North—"

"Oh, yes. The great emancipators! It's more like the great hypocrites. I've had occasion to send Leviticus to Ohio and New York with shipments to and from the farm. He begs me not to. He's treated worse there than in Virginia. My people were abandoned by many the day the war ended. Now, we're despised and abused like we're still slaves. In some cases, worse." Jasmine swallowed hard. "It's not your fault. I know. I know. It's just so unfair. But, you see, I can't make my children go through what I see so many others suffer. Not when they have an alternative. I don't want them to feel the guilt I feel for lying and feeling as though I'm betraying my own people by denying that I'm one of them. Not because I am who I am, but because everyone should be able to live as I do and they don't have that possibility."

***

In the quiet of his hotel room with Maureen, Landry Dawes buried his head in his hands. Speaking on Jasmine's behalf, his wife had just finished her request for them to purchase the church ruins and lands. He took several deep breaths. When he finally spoke, he talked from behind his fingers and palms. "There's a lot to consider besides just agreeing to buy it and to keep it for three forevers. Figuring out the price that's fair. Squeezing out payments through our ribs. Taxes. Protecting it." He shook his head. "And, we'll have to figure out what to do with it after we buy it."

After his last words, Maureen smiled. She said, "Nothing, dear. We don't have to do a thing."

***

Maureen listened to the steady rhythmic snores coming from their hotel room bed. She'd tried to sleep, but a life-long obsession with attacking her problems until they were resolved wouldn't let her rest. The paper lay on the desk in front of her. She stared at the pen and ink as she listened to Landry's nasal sounds. Landry had agreed to his part, now she must do hers.

Her heart went to her hand as she picked up the pen, dipped it into the ink bottle, and began to write.

Miss Stephanie McKenney,
808 Poplar Street, Room 2B
Northhampton, Massachusetts

Dear Stephanie,

It has been over three months since I last took pen in hand to write to you. I apologize for my delinquency in answering your letter. I have no valid excuse. As you are aware, your mother and I are visiting with each other and she's informed me of your up-coming graduation. You have my most sincere congratulations. I expected no less from the very intelligent person you have become. Since I first saw you on the day of your birth, I've had no doubt that you would be a very special woman.

While I would like this to be strictly a congratulatory letter, honesty forbids that. This letter is written out of concern for your mother, my loved sister-in-law. Her heart ache is mine, and therefore I'm writing this letter to spare her from despair and embarrassment and you from possible disillusion.

It is only natural that a young person be curious about their heritage. Your mother says that you are most curious about her parentage, and though I'm sure you're unaware of this, that fact is most distressing to her. Because of the person I know you to be and love and the person that I love who is your mother, I am writing to serve the both of you to the best of my ability.

Many things you have been led to believe about Jasmine's parents aren't correct. I will tell you what I can without doing a disservice to either of you. Jasmine's parents are now both dead, however, they didn't die in the war. In cruel hard fact, your mother was born out of wedlock. It is a fact that neither your grandfather nor grandmother wished divulged. Many unpleasant and damning events could take place if this secret, interred for many years, was exhumed. I ask you to take my word. Past this, I chose to tell you no more for it can provide no good service to any one and could cause pain and suffering to your mother and you.

I pray that you will understand that the secrets involved with your mother's birth were kept from you for good cause and fervently hope that you will choose to wait for your mother to provide any additional information regarding your maternal grandparents if and when she should choose to do so. I also hope that you will keep the receipt of this information as a confidence between we two. I love you both and wish only the best for each of you.

I remain your loving Aunt,
Maureen McKenney

***

June 16, 1886

Maureen opened the letter addressed to her from Stephanie with nervous fingers and read:

Dear Aunt Maureen,

I am sorry for the delay, but must explain that it was difficult for me to accept the information you shared with me in your last post. My shock was greatest, not in the fact of my mother's birth, but in her withholding the facts from me. I went through a few days of bitterness then anger, then, finally, understanding.

There is no doubt that you and mother want nothing but the best for me. This being true I must accept your council. I'll be patient and wait for mother to tell me what she will, but not without difficulty. I thank you for your care and concern for us both.

I have other news. Quite good I believe. My credentials have been accepted by the University of Michigan's Medical.

Maureen sighed with relief, folded the letter and slipped it back into its envelope for reading later. She opened a drawer from in the desk at which she sat. Before she put the letter inside, she hesitated. Something deep inside of her spoke, telling Maureen to remove pen, ink, paper and an envelope from the drawer. Scarcely thinking of the words she wrote, the message that found its way to the paper flowed from her heart, by-passing her mind, directly to her fingers that held the pen. It was a message for someone she knew she'd never know, yet she knew its importance. Maureen's hand moved over the paper smoothly without the slightest hint of hesitation. Words on the sheet were the perfect product of sincerity.

When she finished the letter, she carefully folded and placed it in the envelope and addressed it to:

"To the successor of Landry Dawes who inherits the privilege of painting the cross on Cotton Creek - open before making the decision to sell or dispose of the cross, the church ruins or the land."

She did not smile. She did not frown. She did make a mental note to speak to her husband about what she'd just written. And, she felt an inner peace that would never leave her.

Chapter 19

June 22, 1899

"It's a shame to let this land sit idle." He tried to talk over the noise made by the Olds horseless carriage that bumped and jarred over the rough country ruts that was known as Cotton Creek Road. Edgar Waltham detested riding in the vehicle, but his young wife of one year, Glenda Pearl Waltham, loved driving the "automobile" her father had purchased directly from Ransom E. Olds. It was one of Olds' original prototypes, the only such conveyance in the surrounding nine counties, and another of the many gifts Percy Tuttle Perkins lavished on his favorite daughter. As one of the richest men in Georgia, he could do so at his whim.

The beautiful raven haired woman aiming the "auto" along the red clay tracks pretended she didn't hear her husband speak. She detested the man she not so secretly described to her close friends as, "the slimy toad I married." Glenda was on the deserted back-road for one reason, the sheer thrill of driving. A smile covered her beautiful features and the wind whipping against the curve hiding dress that covered her neck to toe gave her relief from the late June heat.

Edgar tapped her on her shoulder to get her attention.

Glenda snapped her head around and glared at him. "Don't bother me when I drive!" When she turned back to face the road, the smile returned, this time enhanced by the opportunity to rebuff her unwanted husband. To Glenda's way of thinking, Edgar Waltham was a fountain producing gushers of stupid ideas, the trip out to visit a ruined old church being one. She loathed the idea of having to stop and walk around as they agreed, but she'd given her word.

Above all, she hoped that this wasn't one of her husband's latest attempts to have sex outside of their bedroom. Like most properly brought up girls of the time, Glenda's first experience with sex was on her honeymoon. After her first several episodes, she couldn't understand why any woman would enjoy what she considered a disgusting, unexciting experience. However, Edgar might try despite knowing her sentiments. She thought it was a good thing she could probably "whip him" if it came to a physical confrontation. It was bad enough to have to behave like a brood mare from one of her father's stables in the privacy of her bedroom, but anywhere else? No!

"Don't you think you should slow down? This road is rough and you've never been out here before. You don't know what might be around the next bend," Edgar said.

"Shut up, *please*," Glenda said.

"Be reasonable."

Glenda brought the vehicle to an abrupt stop. She glared at him silently for a few seconds before asking, "If you're too scared to ride along, get out and walk. I'll wait for you at the church." It hadn't taken long for her to discover the buttons to push to intimidate and humiliate the man. Ever since she observed his reaction to heights on their honeymoon trip to the mountains, she played his lack of courage like a violin concerto.

"Why don't you behave like a *lady?*" Edgar responded with his only effective weapon.

Glenda looked up toward the heavens and hoped "the slimy toad" would give her a reason for a divorce soon, no matter how much her father might object. "I'll go a little slower." She added with fiendish delight, "You can close your eyes if you wish. I shan't wreck us." She eased the horseless carriage into gear and drove just as fast as she had before stopping.

***

"I wonder why no one ever rebuilt it?" Glenda looked up at the steeple and the white cross on top. She hadn't climbed down from her Olds before she'd changed her mind about coming. The place had a soothing impact on her and she relaxed as she picked a path through the tall weeds. Glenda hiked her skirts up to make it easier to walk through the impediments. Her husband trailed behind her, walking very slowly, though he didn't seem the least bit concerned where he stepped. She waited for Edgar to make some suggestive remark which she was ready to rebuff. He didn't. Arrival at the old church's ruins had the opposite effect on Edgar than it did on her. Waltham became nervous, jumpy. His head twisted around continually as though he was waiting for someone or something to jump out of the weeds or from behind the crumbling walls. She picked at him saying, "Come on, Edgar, there's no such thing as ghosts."

Pausing she continued, "This is a special spot." Glenda stopped at the base of the steeple and stared up at the cross. "Look, the steeple part of it is in remarkably good shape. The cross practically gleams."

"Some nut comes out here every few years and paints it." Edgar wandered around the church grounds several yards from her, alternately looking around at the road and down in the weeds as though searching for something.

"What are you worried about? There's nobody around here. It's been dry for a week and I didn't see any tracks on the road. Besides, why would anyone want to bother us?" She shook her head. "What *are* you looking for?"

"A loose brick. There might be snakes around here." Edgar would continue to search until he found one. Glenda considered him obsessed with the many phobias that passed through his myopic brain. Snakes were one of them.

"Why does he do it?" Glenda asked.

"Why does who do what?"

"Why does the nut paint the cross?"

"Hell, I don't know, Glenda. It's one of those stupid war tales. Take your pick. One is he accidentally killed the preacher and he does it as a penance, so's that's why. Another is the dew dripped off the cross while he was dying from a wound and it brought him back to life. Some folks claim he hid in the church before it got burned and promised the preacher to keep it painted. Another is some man pays him to and nobody's sure why." Waltham shrugged his shoulders and snorted.

"Do you know who owns it?

"No. Not for sure. I've heard a family in Virginia does. It's no one from around here."

"I'd say this is a waste . . . normally . . . but, there's something else here. It's quiet strength. It's a sense of finality. Do you feel it?"

"No," her husband answered. He bent over and picked up a brick, then Edgar walked over to her. "Let's go inside and see what it was like," he suggested, motioning with his hand for her to proceed. He made a quick survey of all the ruins' surroundings before following her up the deteriorating steps to and through the entry.

Inside the opening that once housed the church's front door, the thick oak floors were slowly succumbing to time's ravages. More than half the exterior walls had fallen, all inwardly, a circumstance that surprised Glenda. She guessed it had something to do with the buildings engineering or method of construction. Edgar was right behind her, practically walking in her foot prints. *Typical*, she thought, *the bastard is letting me test the floor for him to find out if the wood's rotten.*

"Stay over to the right, closer to the wall," Edgar said gruffly. The area her husband wanted her to walk toward was the corner formed by exterior walls that still stood. The "L" shape protected the floor there. Little debris was strewn over its surface. However, ominous cracks in the walls made standing close to them seem unwise. Several straight steel rods, used to hang oil lamps from, still extended from the brick work. Each "hanger" had a decorative flat piece of steel attached to the end. It was elliptical in shape and pointed at the end, making the hanger devices look like a spear that had been thrust through the wall's side. High enough to be above the tallest man's head when standing, they were just low enough that a lantern handle could be lifted over the pointed ornament that acted as a retainer on the rod's end. Glenda stared at the ironwork, a soft voice said something that sounded like, "Watch out!"

Glenda twisted her head and said, "Did you hear . . . ." She was unable to get the word 'that' spoken. Movement in her peripheral vision was followed by a horrendous blow to her temple . . . and blackness.

***

Glenda's next recollection was of something on her eye lid on one side of her head. It took several seconds to realize she was lying on the floor of the old church, her husband had smashed her on the head with the brick he was carrying and the something on her eye lid was blood.

Grunts came from somewhere near. She tried to move, but all that would respond was her head which she could move enough to see Edgar had pulled her close to the wall, but the man wasn't in sight. The grunting got stronger followed by her husband's favorite pronouncement when he became upset, "Horse shit!" It was then Glenda realized Edgar was on the other side of the wall trying to push it over on her.

She started to try to move when a voice close to her murmured in urgent tones, "Put your head back as it was, close your eyes, stay quiet, don't move, no matter what!"

She did what she was told; she was too groggy to question why.

The shuffling sound of Edgar's feet on the church floor stopped right by her head. He said, "Glenda . . . Glenda . . . Glenda." His clothes made a rustling sound as he bent over.

She made no response.

He nudged her with his finger. Glenda let her shoulder go limp as pudding. The rustling sound repeated itself as he straightened up. The voice cautioned her, "Be quiet. Don't move." She obeyed.

She felt the toes of Edgar's shoes against her body. He kicked her, but not viciously. He laughed, "She's as dead as old Abe Lincoln." It was all she could do to restrain herself—but she did. The man's shoe tips pushed against her body then slid away. He'd moved five feet away. Glenda heard him, straining, his breathes coming in pants. She opened one eye lid to a slit where she could see above and to her side. Edgar was pulling on one of the lamp hangers as hard as he could.

The voice repeated, "Don't move!" It was surprising, for Edgar showed no sign of hearing the warning. Dirt and mortar began to rain on her and she closed her eyes. There was a strange swooshing noise, followed by a thunderous crash and a short high-pitched scream mixed with it. Glenda felt a couple of heavy objects drop on her body, but nothing of severe consequence. She heard a moan and the sound of someone exhaling slowly.

Her eyes opened wide. The wall had seemingly flown at Edgar, breaking away three foot above floor level. The items she'd felt were a few individual bricks. However, Waltham's shoes were the only thing visible. The wall had crumbled on him, doubling over and folding in on itself, doubling the crushing weight. She struggled to her feet and careened around the pile until she could see the small portion of Edgar not covered with bricks. His face and a small portion of his chest were all that were visible. That was only because the lamp hanger had impaled him, its point driven through the center of his chest. The steel rod separated the bricks in that small area. His wide open eyes had the shocked, vacant, pained look they wore at the second of his death. If she'd moved . . . .

She looked for the person who had been advising her. No, that wasn't right. The person must have been helping her for the wall could not have achieved enough force and speed to make the movement over her body without considerable strength being exerted against the other side.

"Hello. Where are you," Glenda cried out.

There was no response.

"Please come out. I need help." She staggered to the front opening, grabbed the doorless jamb and thrust her head out, expecting to see a horse, or a carriage or a wagon, and a person. Her Olds sat in the tall green weeds, but there was no one and nothing to be seen. The jolt of adrenaline began to fade and her knees became rubbery. Glenda felt her body lean against the door opening and slowly slide downward. Noises popped and lights flashed for a second or two; she was on the threshold of passing out. She murmured, "Please God, help me." Her eyes closed, but she fought to stay conscious. Slowly the noises and lights disappeared. Glenda struggled to her feet, clawing up the jamb. She put her hand to the side of her head. Her palm and fingers came away sticky, wet and red.

Where had the person fled to? Her legs were increasingly stable. Could she dare try going down the stairs? Glenda called out, "Is anybody here? Please, I could use some help." She looked around the yard, listened, saw no sign of a human, and heard only birds and insects.

It took a couple minutes to increase her resolve, but she made it down the stairs. Walking was less difficult. Her dizziness was fading. She was developing a headache, but not an overpowering one. Glenda picked up a limb and used it as a cane to steady herself as she circled the ruins trying to find the source of the mysterious voice she'd heard and who had obviously helped her. No one was visible. She returned to the church's front and leaned against the steeple.

It was then two realizations struck her. She would have to do the rest by herself. She would get no more assistance from whoever spoke to her. Glenda straightened up making the decision to get to her horseless carriage, muster the strength to crank start it, and drive to the nearest help. The other thing she did was promise herself to never tell anyone of the voice she heard. No one would believe her if she told them who she thought she heard speak. At minimum, she was sure it was a representative. Glenda took one last look for her mysterious voiced savior, but as she expected, there was no one there to see.

The spot *was special* and had the strength she had felt when she'd arrived. For sure, it had the power to render a final judgment. Strength flowed back into her faster than blood flowed out. Walking to the vehicle and turning its crank were not as difficult as she had feared. Yes, she told herself, she had new strength. As the vehicle started, Glenda knew her belief in a superior power would never fail.

Chapter 20

November 26, 1954

Landry Junior watched the last of their visitors depart.

The tow truck managed to repair three of the tires on the Packard. Amazingly, the stem valves had all been removed and the truck only carried three inner tube replacements that would fit. But, the car still had to be towed. Young Dawes watched the disgusted and deeply suspicious Doctor Vale and his assistant haul their fancy business suits, now damp with perspiration, into the tow truck's front seat next to Dexter their repairman. Both the Dawes were happy to see them leave—Dexter's other job was cleaning septic tanks—since there was a distinctly unpleasant odor that accompanied the man. Young Landry chuckled when he visualized the professor's eleven mile trip to the repair shop.

Dawes Sr. was placing the final ropes on the ladders that were on the Ford's top. The cross was sparkling white and his duty done for five years, though the shortness of the late fall day made the evidence difficult to see. After several adjustments, tying and retying the lashes, he pronounced them, "Ready to go. You have everything you came with?" He asked his son.

"Yep." The boy walked to the passenger side to climb in. "What time do you think we'll get home?"

Mr. Dawes pulled out his pocket watch. He squinted at its hands in the gathering darkness. It read 4:40. "Figuring an hour to eat someplace and a phone call I gotta make—midnight or some after." After the watch went back in his pocket, he opened the door and prepared to climb in. That was until his son stopped him by saying. "Ahhh, Dad, we got more company."

A beat-up old Dodge pick-up stopped at the edge of the road a hundred feet away. It was too dark to see who sat inside, past the fact that there were two heads visible. "Should we wait or drive down?" Landry Junior wondered out loud.

"They're getting out. We'll just wait here."

The two people advancing toward them were semi-silhouettes. One was short, heavy, and obviously female. The other appeared to be a male of unremarkable size. They'd advanced a third of the way across the church yard before it was possible to tell more about them. Even through the paucity of light, the Dawes could tell their visitors were Afro-American. The man wore a straw hat and removed it as they approached. As they came closer and closer, it was clear that the two figures' focus was on the cross, not on the Dawes.

The younger Dawes said, "Dad, I noticed that Dodge go by a couple times today. What do you think they want?"

"We'll find out soon," his father said.

When they were thirty feet from he and his son, Dawes Sr. raised his hand and waved once. He said, "Hello, folks."

Both visitors responded with hellos as they got within six feet . . . and stopped. The four of them stood facing each other; an awkward quiet dropped a curtain over them. This silence was bred of uncertainty—uncertainty regarding their visitors purpose—uncertainty regarding how their visit would be received. Both waited for the other to break the tension. Mr. Dawes realized it was up to him to snap the impasse.

"Can we help you folks?"

The woman said, "Mizz Autry, told us the man that paints the cross was out here. She said you wanted to know what this place means to some of us. Well, I just wanted to talk to you a minute and tell you my story, if you're interested. Buzz, here, and I saw'd you up there painting away most all day. Didn't want to bother you none."

"It's certainly not a bother. Why didn't you come up when the other folks were here?"

The two blacks looked at each other. The man who the woman referred to as Buzz said, "Didn't know if'n we'd be welcome. Different folks look at different things . . . different." It was as close as he wished to get to the subject of the prejudice he lived with daily.

"Well, you *are* welcome. I'm Landry Dawes," he pointed to his son, "This is my boy. His name is Landry, also. Who do I have the pleasure of speaking to?"

"I'm Henry Bonham, but most folks call me Buzzard or Buzz. This here's Neessa Clark. She's the one wants to talk to you. Mrs. Clark, she lives over to Monticello. I just drove her over. She ain't got no car.

"Buzz, I can speak for myself." The woman had a sad smile on her face. "He just has a bad case of runnin' off at the mouth, Mr. Dawes." She reached in her purse and without looking removed a scrap of cloth. Dawes noted that her fingers grasped the object tightly and he noted an air of indecision in her manner. "I come here . . . I come here." She stopped and dropped her head. "This just ain't so easy."

"She brung you something, Mr. Dawes," Buzz said. He nodded at Neessa, "Go ahead."

"Okay, okay," the woman said as she took a fortifying breath. "I been knowing Mrs. Autry a long time. I worked for her at Fanny and Flora's for quite a spell. That's why I knew about this place." She thrust her hand that gripped the object at Landry Senior. "Here, I want you to have this."

"Thank you." Mr. Dawes placed his hand, palm up, under Neessa's. He was curious and surprised. The woman's hand trembled slightly as it opened and dropped the cloth into his. He spread it open so that it lay flat and he could see what he'd been given. It was a shoulder patch. It had black bands stretched across the top and bottom of its square shape. Between the two black borders, a gold background interlocked by means of castellated edges had a black panther centered and striding across the gold. On the bottom, a scroll banner bore the words "Spit Fire." Landry knew he was looking at a military shoulder patch. He didn't know what group it represented or why he was receiving it. He repeated, "Thank you," and added, "But, I don't understand."

"That there shoulder insignia is my son's. He was a fighter pilot in the War in Europe. I got that back because of this spot, so's I'd like to give it to you for keepin' it up."

"Oh. He was in the 332nd?"

The woman stiffened. "Yes, *he was* a Tuskegee Airman." Her pride was evident.

"That's a very famous fighter wing. I had relatives that fought in Italy. They flew bombers. I heard about that group from them. In fact, the 332nd flew fighter escort for them." Dawes rubbed the surface of the patch. "Would you tell me about this?"

"I'd be pleased to." The woman looked up at the cross. "My son Charlie, he always wanted to fly and he always liked church. At Tuskegee, where he went to college, his nickname was Charlie the Chisel, 'cause he was sharp smart. When the war started, he joined the army, and when he had a chance to get into the Air Corps, he jumped at it. He was a good athlete, had the college learnin' they was looking for and even had done a little flying. But, it was still hard to get in. I fretted just like every mother does that see their boy go to war. He'd say, "Don't you worry, Mama. God will take care of me. I'll be back." He really believed that. I got to see him some when he was in training at Moton and at the Tuskegee base, but in 1944, they went to the war. He was at Ramitelli Air Base; I still don't know exactly where that's at. He told me weren't nowhere near Rome. I didn't hear much from him after he went there. I'd get a letter every two or three weeks. Black lines drawn all over it. But, the one good thing—I knew my boy was alive."

The lady looked uncomfortable, so Landry asked, "Would you like to sit in the car? You look tired."

"No, but that's kind of you. If'n it's okay, I'll just lean on the side. My legs got the miseries. Varicose veins, you know."

"Go right ahead." Dawes said.

Clark walked over to the Ford and leaned against the front fender. "Awww, that's good." She smiled; it was much easier to read her features for the setting sun rays shone on her face and weren't striking the back of her head. "Where was I?" She answered her own question. "Oh, yes. I was telling you 'bout what happened to Charlie. He was a good pilot. Real good. Charlie flew all kinds of planes. I know the numbers, but not much else. I memorized them." Neessa's head held a little higher. "There was P-40s, and P-39s, and P-47's, and last P-51s. That was his favorite. He said he felt like that plane was a part of his body. He shot down three of them Germans. Anyway, months went by while he was over there. April . . . May . . . June . . . July. . . August. Then September. No letter came. He never went longer than three weeks without writing. Four weeks and I know'd something was wrong."

She shook her head. "Then it came. One of those telegrams. You know. The one I got said, 'I'm sorry to inform you that your son, Charles Thomas Clark, did not return from a mission on September 17th. He is officially listed as missing in action and is presumed dead.' I won't ever forget those words. My world was crushed. Charlie was all I had. My husband died in a saw mill accident the year before, my mother and sister burned up in a house fire, and my brother, well, he got himself killed. All that happened in the previous two years. I'd done all the grieving I could stand. I thought sure I'd end up in the crazy house up to Milledgeville."

"That's more than any one person should have to endure." Mr. Dawes said.

"Amen!" Buzz Boykin added.

"Sure isn't fair," Landry Junior said.

"That's just how I felt! It wasn't fair. I was working at Flora and Fanny's back then. Miss Flora saw me crying. She come up and put her arm around me. Asked me what was wrong. When I told her, that skinny little lady hugged me half to death. Miss Flora was a true lady and right good to us colored folk. Anyway, she said, 'Don't you fret, yet, Neessa. They didn't say killed in action, so they don't have his body, and that means there's still hope. Keep hold of that.' She stepped back and looked at me for a few seconds then she said, 'Take your apron off.' Miss Flora bundled me into her Studebaker, and off we go, out to here. When we got here, she say, 'You go talk to Him, Neessa. Tell Him how much you need your boy. Take your time. Let Him see your heart. This place has power other places don't have. Believe me, I know. *I know*.' She practically shoved me out the door."

"Well, I come up here, kneeled down next to the steeple and looked up at the cross. It looked so strong. I prayed. Don't ask me what I said, 'cause I ain't got no idea. What I do know is I showed what was in my heart like Miss Flora said. I asked. I promised. I begged. I don't know how long I was there, but finally something changed. It snapped just like that. Don't know why, but I looked at my watch. It said 1:45. Right then, I didn't feel so hopeless no more. Oh, there wasn't no flashing lights, or voices, or Dixieland bands playing. No angel come sit on my shoulder. But when I got up . . . somehow I knew there was a chance."

"And was there?" Mr. Dawes asked.

Neessa smiled. "Yes. Miss Flora took me home directly. She told me to stay there until I wasn't feeling poorly. Said she'd pay me like I was at work. Miss Flora was a fine lady. Yes, she was. When I got to my house, I made a pot of coffee and I waited. I didn't know what for, but I knew that's what I was s'possed to do. Sat there all that day, all that night, and most of the next—drinking my coffee and napping some. There was this knock at my door come late one afternoon. It was another telegram. It said, 'I'm pleased to inform you that your son, Charles Thomas Clark, has been located and is no longer considered missing in action. He is convalescing in a military hospital.' That was the best thing I ever heard."

"Hallelujah!" Buzz shouted.

"How badly was he hurt?" Dawes asked.

"Oh, he was bad hurt. Got some of them German bullets that went clean through him. And, his parachute got hung up in some trees. That beat him up more. He had it rough and can't throw a baseball no more—other than that, he's just fine now. But, but I gotta tell you the rest. After he come home, we was talking. He was telling me how he got back to the hospital. Charlie said there was these Italian farmers that come across him while he was hanging in that tree. He figures he'd been in it for days, kind of floatin' in and out of consciousness. They cut him down and knew he was in real bad shape. They took him to some Army soldiers. 'Bout then he passed out again. When he came to, he was so weak he couldn't move or even talk. There was a blanket over his head."

"And then Charlie told me, 'Mom, they thought I was dead, but I heard this one doctor say, "What time is it?" Someone answered, "It's 1:45." That doctor said, "I've got time, I'm going to look at a couple, just to be sure." He pulled the blanket back off my face. He said a nasty word, Mom, then, "This one's still a little alive." Then I passed out and didn't wake up until I was in the hospital.'

"Mercy, a bolt of electricity went through me. I asked him what day it was when he heard the time and we figured that it was on the 22nd of September. And you know what, that was the same day I was here." Neessa Clark looked up at the cross and said, "Thank you." She began to cry.

Landry Senior walked to her and put his hand on her shoulder. He said, "I thank you for telling me about your boy." He held out the patch. "I think you should keep this."

"No, sir!" The woman was adamant. "I made a promise if'n I could find out who kept this place for all us folks, I'd give him something that meant as much for me to sacrifice as you and all your family done here. Charlie and I agreed you should have this. That means a powerful bunch to both of us, so you gotta have it. I hope you understand."

"I do. I promise I'll keep this and it will have a special place in our home." Mr. Dawes gently stroked her shoulder a couple of times before stepping back and respectfully folding the insignia patch. He reverently placed it in his pocket.

"Buzz, I think we should be going," Neessa said. "Okay," he replied and took a step toward the pickup. "Please, don't leave yet." Landry Senior took a step after them. "What does Charlie do today? I'm interested. He seems like a good, strong man."

They stopped and faced him. Neessa and Boykin looked at each other. Buzz shook his head and murmured low, "No."

Neessa stared at him for several seconds before swiveling her head to look at Landry Senior. "My son lives in Atlanta. He works there and he helps the pastor at one of the churches. The preacher is Dr. King."

"Dr. King?" Landry shook his head. "Sorry, I don't know the name."

"His name is Dr. Martin Luther King. Someday, I think you'll hear about him. There are folks hereabouts that know him, they know my son works with him, and they don't care much for that. For honest, that's why we didn't come up earlier."

"Well, I wish your son well in whatever he does and please thank him for the patch."

After "Goodbyes" Landry and his son watched the two people get into the Dodge and disappear down the road into the woods and the coming night.

Chapter 21

November 26, 1954

The last light had vanished when the Dawes drove into Flora and Fanny's parking lot. The headlights shone against the dozen cars already at rest on the gravel and made two bright white spots on the buildings side as the front bumper came close. Mr. Dawes noted that his son had taken time to clean up in the creek, changed his shirt, and combed his rebellious hair. The boy sat bolt upright, stiff and alert. He chuckled to himself and shook his head slightly. It was truly amazing what effect estrogen could have on young men.

Before Landry Senior could reach to the dash to turn the ignition key off, the door on his son's side was already open. He said, "Slow down, you don't even know if she's there."

"Who?" His son tried to sound disinterested. It was a very poor attempt. He did let the door close.

"Miss Cleavage. The redhead. The waitress. She might not be working tonight."

"Her name is *Julie*. She told me she is working until nine."

Mr. Dawes marveled how quickly the young changed perspectives given the right stimulus. "Sorry. But, can I give you a piece of advice?"

"Uh-huh." Junior's agreement was obligatory.

"You'll do better if you don't charge in there like a bull in heat. Take your time and keep control. Count to twenty before you get out."

The boy counted half under his breath, "One . . . two . . . three . . . four . . . five . . . six . . . seven . . . eight . . . nine . . . ten . . . eleven . . . twelve, thirteen, fourteen, fifteen, sixteen, eighteen, twenty." The passenger side door swung open again, fast and hard. Landry Junior was half-way to Flora and Fanny's entrance before Mr. Dawes managed to open his door and call after his trotting son, "Find out if they have a pay phone and where it's at."

"Sure." Young Landry's word coincided with his hand hitting the restaurant's front door latch.

Dawes Senior watched the hormonal wreck disappear inside. He leaned over on the bench seat and opened the glove compartment. Landry quickly found what he was searching for; a small black notebook. His fingers brushed against another item he wouldn't need now. The tips of his fingers hesitated on it. Maybe he should look because he had seriously considered— His mind was made up. He removed an envelope, too. Dawes stuck them in his coat pocket, a coat he'd need to shield him from the chilly November evening.

***

Julie and young Dawes were chatting and laughing as Mr. Dawes found a table. It took a few minutes for his son to remember they'd come to the restaurant to eat. With great difficulty he tore himself away from the redhead. Landry Senior noted that Julie wasn't dressed for work. She wore brown and white saddle oxfords, fuzzy white socks, one of the poodle dresses that were in style and a green sweater that wasn't designed to hide her curves. He doubted his son's eyes ever went much farther down than to the color green. Julie had definitely prepared for Landry's visit; her hairdo and makeup were different than before. As his grandfather was fond of saying, "She shined up like a polished cow bell." The father could read the son's lips well enough to see, "I'll be right back," flow from them as he left the girl.

When Landry Junior was a few feet from his father he said, "Dad, they don't have a pay phone here. But, Julie talked to Mrs. Autry. You can use the phone in the office if it isn't long distance or if you can reverse the charges if it is." He leaned on the table with both hands, but made no attempt to be seated.

"Good. It's a local call. Thank Julie and Mrs. Autry and tell them I'll place the call as soon as I finish. What do you want to eat?" He smiled at his son.

"Well . . . Uhhhh."

"Don't say anymore. I see Julie isn't dressed for waitressing." Mr. Dawes removed his billfold and took out a twenty. He stuck it between his son's fingers. "You earned that today. Mind going over and sitting with the redhead? You can eat with her. I need a break before I have to listen to you snore all the way home."

"You're the top banana, Dad." He started away and turned back quickly. "I'll get Irene to come over, she's the night waitress. Oh, and Julie says stay away from the liver and onions or the boiled okra. But, the fried okra's good and so are the pork chops, taters, and milk gravy." Smoke rose from the boy's footprints as he retraced them back to Julie.

Julie disappeared for a few seconds then reemerged from what Mr. Dawes guessed was Autry's office. The two "mightbe" lovers were laughing and talking as soon as their rears found their chairs at a table they selected in the restaurant's rear corner. He hoped his son remembered to eat. "There's no fool like an old fool, unless it's a younger one," he said.

"There's plenty of both of those around. I'm Irene. What you want to eat?" The waitress looked at him like a bad check. She was thin . . . no, skinny, with a face that could have been cute if her perpetual frown hadn't warped it. Irene was not the type to believe in the benevolence of her fellow man.

"Do you have a menu?"

"Yeah. Do you need it?"

Dawes couldn't help but smile. "I guess I don't. Pork chops, fried okra, mashed potatoes with milk gravy. Do I get anything with that?"

"Cornbread or grits and indigestion. I'd drink coffee. The roaches been in the tea and Maylyn makes the lemonade so strong it'll eat the enamel off your teeth." Irene was bitter, but honest.

"Cornbread and coffee."

"It'll be a few. Maylyn told me she's gonna stretch the time out so Julie gets some sparking time with your boy, but you aren't supposed to know that. Oh, the peach cobbler is what you'll want for dessert. It ain't the only thing worth having, but it's the best."

Irene walked away. By the time she was half way to the kitchen she was a slender pole indistinguishable from the clothes rack next to the front door.

***

She smiled, "You just take as long as you want, Mr. Dawes. I've got to see to the kitchen anyway. My evening frycook is messy." The door closed behind Maylyn Autry as she exited the office.

Landry looked around the small room. He wondered if it was an enlarged closet. A desk, a table, a file cabinet and two chairs left little space for humans to occupy. Though he felt like an intruder, Landry maneuvered around and behind the desk and sat in Autry's chair. The clutter of empty boxes and cooking paraphernalia between the desk and table made getting to the other chair a daunting task.

He wiggled in the chair to be able to reach the notebook in his coat pocket. Tossing the black leather object on the desk top, he stared at it for several seconds before picking it up. He didn't like reexamining his decisions, but felt obligated to take a last look at one he'd made earlier in the day. Landry told the walls, "No way," picked up the book, and thumbed through the notes to one of the last entries. It said, "Carlson Combs, real estate agent, Eatonton. Phone number is Azalea 47986. AZ for Azalea."

Landry pulled the phone to him, stuck his finger in the dial to "A" and spun it. After repeating the process six more times he marveled at modern communications. His farm outside Eufaula was serviced by a small county-wide company and was still using operators to connect each call.

The city itself had dialing. Even the old home farm near Troy had dial calling, but he was sure that the nearness of the Mobile & Girard Railroad helped promote progress there. It wouldn't be long before he had it at home. Hell, a television station in range of his place was a possibility in the next few years, if he wanted to pay for a fancy enough antenna!

"Hello." The voice came through the handset that pressed against his ear.

"Hello, may I speak to Mr. Combs?" Landry said.

"Speakin'"

"This is Landry Dawes. You wrote to me about someone wanting to buy property I own. I promised I'd call when I got up here in Eatonton."

"Oh, yes. Did you get the offer I mailed to you?"

"Yes, I did. That's a lot of money. Particularly for some land that doesn't appear that special."

"It is, but the person wanting to buy it is just set on getting it. Truth be told, the offer is fifteen percent more than I recommended and that was on a par with some of the best improved pasture around here." Combs waited for a response, briefly. When none came he said, "Could we meet in my office tomorrow and get this deal done?"

"Whoa. The price is fair and all, but I'm not interested in selling."

The phone was silent for several seconds. "Mr. Dawes, you got to know that deal is for more than the property is worth."

"Yes, I agree that it is."

"Well . . . ," the man hesitated. He cleared his throat. "Well, what would it take for you to sell it?"

Landry chuckled, "Look, I don't think you understand, but—"

"Mr. Dawes, my client has his heart set on getting that land. Mr. Waltham is an extremely wealthy man, I'm sure he'd consider paying more. Why don't you give me a figure? I'll see if he's willing. I'd hate to disappoint him."

"Waltham? He's from around here, right?"

"Yes. His family has been here since the 1850's."

"Uh-huh. Well, I guess you'll just have to disappoint him, because I'm not going to sell. The price doesn't have anything to do with it." The scowl on Landry's face told how he felt about the Waltham name.

The phone was silent.

"I don't want to waste more of your time. I'll—"

"Hold up just a second." Combs was buying time for some reason. "You said you wanted to keep the church ruins. Would you sell the rest, if Mr. Waltham made you the same deal and let you keep that and the two or three acres around it?"

"I'm sorry, but that wouldn't change my mind."

"Well, what about—"

Landry cleared his throat. "Look, Mr. Combs, *'no'* is a two letter word and it's easy to say. I can say it over and over and over and never get tired. Sorry, the property just isn't for sale."

Combs was quiet, again, for several seconds. Finally, he said, "Well, Mr. Dawes, you are an interesting fellow. I can assure you if you change your mind, Mr. Waltham will be ready to deal."

"That's good to know, but if you'll excuse me, I have a long drive home tonight. Bye."

***

Dawes was at the office door as he stuck the notebook in his pocket. His fingers touched the envelope and he stopped. Curiosity tugged at him. With his other hand he removed his pocket watch. Seven-thirty. His prognostication that they'd arrive home around midnight was all wrong. It was looking more like two. He shrugged his shoulders; a few more minutes wasn't going to make any difference. The watch went back into his pocket and he maneuvered through the obstacle filled path as he retraced his steps to the chair behind the desk. Before he sat down, he placed the envelope on its surface. Landry wondered how many times he'd looked at it in his home desk drawer where it normally resided; hundreds for sure; maybe thousands.

Slowly, he lowered himself into the chair. Was he doing the right thing? When he decided he wasn't going to accept the agent's offer, the reason for reading the message inside the envelope ceased to exist. The instruction written on the yellowing paper said,

"To the successor of Landry Dawes who inherits the privilege of painting the cross on Cotton Creek - open before making the decision to sell or dispose of the cross, the church ruins, or the land."

Those instructions were always considered sacrosanct. When Landry IV was given the letter by Landry III, it was with the most gravity and solemnity he could muster. Part of that was taking an oath that he would not sell or dispose of the church ruins and its lands without first reading the message. His dad assured him that the ritual started with the first Landry Dawes and was passed down, father to son. Someday, it would be his responsibility to indoctrinate Landry V.

The question he faced now was one on which he had no clear guidance. Was he not to read its words unless the fateful decision was in the balance? Landry couldn't remember anything in his father's prolonged lecture barring him from looking inside. It was the self-supported solemnity accorded the document that locked the unsealed paper from his view. Was there a dark family secret contained in its yellow folds that should not be known unless the property was to change hands?

He wondered if his father and his father's father struggled with the same moral dilemma. Had their hands shaken nervously as they removed the letter from the envelope? Did guilt fill them as they unfolded the paper? Were their eyes reluctant to read the first words? Those were his feelings as he did precisely those steps.

It took a couple of moments to summon the courage to begin reading, but he did. The pen strokes written with a bold strong hand captured his eyes and in his ear for he heard the imagined voice of his great-great-grandmother saying the words to him:

Dear Descendant,

I am writing this letter in the hopes that it will act as a guide for you if you are faced with the necessity or desire to turn over the Cross on Cotton Creek, the ruins surrounding it, and the lands that it occupies, to another outside our heritage. While there may be no recourse for you I wish you to understand what I believe is the true meaning of painting the cross and keeping it as a beacon. I implore you: Don't relinquish your birthright. You'll see in time what you're nourishing isn't an object or a monument. Rather you are sustaining belief itself.

So many gave so much to the hallowed ground you keep because of their belief in the God it represents. The Hurleys – Marcus and Marian, Samuel and Louise Jones, and my beloved brother Stephen McKenney, blessed the land with their blood. Jasmine McKenney, Stephen's wife, endured great personal hardship to acquire and keep the property and has entrusted it to our custody. Their belief in each other, in man's duty to others, and in God, makes the Cross on Cotton Creek a special place.

Its power will grow through the years. Others will come, have their belief fortified or awakened and each will leave with more strength. In turn, their renewal or awakening increases the power of the place by making it easier for others to believe that they, too, can receive a blessing beneath the out-stretched arms of the Cross. And if it is just that small bit easier for them to believe because of its history and its mystic, it is the removal of one more barrier between them and finding God, perhaps for the first time.

Is the placed blessed by God? I truly don't know, though I believe and hope it may be. I do know that God will answer prayers whether they are made beneath a cross over a ruins or not. What is important is that those who go there go because they are desperate, and if it is easier for them to believe their prayer will be heard there, then it will be.

By continuing to paint the cross, our family has the honor of letting people know that God can be found even in the midst of ruin and despair. That is the true power of the Cross at Cotton Creek.

Some day may we all rest together?
Maureen McKenney Dawes

His eyes were no longer captive. His heart was. At the bottom of the page, inscriptions answered his questions. In sequence appeared:

Dear wife your wish has been kept and is forwarded, Landry Dawes
Landry Dawes II, Your trust is maintained
The covenant is kept and passed, Landry Dawes III

Landry folded the precious instrument of strength and returned it to the envelope. He'd add his name someday . . . and do it proudly. As he rose from the chair, he felt different. It wasn't until he opened the door and saw his son and Julie engrossed in their conversation that he realized what that difference was. What he and his son inherited wasn't a responsibility and a duty. It was a pleasure and a privilege. His trip home would be a short one.

About the Author

D.L. Havlin is an eclectic author whose novels, novellas, and short stories mirror his rich, varied background. Born April 18, 1941, he's packed three lifetimes of experiences into one brim full existence. He believes, "The one big advantage writing at an advanced age provides is that life is what you know and not what you project it might be."

Schooled in Ft Myers, Florida, Anderson H.S., in Cincinnati, Ohio, and the University of Cincinnati, his widely varied career included: systems analyst, procedure writer, production manager, materials manager, licensed boat captain, fishing guide, high school football coach, product sales manager, manufacturing plant manager, world-wide divisional customer service director, chemicals distributor general manager, call center tech service rep, president and general manager of a small manufacturing company.

A deep love for nature and especially wild Florida often furnish settings for his work, but his travels make places such as Kiev, Singapore, London, New York, Modena, or Saxon-Hausen backgrounds for his stories as well. His unique combination of a vivid imagination and his ability to weave intricate plot lines, seasoned by his life-time exposure to fascinating story possibilities and his knowledge of human nature, provides the heart-felt, enjoyable reading his novels provide.

He answers, "Why do you write?" by saying, "To entertain—that's first, but to provoke thought is a close second. I firmly believe both are done through the heart, for the mind is seldom opened until it is emotionally conditioned to respond."

Printed in the USA
CPSIA information can be obtained
at www.ICGtesting.com
LVHW011335051023
760085LV00063B/1785